learning TO FLY

OTHER BOOKS AND AUDIOBOOKS

BY CHALON LINTON

Regency Romance

Standalone

An Inconvenient Romance

Christmas Grace (contributor)

A Tangled Inheritance

A Christmas Courting (contributor)

Adoring Abigail

Everly Series

Escape to Everly Manor

Forever, Phoebe

Chiara's Choice

Contemporary Romance

Flying in Love Series (Air Force Romance)

Flying in Love

Fly Home to Me

Learning to Fly

learning TO FLY

an air force romance

CHALON LINTON

Cover images: *Sleeping Lady Ridge Sunset* © Ron Castle Photography; *Plane,* courtesy Alamy Stock Photography

Cover design copyright © 2024 by Covenant Communications, Inc.

Published by Covenant Communications, Inc.
American Fork, Utah

Library of Congress Cataloging-in-Publication Data

Name: Chalon Linton
Title: Learning to fly / Chalon Linton
Description: American Fork, UT : Covenant Communications, Inc. [2024]
Identifiers: Library of Congress Control Number 2023951559 | ISBN Number 978-1-52442-532-6
LC record available at https://lccn.loc.gov/2023951559

Printed in the United States of America
First Printing: July 2024

30 29 28 27 26 25 24   10 9 8 7 6 5 4 3 2 1

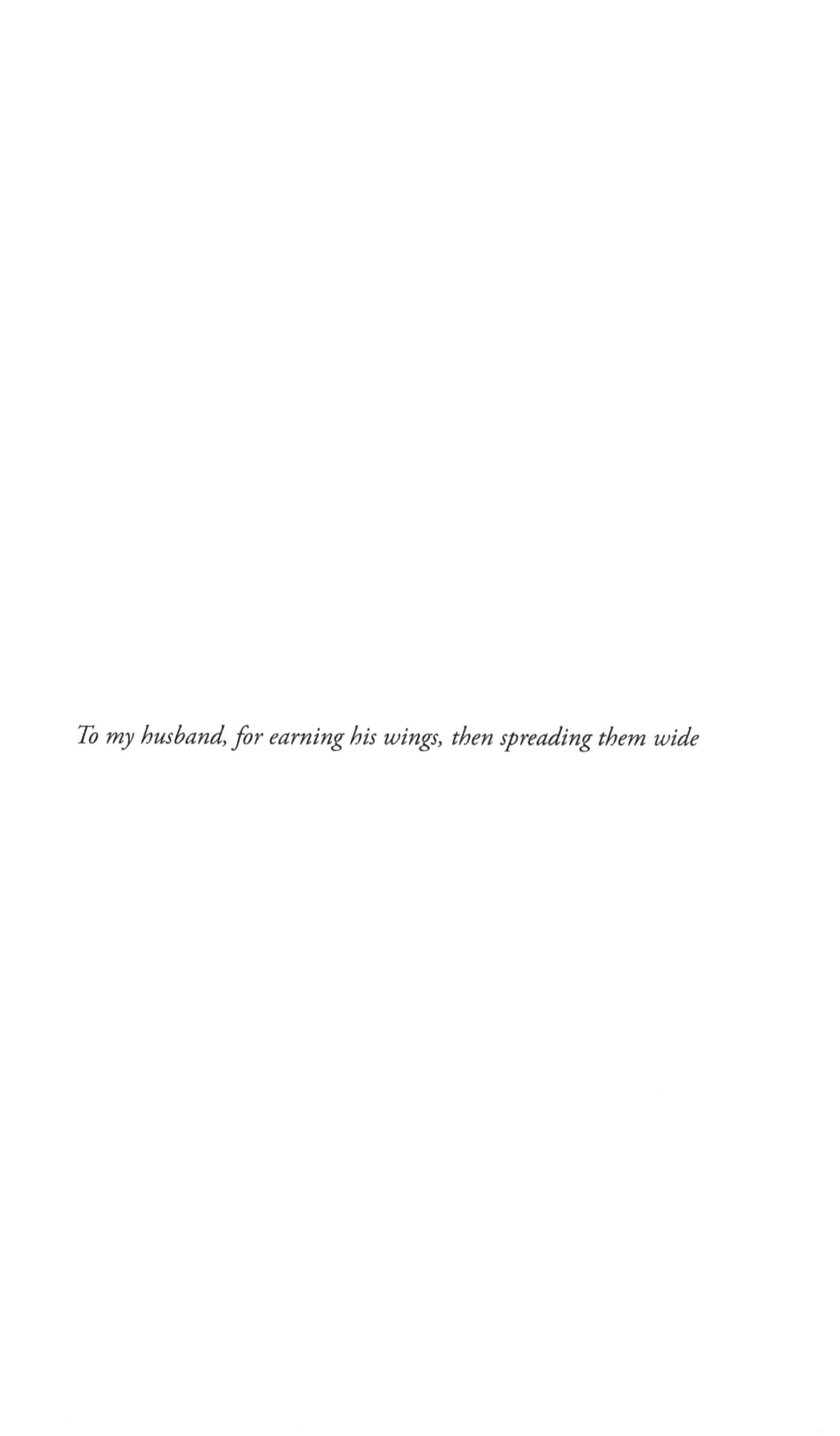

To my husband, for earning his wings, then spreading them wide

ACKNOWLEDGMENTS

My husband and I had been married for three years when he began Undergraduate Pilot Training for the United States Air Force. Our first daughter had been born the week before his start date. To say it was a difficult year is a massive understatement. Air force pilots are tried and tested; high regards to all who graduate with their wings.

Writing this novel transported me back to the sights and sounds and smells of Del Rio, Texas. There are places, vistas, and most importantly, people, I'll never forget. Mandi and Andrea loved on my little girl, and Karrie gave me good mothering advice. While it was one of the most difficult years, it was also a year full of blessings and friendships. I am honored to share a piece of this time of my life with you through Andrew and Kasie's story.

I am grateful for the vision of Covenant Communications to bring wholesome stories to light. Their support of this series has been another blessing in my life. Kami Hancock is a wonderful human who supports and strengthens me in this endeavor. I am grateful to Emily Remington for the cover design. Shara Meredith jumps in to every book launch with enthusiasm and glittery pom-poms. My support team is the best, and I feel so honored to work with them.

My beta readers are so amazing. They dive in with short notice and help me make the most of every page and scene. Andrea, Melissa, Denali, Laura, Tiffany, Anneka, and Heather, thank you, thank you, thank you.

My relationship with God has helped me weather the storms. I am grateful for His presence in my life. My family is my rock and my joy, and my husband, Todd, is my forever. Thank you, Todd, for inviting me to be your partner on this journey all those years ago. I love walking by your side.

CHAPTER 1

I STOOD IN THE RELENTLESS Texas sun and watched yet another plane fly overhead. I'd read that the temperature topped out at the mid-60s in January, yet on January 23 I stood fanning my face with my hand, grateful to allow the three movers hired by the military to do their job. They carried armloads of boxes into the cookie-cutter duplex I would call home for the next twelve months. Life on a military base would be a new experience for me. My brother, Tucker, was an air force pilot. I was simply the doting aunt who would care for my nephew for a year with the perk (intended sarcasm) of living in Nowheresville, Texas.

Tucker was older than me by four years. I was twenty-three. He stood just under six feet. I could claim five-six in my tennis shoes, though we still resembled one another: round cheeks, black hair, and naturally olive-toned skin. The layers of my hair reached barely past my shoulders, and Tucker sported his military haircut. We both had brown eyes, but Tucker's were a shade lighter. Precious Noah had inherited his father's eyes and his mother's thick brown hair. He was a beautiful baby.

I still called my nephew a baby, even though we had celebrated his second birthday almost four months ago. Tucker's wife, Stacy, had died seven months ago. She had contracted stomach cancer, and by the time it was discovered, the cancer had spread through her stomach wall. She was diagnosed in March and gone by June. Mom and I had worked together to make Noah's birthday spectacular—loads of balloons, a cake covered with frosting roads and matchbox cars, and gifts stacked taller than Noah himself. Tucker had sung along with my parents and me, but then, like now, his smile was forced.

Before Stacy passed, she had cuddled her baby and made Tucker promise to teach Noah about God. She had also made Tucker promise to continue living. To raise Noah with joy instead of sorrow. "Noah needs to see his Daddy have faith to do the hard things," she had said. Tucker was still working on the living-with-joy part, but I hoped I could be a boon and support while he worked through his grief.

Moving with him and Noah to Laughlin Air Force Base was a huge sacrifice for me. Last August I had graduated from California State Northridge with a degree in theatre studies. The day I'd decided to major in theatre, my dream had rooted deep. After graduation I would work and save up, then spend a year in London to learn more about the industry and make contacts. I'd sent out internship applications and started making connections, but after Stacy passed, conversations with my parents and lots of prayer helped me see the Lord had a different plan for me. Spending a year in Del Rio, Texas, living on a military base was a sacrifice I was willing to make. It was one I *could* make, and it would help my parents and Tucker and Noah. Once the year ended, I'd head overseas and pursue my dream.

Sweat dripped off the forehead of a muscled mover as he hefted another stack of boxes into the house.

"That one goes to the kitchen," I said. "Thank you! Lunch will be here soon!" I wandered inside and imagined what the house would look like once the unpacking was complete.

Tucker walked through the front door holding a sleeping Noah. I rushed forward to meet him. "Sorry I took so long," he said. He passed my nephew into my arms. "They were still making the food when I got there. I'll grab the food and the portable crib so we can lay him down."

I rocked Noah in my arms, and Tucker soon returned with the portacrib in one hand and a bag of food in the other. "Where should we put him?" I asked. I was still adjusting to my new role, figuring out how to take care of a toddler.

"How about the main bedroom closet?" Tucker said. He set the food on the counter, and another airplane screeched overhead. Noah wasn't fazed by the noise, but it would take me some time to adjust to living beneath the flight pattern. "The movers are unloading the couch right now. Let's get Noah set and then offer them lunch."

I followed Tucker to the largest bedroom. Tucker clicked the bars on the crib into place and set the mattress in the bottom. He grabbed the blanket from the diaper bag and spread it out, I laid Noah down carefully, and we backed slowly out of the closet.

I left the door open a crack. "Do you want to tell the movers lunch is here? And don't forget the drinks in the refrigerator."

"I'll do that." Tucker stood with his hands on his hips. He wore jeans and a flannel with a pair of Chacos. Before I could react, he pulled me into a hug. "Thank you, Kasie."

We'd been through this before. I poked my fingers into his sides, and he jumped, like I knew he would. "You're welcome. Now, let's keep your movers happy."

We walked to the kitchen, and I quickly cleared a few boxes of kitchenware from the table. "Let's spread it out here."

"Did you tell Mom and Dad the movers arrived?" Tucker asked.

"Yep," I said. "Mom said to send pictures of Noah."

Tucker cracked a small smile. "Shocker."

My parents are the epitome of good people. Before Stacy's diagnosis, they had partnered with a nonprofit missionary coordinator to serve in Mexico. They were able to delay their scheduled trip for a handful of months and had immediately relocated to Arkansas, where Tucker's family had lived, to offer support. However, because of tax implications for the donations they had collected, they were able to postpone their service for only so long, so I found myself filling the role of caregiver for Noah and backup for my brother in his new duty station.

Tucker told the movers lunch was ready and they eagerly loaded their plates with food and headed outside to eat.

In his previous assignment, Tucker had flown a C-130, a military transport plane, at Little Rock Air Force Base. After Stacy's funeral he had requested to be reassigned as an instructor for new pilots, with the hope that he could limit his deployments, work more regular hours, get most weekends off, and have more time with his son.

I grabbed one of the remaining burritos from the table. Tucker had told me one benefit of living on the Mexican border was the mom-and-pop restaurants with legit Mexican food. I was excited about that part. The rest—a year in Texas instead of London, a serious change of social scene, and living away from everything familiar—I wasn't so excited about.

I glanced out the front window to see the movers sitting on the front lawn under one of our two trees. Base housing fit the definition of utilitarian. Basic. The homes were not going to win any awards for architecture or style. But by my choice, Laughlin Air Force Base would be home for the next twelve months. I planned to be happy and figure out what God had in store for me here.

Tucker pulled several drinks from the refrigerator and carried them outside. He passed them out to the movers, chatted for a moment, and then came back inside. "They said they should be done in about ninety minutes," he said.

I clapped my hands and rubbed them together. "Then the fun begins."

Tucker scoffed and stuffed a bite of his burrito into his mouth. "Have at it, Kasie." He had given me free rein to decorate the house how I wanted. We couldn't paint the white walls of base housing, but I planned to get creative.

"I'm thinking orange slipcovers for the couches, with purple and teal pillows." My years in theatre had trained me to keep a straight face.

Tucker scoffed again, and I saw a bit of a smile. "My couches are just fine, thank you."

"Fine," I huffed with dramatic flair. "I'll use the orange and teal in my bedroom."

Tucker had only qualified for a two-bedroom because his only true dependent was Noah. However, he had reached out to his commander, and due to the circumstances, he'd received approval for a three-bedroom house. Tucker would take the main bedroom and bath since his work hours would vary between early mornings and late nights. He'd also requested special accommodations to get me permissions on base. His commander had been understanding, and I could now brandish my own military ID. It stated my civilian status rather boldly, but still.

Two hours later Tucker and I stood in the carport and watched the moving truck pull away. The hum of a low-flying plane buzzed overhead. We looked skyward to see the blue underbelly of the aircraft. "There's a T-6," Tucker said.

I offered my customary nod and half smile, the one I shared anytime Tucker started talking in military-speak.

"It's the plane I'll be flying," he said. His hands motioned while he told me all the features of the airplane.

"Hi, y'all," a happy voice called. We turned to see a woman carrying a plate filled with brownies across the lawn. Her cute brown bob cut framed her full white cheeks, and she wore skinny jeans and a loose sweater. "Looks like your movers finished. Did everything arrive in one piece?"

Tucker's expression turned from excited to polite. "The furniture looks good so far, but we haven't unpacked much else," he said.

"My name's Hope Nottingham. We live right next door." Hope had an endearing Southern accent. She extended her free hand.

I shook it first, but Tucker replied. "Nice to meet you. I'm Tucker Foster, and this is my sister, Kasie."

"It's nice of you to help them get settled, Kasie," Hope said. "We've been here a year and a half, and I finally threw away my last box a week ago." She laughed. "I'm sure it's nice to have an extra set of hands to unpack." She smiled politely, then turned to Tucker. "What's your call sign?"

"Tuck."

"Are you gonna be an IP, Tuck?"

I'd learned *IP* meant Instructor Pilot.

"I'll be instructing in the T-6," Tucker said.

"Maybe you'll be in the same squadron as my husband, Ian. Bowman's his call sign," she said. "Come to think of it, I think he mentioned a new arrival."

"How did he get his call sign?" I asked.

"Ah, 'cause our last name is Nottingham, like Nottingham Forest in *Robin Hood*. When Ian got the top shot award, they came up with Bowman, like the archers from the story." Hope seemed to remember the plate in her hands. "I hope y'all like chocolate. Brownies are my specialty." The frosted chocolate squares looked delicious. These were far more deluxe than the boxed brownie mix I defaulted to. My mouth watered.

Tucker took the offered plate. "Thank you. I'm sure they won't last long."

"Did I see you have a little one?" Hope asked.

"My nephew, Noah," I said. "He just turned two."

"Ian and I have two kids," Hope said. "Cole is seven, almost eight, and Rebecca—we call her Becca—is three. Maybe your wife and I can set up a play date once you're settled."

I nodded and stole a glance at Tucker, whose jaw tightened. Telling others about Stacy was always the toughest part for him. I touched his arm. "Maybe you can take those brownies to the kitchen and check on Noah?"

He offered Hope a mumbled thanks for the treats and walked into the house.

Poor Hope. She twisted her hands. "I'm sorry. Did I say something wrong?"

"Tucker's wife passed away not long ago," I said. I spread my arms wide. "That's why I'm here." I smiled. "I plan to live with Tucker for a while to help take care of Noah."

"Bless you," Hope sympathized, reaching out to set her hand on my arm. "I stay home with my kids, so we can get the kids together sometime. And you let me know if you need anything."

I pulled my phone from my back pocket. "Can I get your number?" I asked. I knew no one in this tiny town. It would be nice to have a contact.

Hope listed her cell number, and I sent her a text so she would have mine as well. "Anytime you need help watching little Noah, you just holler," she said.

I scanned the quiet street and laughed. "I don't imagine I'll have much of a social life."

A knowing glint flashed through her eyes. "Oh, I don't know about that. There are plenty of eligible bachelors here. In fact, Ian's cousin is a student right now, and he's single. He'll be moving to Ian's squadron in a couple of weeks. It's uncommon for them to pair students with family, but they don't like pushing students back to a later class. As long as they don't fly together, Lieutenant Colonel Haggar said he trusts Ian to be fair." Hope waved a hand. "I may be partial, but that family has some good genes."

I laughed. "I'm not sure I could cut it as a military spouse." While I appreciated Hope's scheming, I'd tried dating a prospective pilot before, and that hadn't worked out so well. I would be keeping my distance from the eligible bachelors on base.

"You get used to it." Hope waved her hand again. "Military folks are a lovely group of people. They really take care of their own. And you're here, so you're one of us now."

Her words bolstered my hope that I could make something positive come from this difficult transition. "Well, first things first," I said. "I'd better go unpack. It was nice to meet you, Hope. Thank you for introducing yourself, and thanks again for the brownies. I'm sure I'll be calling with all sorts of questions."

"Good." Hope smiled.

Her positivity was well and good, but Tucker chose the military life, not me. My adventure was not meant to be next to a runway. My adventure involved a stage, a set, a cast, a crew, and an enraptured audience.

I headed back inside to have a brownie and start the enormous task of settling in to my new situation.

For the next week, Noah seemed bountifully entertained with my goofy faces and silly voices. Tucker and I worked to get the house in order, and I called Mom to brag when I moved the last of the boxes into the storage unit in the carport.

Tucker began to work regular hours, and we quickly settled into a routine. Every afternoon when Noah napped, I cleaned, prepped dinner, searched theatre groups, or texted Mom or my friend and old roommate, Annabelle. After Noah's nap, I would strap him into the stroller for a walk, often to the park.

February arrived and I found myself at the park again while Noah clambered over the playground equipment, making laps up the stairs and then down the slide. When he tired of the slide, I lifted him into the infant swing and pushed him from the front. Whenever he swung forward, I pretended like he kicked me and jumped backward. He giggled and giggled and won my heart again. These simple moments reinforced the rightness of my decision to come to Texas.

"Hi, Kasie." Hope walked up holding her little girl's hand. She looked at Noah. "Oh, he is a cutie."

"And he uses it to persuade me to give in to him all the time." I laughed and squatted to the little girl's eye level. "Hi, Becca," I said. "I'm Kasie." I held out my hand for a high five.

Becca ducked behind Hope's legs. Then, slowly, she peeked her head out, puckered her lips, and looked at my hand. She tentatively reached forward and tapped her palm against mine.

Hope laughed. "She's a bit shy." She looked at Becca. "Do you want to swing, darlin'?" Becca nodded, and Hope lifted her up into the regular swing next to Noah. "Hold on tight now."

Noah had begun to squirm, so I returned my attention to him, jumping away from his kicking feet as he swung back and forth in our imaginary game.

"Ian said your brother has adjusted well to IP life," Hope said. "The squadron has been shorthanded for a while, so I'm glad."

"I'm still learning how everything works, but I think Tucker's happy to fly and be able to see his son every night." I grabbed Noah's little feet and pretended to tickle them before releasing him again. "It would be hard for him to have to deploy with Noah at this stage."

"It's true they love their airplanes, but this is a different assignment. They get lots of hours, but it's hard on them. When his students fail or wash out, Ian blames himself. And, if you hadn't noticed, we sort of live in the middle of nowhere." Hope motioned toward the dirt strip running from the end of the cul-de-sac to the tall barbed-wire fence.

"I had noticed that part," I said with a smile. Noah began to push against the front of the swing and tried to wrangle his leg out. "You ready for a nap?" I stopped the swing and lifted him into my arms.

"I done, too, Mama," Becca said. She had a slight Southern accent that mirrored Hope's.

Hope slowed Becca's motion, and Becca jumped down and ran to the slide.

"Why don't the three of you join us for Sunday dinner?" Hope said. "I'm making a pot roast, and I'll have plenty to share."

"That would be nice," I said. I asked her a few more questions about where she shopped and if she attended a local church congregation. She gave me the details of the services at the base chapel, and I told her I'd check with Tucker about dinner and get back to her.

Tucker wasn't excited about the idea. Outside of Noah, he wasn't excited about much lately. But when I told him I was fine going by myself, he said he would go. I texted Hope that we could come for dinner and offered to bring dessert.

On Sunday we attended the church service at the base chapel and spent a few hours at home, sorting through file folders of Tucker's flight records and Stacy's medical bills. The military medical insurance had covered all her treatments and care. A huge blessing during such a difficult time.

Five o'clock rolled around, and Tucker grumbled about how he'd rather stay home.

"I didn't force you to agree to it," I said. "You don't have to stay long. Or you can text Hope and tell her you changed your mind." I picked up the plate of snickerdoodle cookies I'd made.

With a heavy sigh, Tucker lifted Noah into his arms, and I followed him out the door. "Noah only napped for forty minutes after church, so we'll see what happens," Tucker said.

I tried to stay positive. "I'm glad you have a friendly neighbor. Plus, I'm ready for some adult conversation." While I loved my nephew, living with a toddler proved to be a huge adjustment. My vocabulary had simplified, and I had teased Tucker that trying to decipher Noah's words should count toward linguistics credits.

We arrived at the Nottinghams', and Hope welcomed us in. Tucker introduced Noah and me to Ian.

"You two resemble each other," Ian said. His white head was shaved bald, and he had a wide smile. He was taller than Tucker. Thicker, too, and his friendly blue eyes matched Hope's.

"I don't always consider our similarities a compliment," I said, throwing a teasing smile to my brother.

"I'll take those," Hope's son, Cole, said, and he reached for the cookies. I handed him the plate.

"You don't get one till after dinner," Hope called after him as he darted to the kitchen.

Tucker set Noah down, and Noah immediately toddled to where Becca sat on the carpet, stirring an imaginary mixture in a toy bowl.

Cole appeared again, with his hand wrapped around the wrist of a man he dragged behind him. Ice streamed through my veins. I knew that face. I knew that man. I'd kissed those lips. *Andrew Stoll.* The dozens of bandages I'd placed on my heart unbound at once, and fissures of pain, excitement, and confusion splintered outward, making time stand still.

"Mama," Cole said. "Andrew ate a cookie even though I told him you said not to."

A sheepish grin filled the face I knew so well. It had been twelve months, and while his dark golden-brown hair was buzzed short on the sides, his smooth white skin and hazel eyes had not changed. They were as arresting as ever.

With his free hand Andrew wiped the crumbs from his mouth. "I couldn't resist," he said, and a flash of his adorable dimples pricked my heart. It was then he noticed me. His smile fell away, along with his joviality. "Kasie?" My name on his lips felt like a warm whisper. "What . . . what are you doing here?" The shock filtering through his wide eyes anchored my feet to the floor.

Hope smacked Andrew's arm. "That's no way to talk to my guests." She offered an apologetic smile.

The phrase *small world* seemed too cliché for this crazy turn of events. Yes, I knew Andrew had wanted to become a fighter pilot. And yes, he knew my brother flew for the air force, but to be standing in the same state, on the same base, in the same house . . . for Ian's cousin to turn out to be *Andrew*—this couldn't be real. My stomach turned, and I couldn't form a single word.

"Andrew, as in . . . ?" Tucker turned me, heat in his eyes. The question died on his lips. He knew how my breakup with Andrew had turned me inside out.

I had been the one to end things, because I had prayed, harder than I had for anything before, and I'd just felt . . . off. I'd taken that to mean we shouldn't be together. Andrew had begged for me to stay, to try. He was convinced we could make a long-distance relationship from England to wherever he ended up work. So many of my choices had been grounded in prayer. And every other time I had prayed about a decision, peace had filled me. But not this time. When I'd prayed about continuing with Andrew, turmoil had churned through my chest. I had lost sleep night after night, and my appetite had waned. I couldn't deny the answer I had received. But it had been hard. So very hard. Harder than anything I had done before—or since. Breaking up with Andrew had jolted my world, and it had taken a long time for me to regain my footing.

"Hello, sir." Andrew turned to my brother and offered his hand. "Kasie and I attended Cal State Northridge together."

"I know who you are," Tucker said bluntly. He gripped Andrew's hand while he eyed him up and down.

Poor Hope. She'd had the best intentions and was now caught in a Texas twister. She looked between us and then stepped closer. "Andrew, I told you about Kasie, remember? She's here helping her brother take care of little Noah." Her voice wavered with uncertainty.

Andrew offered a smile, but I could tell it was forced because his dimples didn't appear. "You never told me a name, so I never imagined . . ." He stuck his hands into his pockets. When Andrew and I had dated, he had oozed confidence. Now, as he stared at me, hesitancy filled his gaze.

That same hesitancy churned my insides. Words fumbled around in my head, and I forced myself to look away from Andrew's handsome face. Guilt wormed through me. Our history, the one without a happy ending, had, after all, been my doing.

Hope clapped her hands together, and her eyes lit. "Well then, isn't this a fun coincidence?" Her exuberance fell as flat as the Del Rio landscape.

I finally grasped a sentence. "We were in the same advanced writing class," I said.

"That's an understatement," Andrew said, bitterness lacing his words. His tone changed to matter-of-fact. "Kasie and I dated." His jaw tightened. He looked at Ian, then turned his eyes back to mine. "It didn't work out, and we broke up last February." Remorse and anger framed his words. "In fact, it was exactly a year ago today." His gaze kept me frozen in place. Dread pooled in my stomach as blips of that awful conversation flashed through my mind.

I'd been in tears. Andrew, too, had cried. We'd seemed to fit so well together—in class, on campus, dating—until we didn't. Our futures diverged like the paths in Robert Frost's poem. Andrew's future headed one direction and mine the opposite.

"I remember," Tucker said. He crossed his arms, poised like a bouncer to an exclusive club.

Ian grimaced. "Uh oh. That doesn't sound like a ringing endorsement." He appeared entertained, but I couldn't find the words to explain why this was not a happy coincidence. Tears threatened, and I blinked excessively to keep them at bay.

Andrew could rock a room with his presence. He had been dashing and charming and ever the gentleman, but I had walked away. Now he stood watching, waiting for me to establish the expectation. Ever the gentleman.

Hope looked at her husband, her eyes begging him to intercede. My stomach churned, and if my hands weren't twisting in front of me, it would be obvious that my fingers shook. Hope nudged Ian, but Andrew spoke first.

"I thought you were heading to England." His eyes remained on me.

My stomach dropped. My London theatre dream was one of the reasons I had given as to why we should break up. "Some things . . . happened," I said glancing at Tucker. "Plans changed."

Hope put her arm around my shoulder. "I told you why Kasie's here," she told Andrew. "Little Noah's mother has passed on, so Kasie's stepping up to help."

Andrew's eyes penetrated my defenses. I ached for what once was. Andrew hadn't agreed with my decision, but no matter how hard he had tried to change my mind, I couldn't deny the sourness that had accompanied thoughts of staying together. We weren't right together. But standing here, seeing him look at me with resolute disappointment, my heart pinched, and my confident certainty fell in tandem with the tears now dropping down my cheeks.

Andrew inhaled deeply and his jaw relaxed. He turned to Tucker. "I'm sorry for your loss," he said.

Tucker turned somber for a single moment. Then a spark of realization lit his eyes. "Wait. You're here for training?" he asked. My family shares everything. My parents and Tucker knew all about Andrew and how my heart had shattered when I had broken things off. Andrew's dream lay at the core of it all. His dream versus mine. He dreamed of flying for the military. Laughlin Air Force Base was a pilot-training base. Tucker was an instructor, who if he hadn't had his own tragedy, would have been stationed far away. But here we were. Tucker and Andrew and me. God must have a sense of humor.

"Yes, sir. Halfway through. I start T-1s tomorrow." Andrew's smile turned sincere, maybe a bit prideful. And I was glad for it. Glad his dream had taken root. Or maybe more fitting, his dream was taking flight.

"Andrew's actually in our squadron," Ian said. "We'll meet all the students in our new class tomorrow."

Tucker's lips pressed closed. Silence reigned until Cole spoke. "Mom? Since Andrew had a cookie, can I have one too?" Bless his heart.

"After dinner, hon." Hope turned a cheery smile to the group. "Should we eat?"

"Tomorrow will be a long day," Andrew said. "I should go."

Hope's smile fell. "But you haven't eaten," she said.

Cole grabbed Andrew's hand and swung it back and forth. "What about playing Legos?" Cole asked.

I couldn't change much about tonight, but I could let Andrew spend time with his family. "I think I'll head home," I offered. "My head's really throbbing." A total truth. I forced a smile and moved toward the door.

Tucker moved toward Noah, I assumed to follow me. Hope seemed defeated.

"Kasie," Andrew said. "You should stay with your brother. I'm not very hungry, so I'll just grab a few cookies for the road and head home to get ready for tomorrow." He squatted down in front of Cole. "How about if I play Legos extra long next time?"

Cole offered a dramatic sigh. "Okay," he said.

"Thank you, Hope. Ian." Andrew leaned forward and gave Hope a hug. He waved goodbye to Cole and Becca, nodded at Tucker, held my gaze for a long second, and then he was gone.

Ever the gentleman.

CHAPTER 2

I ACHED. MY HEAD. MY limbs. My heart. Dating Andrew had been a good thing, a great thing. I'd thought it was everything love was supposed to be, until fear and uncertainty had started squirming in. I would graduate the same semester as Andrew, and as the blessed day neared, the conversations about our relationship had grown serious. He had asked if we had a future together. We'd decided to pray about it. His answer was yes, mine was uncertainty.

After the breakup, every day on campus had me on edge. I had avoided all the places we had walked and studied and kissed. I had assumed I would heal with time, but I don't know that I ever really did. My roommate, Annabelle, was also a theatre major. She had compared our breakup to a Greek tragedy. Stacy was diagnosed a few weeks later, and all of my energy and emotion had turned to processing her illness and then mourning her loss.

The combined emotion about our dating relationship, our breakup, and the fallout resurfaced as I bumbled my way through dinner. I sniffled into my napkin and focused on feeding Noah potatoes and carrots. Tucker, Hope, and Ian didn't push me for an explanation. Instead they turned their attention to Cole and Becca.

I forced myself to eat, mostly to keep my mouth full and avoid talking, but my mind was elsewhere. For the next year I would call Texas home. If Andrew was halfway through training, our time here would overlap for at least the next six months and the statistical probability that we would run into each other again had bloomed astronomically, especially with Ian being Andrew's cousin. Six months that I'd imagined would be filled with cacti and only the sounds of planes screeching overhead now promised overthinking about the neighbors and their relations and when and where I might run into Andrew.

I thought on this way more than I should have through the rest of dinner and long after.

The next week, during one of Noah's naps, Annabelle and I finally caught up with each other. Her shock as I related Sunday's events made mine feel more justified. "No way! Andrew, as in *the Andrew*, is on the same base as you?" she asked.

I ran my fingers through my hair. The surreal scene had played on repeat for the last five days. My stomach tumbled with every replay. The shock I'd felt, the stabbing ache in my chest, the pain that had washed over Andrew's features as he acknowledged my presence.

"What are you going to do?" Annabelle asked.

"What can I do?"

"Kiss him again—you know, for old time's sake." Annabelle always had been one to swoon over kisses.

I couldn't deny that in the year since our breakup, I'd thought about Andrew's kisses way more than I should have. Nowadays my kisses involved slobbery snuggles with Noah. Thankfully, Noah included a hearty amount of giggles, a fascination with the lizards that seemed to multiply in our yard, and a natural inquisitiveness that I loved to observe. There were also moments that made me doubt I was the best to be caring for him, like when he popped a full grape into his mouth and gagged a few times before I could swipe it out. The stupid grape had me in tears.

"I think I'll just hole up in the house for the next few months," I said. "Noah will keep me entertained."

"Hey." Annabelle switched to her no-nonsense tone. "You made the choice you felt was best. There's no reason you and Andrew can't live peacefully in the same neck of the woods for a few months."

I agreed with her in theory, but I knew how my anxieties worked. Luckily, she changed the topic and updated me on the Shakespeare play she had auditioned for. "The director is really amazing. I'm so glad I got a part," she said. "I feel like I can learn so much from her."

"That sounds like such a great opportunity," I said. We chatted a bit more about several other people from our program, and I said goodbye when I heard Noah calling out from his crib.

"Hey there," I said, lifting him over the bar. "Did you have a good nap?"

Tucker's long work hours meant some days passed without him seeing his son awake. Thankfully they didn't train on the weekends, though Hope warned me that if the class fell behind schedule, those would be gone too.

Andrew would have started in Ian and Tucker's class by now. He'd been on my mind for days. And, really, who was I kidding? I'd thought of him often since our breakup, long before he'd walked out of Hope's kitchen. Without fail, whenever I replayed the scene in my head, heat washed over me, from my scalp to my toes. It wasn't burning regret, nor was it a scalding warning but warmth and deep joy mixed with sadness. How I could feel such opposite emotions at the same time, I didn't know, but both extremes threaded through me. Since our run-in, I had worked to keep busy, playing with Noah, reading scripts on an indie website, and keeping up on laundry and meals. When I stayed occupied, I couldn't focus on the turmoil interacting with Andrew had caused.

Sunday church promised adult interaction. My time in Texas was meant to lift some of Tucker's load, but after Noah ripped his bowtie off for the fourth time, I gave up, tossed it into the diaper bag, and passed him back to Tucker. The pastor wrapped up his sermon, and as I tried to recall the highlights, the message felt as tangible as air. I was looking forward to sharing Noah's squirminess with the nursery workers and enjoying Sunday School sans toddler.

When the pastor concluded, Tucker stood abruptly. "I'll take Noah to nursery," he said.

"Thanks." I handed him the backpack that served as a diaper bag, and he swung it over one shoulder before sweeping Noah into his arms.

"Hey, Nono," Tucker said as he wiggled his nose against Noah's neck. Stacy had adopted the nickname for her son, one I never used so it could be sacred for their little family.

I eyed my brother as he made his way toward the doors. He'd never been loquacious, but since Stacy's passing, he'd spoken only the most vital words. I worried about him but had no idea what to do to help him. I'd have to call Mom later and hit her up for advice—again. Maybe she could help me sort what I should do for Tucker and how to function knowing Andrew was on base.

I straightened the long sleeves of my dark-blue dress. Small ruffles circled the cuffs and tea-length hem. Noah's wiggles had my clothes all twisted up. I adjusted the elastic waist on my hips and ran my fingers through the ends of my hair before setting off for class, where only a few empty chairs remained. Resigned to the fact that Tucker and I would sit separately, I scanned the room for a seat I could slip into without disrupting the discussion.

A waving hand caught my eye. Hope motioned to the empty seat beside her. I offered apologies to several people as I pushed past them to reach the spot. Hope sat beside Ian, and I hadn't noticed before that on Ian's far side sat Andrew, looking rather dashing in his charcoal pants, blue shirt, and flowered necktie. My breath caught. I wasn't ready to face him again. I hadn't shored my defenses, nor had I prepped my heart to see his hazel eyes and contagious smile. I forced myself to sit and to breathe. Andrew didn't acknowledge me, which I should have been grateful for, but my traitorous heart felt a pang of disappointment.

I should have realized we might meet at church. Our faith had been a talking point while we dated, along with our similar upbringings and the fact that my brother had already achieved Andrew's dream of becoming an air force pilot. The baffling irony that we now shared a row at an obscure air force base in Texas had me opening my Bible and whispering a hasty "Thanks" to Hope.

She smiled, put her arm around me, and squeezed. I felt her sincerity, whether from her Southern hospitality or the fact that she was simply a good person, and was grateful our paths had crossed.

The instructor led the class in a discussion on the first commandment to love the Lord our God, then talked about the second commandment to love our neighbors. Despite the emotional upheaval of the past year, my faith remained solid. I loved God, though I didn't always know best how to love others. I hoped my love for Tucker was evident in my willingness to uproot to Texas. Familial love came rather easily, but I tried to be a good person outside of my family too. I didn't mince words, for the sake of honesty, and I donated to various charities. But I'd always been intrinsically selfish. Something Andrew would probably agree with me on. Before our breakup he had agreed my dreams were important and wanted me to reach all I aimed for, but he had questioned why I couldn't explore another route—one he might be a part of.

My attention was brought back to the present when class ended and the parishioners began to filter out. "Thanks for letting me sit by you," I said to Hope.

"Of course," she said. She turned to Ian. "Wanna go grab the kids?"

"Sure thing," Ian said before moving past us to the door.

"I love the dress," Hope said, pointing at me as we stood.

"I splurged to buy it when I graduated," I said.

"Totally worth it," she said, a gleam in her eye. She turned and looked over her shoulder. "Doesn't she look great Andrew?"

Andrew had been avoiding us, looking absently around the room while waiting for the parishioners on the other end of the row to exit. At Hope's words, his eyes widened. "Yes, she does," he said.

I never quantified forced compliments.

He shifted into a military stance, his feet shoulder width apart and his hands clasped behind his back. His face was all kinds of serious, and while his eyes were technically looking at me, he was doing his darndest to avoid really looking at me. "Did Tuck not make it today?" he asked, all businesslike.

"He's here." I hadn't seen Tucker slip into class but looked around to be sure. "Maybe he had to stay with Noah in the nursery," I said, though Noah usually toddled in without issue to head for the toys.

"Well, I'd better get my kiddos home to feed them." Hope turned her no-nonsense gaze on Andrew. "You still planning to come later?"

"Yes, ma'am," Andrew said with a tip of his head.

"I'll talk to y'all soon, then," Hope said before heading to the door and leaving Andrew and me in the uncertain middle of not knowing whether we should run away or continue awkward conversation with the excuse of being polite.

I opted for awkward. "'Ma'am?' Is that because of her Southern accent?" I asked Andrew.

"No, ma'am," he replied. A teasing grin replaced his serious expression. I much preferred his grin. I'd missed it with a fierceness I hadn't realized before. "Military training," he said.

"Ahh . . ." I nodded, feeling ridiculous that as two adults we seemed unable to carry on a conversation. Sure, we had a past, but shouldn't that mean we had something to talk about? "How's the flying going?" I asked. Inwardly, I knew how ridiculous I sounded. Like a parrot squawking mundane repetition.

He relaxed his stance the slightest bit, his hands falling to his sides. "We're only in academics now, and it's pretty much like I expected," he said with a shrug. "Lots of new stuff to learn and not enough time to learn it."

I fiddled with the ruffled sleeve of my dress, waiting to know what to say. Nothing came. I'd never been good at improv. "I should go check on Noah," I said and turned to leave.

"Kasie," Andrew said quickly.

"Yeah?" My breath caught. I faced him and focused on the contours of his face. The handsome line of his nose, his jaw that gave his face the perfect proportion of solid and touchable.

He blinked and his lips twitched. "You do look nice today." This time his words rang sincere.

Stupid heat flooded my cheeks. I had been the one to walk away. Why could I not be immune to him? "You do too," I spit out.

He raised his arm but then lowered it to his side. "We . . . we should talk." A familiar yearning filled his eyes, along with a look I couldn't decipher.

"Do you think that's a good idea?" I asked.

"I do," he said. He took a breath, and I watched his chest rise and fall. "We're going to keep running into each other, and this is obviously"—he waved his hand between us—"hard."

"I don't want it to be," I said softly, truthfully. We had once talked easily. It was one of the reasons we were drawn to each other. Hour-long conversations felt like minutes. Happy discussions mixed with harder topics. Talking with Andrew had once been as natural as breathing.

"I have to run to a study group right now. How about I swing by when I'm done at the Nottinghams'? We can go for a walk or something?" A hopeful glint touched his eyes.

"Okay. Just text me and I'll come out. You still have my number?" I asked.

Andrew flinched, hurt touching his features. "Of course I do."

His reaction had me feeling all kinds of confused, and I could only nod before I turned away to find my brother.

Tucker stood waiting for me outside while Noah squatted and tried to touch a grasshopper that cautiously avoided his grasping fingers. "Ready?" Tucker asked.

I nodded and tried to focus on Noah and Tucker rather than on my recent, and now pending, conversation with Andrew.

"Did Noah have a hard time?" I asked Tucker when we pulled out of the church parking lot.

"Overall he did well. He acted a little uncertain at first, so I stayed with him." Tucker glanced in the rearview mirror, and I followed his gaze to Noah's heavy eyes.

"I wondered why you didn't make it to Sunday School," I said. "He should be fine next week."

"Yeah." Tucker turned onto the main road leading back to the base. "Sorry to leave you alone."

"I managed," I said.

Tucker hesitated. "I saw Andrew walking out." Accusation filled the creases of his eyes.

"I sat by Hope and Ian," I said. "Andrew was farther down the row."

"Sounds convenient." He kept a straight face and looked at the road.

I scoffed. "Trust me. Nothing will happen between Andrew and me."

"You sure, Kas?" Tucker asked. He held the steering wheel with one hand and rolled down his window.

My natural instinct to glare at my brother almost won out, but he posed a fair question. "Yeah," I answered. "I'm sure."

"You sound like you're trying to convince yourself." Tucker pulled into the carport. "I know you liked him a lot and the breakup hit you hard. And I know this isn't what you bargained for when you agreed to come to Texas."

"I admit it's strange being near him again," I said. "But ending it was the right thing to do."

Tucker turned off the car and turned to face me. "I don't want to see you get hurt. If I remember right, Andrew didn't want to break up. You were pretty devastated when everything went down."

"I know," I said softly. "I have no desire to go through that again," I told Tucker. "That's why nothing can happen. Besides, I'm here for Noah and Andrew is in training. He's going to swing by tonight after he has dinner at the Nottinghams'. We'll get everything out in the open, and then I plan to keep my distance."

Tucker stared at me for a long minute.

"What?" I asked, masking my worry with a laugh.

Tucker shook his head and clicked off his seat belt. "I hope you know what you're doing."

It was a rare occasion when I completely agreed with my brother.

I tried to keep busy after church so I wouldn't fret over my upcoming conversation with Andrew. I asked Tucker if I could reorganize some things in the kitchen, and after Noah woke from his nap, we connected with my parents via video chat. Noah's attention span lasted for only a few minutes, but Mom loved seeing her grandson. Tucker gave his update, and then I took my laptop and disappeared into my room for privacy.

Mom and Dad were currently in San Diego completing training for their service mission.. They would be there for another three weeks before heading to Mexico. "I'm worried about Tucker," I said. "He's good with Noah, but his smiles seem forced, and when Noah's not around, he doesn't say much."

"It's been less than a year, Kasie. It can't be easy for him," Dad said.

"I know, but I don't want to miss anything—if he needs a break or if he needs me to push. I just I wish I knew what to do. I don't think I'm cut out for this." The uncertainty made me question everything.

"He misses his wife, but you aren't meant to fill the hole left by Stacy's death." Mom's eyes glistened with tears. "His sister is exactly what he needs. Listen when he wants to talk and allow him space to mourn."

Dad nodded. "Moving is hard, and so is a new assignment. And your brother is adjusting to a lot more than a new base. It might help to get out and make friends. Be social when you can, but don't push him too hard."

"We did go to the neighbors' for dinner last Sunday," I said. My stomach pinched, and I told them all about the Andrew incident.

"Wow," Mom said. "That sounds like . . . just wow!"

"I guess God is trying to teach me something." I attempted a laugh, but it was stilted.

Mom smiled. "Ah, Kasie, God loves you, and you know you're doing a wonderful thing. We pray for all of you. And I'll add an extra plea that having Andrew near will be for the best."

We hung up, and I thought on Mom's comment. Maybe it was good for me to see Andrew again. We could be in each other's orbit and recognize that our breakup was the right thing. Dad had suggested getting out, meeting more people. The Nottinghams were a blessing, and I could make connections at church too. Then Andrew's image came unbidden into my head. It made sense that I would think of him, as my social connections in Texas were currently limited, but I didn't want to think of him, because when I did, my stupid heart fluttered. Andrew had a plan for the next six months, and the military had a plan for him in the years to follow. His plans differed vastly from mine. Social engagements should not include Andrew, but ironically, he was the only one penciled into my schedule.

I tried to put him from my mind for the rest of the evening.

After dinner, Tucker helped me clear the table.

"I can do the dishes tonight, and then I'm going to step out for a bit and talk to Andrew," I said.

"Thanks, Kas." He scooped Noah out of his high chair. "Should we go take a bath, Nono?"

They disappeared down the hall, and my nerves began to skitter as I finished the dishes.

I dried my hands, slipped on my shoes, and headed to the street. I figured it would be better to pace on the road than circle the living room while I waited for Andrew to finish next door. The sun dropped low, painting the horizon in yellow and orange. After my second pass by the Nottinghams' house, the front door opened. Andrew stepped out but immediately turned back as Cole called, "Wait, Andrew!" and came running out of the house. "I haven't shown you my hundredth day of school outfit."

Andrew noticed me and raised a hand. Then he turned back and knelt in front of Cole. "Can you send me a picture?"

Cole's shoulder's fell. "I wanted to show you."

Hope appeared in the doorframe, wiping her hands on a dish towel. "How about we show Andrew the next time he comes over?" she suggested. She looked at Andrew and spied me on the street. "Hi, Kasie," she called.

Cole's lips turned down in a pout.

Andrew placed his hand on Cole's shoulder. "Can you show me your cane?" he asked.

Cole's eyes shot wide, and he turned to Hope. "Mama, I don't have cane!"

Andrew realized his misstep. "Well, I asked because I have a stick you can borrow that works like a cane. I'll bring it by tomorrow, and you can show me your costume then."

Cole placed his fist against his hip. "Do you promise, Mr. Andrew?" I loved his Southern manners.

Andrew held up a finger. "As long as your dad doesn't keep me late at work, I'll bring it by." He lowered his voice to a loud whisper. "So tell your dad to let us go home early tomorrow." He winked at Cole.

A grin filled the boy's face. "I'll tell him right now. Daddy!" Cole turned and dashed past his mom into the house.

Hope laughed. "Do you really have a cane?"

Andrew stood and shrugged. "I'll figure something out." He had always been good around children.

He rubbed his hands together, then hooked his thumb over his shoulder toward where I stood. "Kasie and I are gonna chat for a bit," he told Hope.

She flung the dish towel over her right shoulder and shooed us away. "That's right. You two figure things out so we can all get together without all this awkwardness."

Andrew leaned forward and wrapped her in a hug. "Thanks for dinner."

"Go on, now." Hope shoved him away.

Andrew walked toward me, and Hope gave me a quick wave before retreating inside her house. My stomach churned, not with pain but uncertainty. My brain still couldn't grasp the fact that Andrew and I were here. Together.

"Do you have any walking sticks I can shorten to about . . . three feet?" he asked, holding his hands the appropriate width apart. "I sorta promised Cole I'd bring him one."

I shook my head, uncertain how I should act around him. "There are some trees around the park. You can probably find a branch that will work."

Andrew tucked his hands into his jeans pockets. "How close is the park?"

"It's on the next street over." I pointed east.

"Mind if we walk there? I don't know when else I might be able to find a cane."

"That works," I said, falling into step beside him. "You could have told Cole you didn't have one."

"I could have, but then I wouldn't be the favorite cousin." His signature aura returned with his grin.

The air held a snap of crisp coolness, and I raised my shoulders and inhaled deeply. "This is strange, right?"

Andrew paused. His eyes roamed my face, and I couldn't hold his gaze. Instead I focused on my feet. "We used to do this all the time," he said as he resumed his pace with me.

"I wasn't talking about the walk, but I think you know that." We had gone on walks. Often. In a roundabout way, it was how we had met.

On a cold February night I'd been walking home from a late rehearsal, and Andrew had been walking home from taking a test. He had glanced at me once, then again. "I think we're in the same creative writing class. Mr. Cane, on Tuesday and Thursday?" he had asked.

We walked together that night and made the connection that we lived in the same building. Then we began to notice each other more and more. One time we met up as he headed to the on-site gym. When I told him I went on power walks for my workouts, he asked if he could join me, and it became a habit. We began walking early every morning, and the walks had led to deeper conversations, which had then led to dates. Annabelle had warned me that I was falling head over heels. She'd been right.

Dusk was falling quickly, and a few bright stars appeared overhead.

"Do you ever wonder where we went wrong?" Andrew asked.

"Maybe we didn't go wrong. Maybe we weren't ever meant to be," I said as guilt rolled through my gut. "You said you understood."

Andrew's feet stopped moving. "I can't argue when you tell me breaking up is an answer to prayer. I'm not going to challenge your faith like that. But that doesn't mean all my questions are answered." His solemn words soaked through my defenses. "You know I hoped for more."

"I know," I admitted. What more could I say? He had imagined a future for us. I'd liked him—loved him, even—but the future he'd envisioned swung far opposite from what I had planned for myself, plus the whole *it had felt wrong* part of the equation.

He sighed and began to walk again. "I thought you didn't want to be restricted to life on an air force base." One of the reasons I'd given him for ending our relationship.

I kept my eyes trained on the road ahead and worked to keep emotion out of my voice. "Plans change."

We rounded the corner, and the blue play structure of the park came into view. "What happened to going to London?" he asked.

"Stacy got sick and Tucker needs help, so I'm here to take care of Noah." I glanced at the huge Texas sky overhead. "London isn't going anywhere."

My theatre arts major had garnered bountiful sympathetic looks and dismissive write-offs from a host of people. Annabelle and I had started keeping a tally of people's reactions when we shared our major. Derision far outweighed support. The prevailing thought was that people couldn't support themselves in theatre arts. I knew it would be hard, but I wasn't afraid of the challenge. Outside of my field, only a select few took time to appreciate the combined intelligence, vision, and work required to create a masterful production. Andrew had taken the time to understand. He'd asked questions about my classes, come to the productions I'd been involved in, and been my biggest cheerleader, even during the times my family wondered where my degree would lead me. I had clung to him while grasping for my goals and dreams and big plans, none of which could have happened if we'd gotten married. It was one of the reasons his request had shaken me. I had known from day one that Andrew aspired to be a pilot. He'd known I aspired to the London stage, but he'd asked me to consider tweaking my goals. When we'd talked of his ROTC commitment, I had known he would end up on a base, wearing a uniform, and perfecting his salute. Even though we had both known our paths diverted, we had continued reaching across the void. We had tried to hold on to each other, until . . . until I couldn't reach anymore and that void had swallowed me whole.

"You sacrificed a lot for your brother," Andrew said. "I . . . never mind." He didn't need to finish his sentence. He thought I didn't know how to sacrifice. Or maybe he wondered why I wouldn't make the sacrifice for him.

"Like I said, plans change. I still dream of London, but Stacy's death reframed my options. I have zero regrets," I said. So far.

"About us?" he asked. His eyes dimmed, sorrow washed over his face, and my heart ached.

"Sorry. That didn't come out as I intended. I only mean that I know I need to be here." I stuck my hands in my pockets and looked up at the flashing lights of a plane cutting through the dark sky.

We reached the park, and Andrew picked up a stick near the base of a tree. He stared at the stick in his hand, his voice tentative. "Do you have regrets about us?"

I picked at the bark on the tree and tried to process his loaded question. Breaking up with him had almost broken me. It was the hardest thing I had ever done. Ever harder than moving to small-town Texas instead of big-city London. "Andrew . . ."

He hit the stick against the base of the tree trunk. "You don't have to answer." He took a few steps, dropped the first branch, and lifted another one to examine. "What about this one?" He turned the crooked branch from side to side. "Or here's another one." He picked it up, too, and walked closer. "What do you think?"

"The one in your right hand." I pointed to the crooked stick.

Andrew's eyes narrowed. "Really?" He looked between the two sticks in his hands. "I would have picked this one." He held up the stick in his left hand.

I shrugged at yet another reminder of why we hadn't worked as a couple. Either stick would work—we just viewed them differently. "I figured the right one isn't as thick, so it would be easier for Cole to hold."

"Good point." Andrew tossed the extra stick back to the base of the tree and held the other triumphantly in the air. "The winner!" His smile revealed his dimples, the ones I'd been such a sucker for. "Should we go all the way around the block?" he asked.

"Sure." It was nice out, and truthfully, I needed time to think before Tucker assailed me with questions.

"Have you dated anyone . . . you know . . . since we broke up?" Andrew asked.

I stared at his hands turning the stick around and around. He had always been a fidgeter. "I've been on a couple of dates, but nothing serious." None of the men I'd gone out with had conjured enough interest to entertain even going on a second date. I hated my next question, but I knew I needed to ask. "Have you dated?"

"I went on one date." Andrew looked at me and gave a halfhearted shrug. "All I could think of was the fact that she wasn't you."

My feet stopped moving. "That's not fair," I said.

"Maybe. But it's the truth." Andrew stopped beside me. "And I always promised to tell you the truth."

I believed my words. Comparisons don't belong on dates. But Andrew's comment pricked like an irritating hangnail because I knew exactly what he meant. I hadn't intended to compare my dates with him. It had simply happened. The first man I had gone out with had walked into the restaurant and let the door swing back into my face. The second had talked about how I should cook for him so he could know my true character. And the third, well, let's just say he liked to talk about his guns—a lot—and he hadn't been talking about the kind of guns you load bullets into.

We started walking again, and Andrew swung the walking stick in his hand.

"Does it bother you? Me being here?" I asked.

"It's strange." Andrew's feet slowed to a stop again, and he turned to face me. "But I think you're brave. You always were. Brave and beautiful."

His dimples tempted my resolve, and my heart skittered in my chest. Why did my heart choose to recall the tingles and butterflies Andrew could conjure, rather than the logical reasons I'd had for walking away?

"Tucker and Noah are lucky to have you." His smile fell. "I'm sorry things didn't work out like you planned. I truly am . . . but I'm not gonna lie. I'm not sorry you're here."

"You're not?"

"Not in the least."

His words felt right, like maybe I'd been looking at it all wrong. Maybe we were supposed to be here together. For what reason, I could never guess, but allowing my anxiety to overshadow the circumstance we'd found ourselves in would make for a miserable year.

Andrew scrubbed his free hand through his short hair. "Pilot training is proving to be the most intense year of my life." He tapped the stick against the toe of his shoe. "Things are tough. People have washed out, and I thought I might be one of them. But I'm still here, and I'm that much closer to getting my wings."

Before I considered the implication of my actions, I reached forward and touched his hand where it held the stick. "I think you're awesome for being here and making it this far." Heat flashed up my arm, and I pulled my hand back and folded my fingers into a fist.

Andrew looked at where I had touched him. He didn't speak. We didn't move. The sun had tucked into the horizon, and the streetlights flickered on, illuminating us in a dull yellow haze.

My head and my heart couldn't agree on an emotion. "I'm sorry, Andrew," I whispered.

His head raised and he met my eyes. "I was motivated before, but with you here, I feel like I have something to prove."

"You don't have to prove anything to me."

A smile flickered across his lips, and that small movement infused me with a flutter of light. "Actually, I'm going to prove you wrong," he said.

I tilted my head, and a funny feeling flitted through my stomach, like a joyous rush from the high jump into a pool, and when his dimples appeared, I knew I would believe whatever he said. I should have looked away, or maybe I should have run home, because the words he uttered next went against everything I'd been trying to convince myself of for the last twelve months. "I'm going to show you that we can work. You can live your dreams and I can live mine. And we can do it side by side."

My arms wrapped around my middle in an unconscious effort to brace myself, to hold my soul together. Because if there was one thing I knew about Andrew, it was that when he set his mind to something, he didn't hold back.

CHAPTER 3

March brought rain, but it was rare not to hear the constant buzz of planes still circling overhead. No matter how many times Andrew's declaration crept into my head, I pushed it aside. There was a lot of pushing going on, because his words cycled over and over and over, like the one song that plays on repeat day after day in your head, even when you try to replace it with something else. My priority was Noah, and my focus needed to be on him.

Yet Andrew's avowal of changing my mind pinged through my head every morning. I wondered if today would be the day he'd try to prove me wrong, if he would make some grand gesture or if we'd have an accidental encounter. I'd seen Andrew at church the Sunday after we had talked and promptly acted like a thirteen-year-old girl by purposely avoiding him. I'd even ducked into the bathroom and hid until I knew Sunday School had started and I could sneak in without notice. And in the final minutes of class, I had scooped up my purse and headed straight for the car to wait for my brother. I didn't run because I didn't want to see Andrew; my reasons were quite the opposite. I ran because when he stood there, a reality only yards away, I wanted to run to him. We'd shared some serious snuggles when we dated. One of my favorite things had been to curl up next to him. He would wrap his arms around me while I snuggled against his solid chest and listened to his heartbeat. I'd forfeited my chance to listen to that warm, steady rhythm, and neither of us needed more confusion. It was better, easier, to run away, so I did. But I should have known Andrew wouldn't wait too long.

Monday morning Noah and I returned from a walk to find Andrew standing at the front door. I hadn't seen him in his flight suit before, and he wore it well. Too well. I hoped the sun from our walk could count as cover for the blush I felt creep over my cheeks.

"I thought you guys had a late night," I said. Not a very hospitable greeting, but the rightness of Andrew at my house fought the wrongness of the joy I felt seeing him.

"I have a thirty-minute break and wanted to drop this off." He held a magazine out, and I stepped forward to take it. Andrew squatted by Noah's stroller to give him a high five.

I turned the magazine in my hand. *Stage Presence* was a popular theatre publication. I had subscribed to it in college, but one month when my finances were tight, I had let the subscription slip. He had remembered.

He stood and pointed at the periodical in my hand. "Did you ever restart your subscription?" he asked.

"No," I said softly.

"Good." He grinned. "I paid for two years, and it should start arriving next month. I ordered this one off Amazon."

"How did you know?"

"I listened to you, Kas. Even when I didn't like what you were saying, I still listened." He raised his hand for another high five from Noah. "You keeping an eye on Kasie for me? Chasing all those other guys away? I'm counting on you, man."

I should have corrected Andrew, but watching Noah giggle and raise his palm to meet Andrew's hand was adorable. I couldn't help but smile.

"Nice one," Andrew said, making explosive noises as he touched his knuckles back to Noah's palm and then wiggled his fingers. He stood straight and turned to face me. "Sorry, but I've gotta run. I'll call you soon," he said, touching my shoulder and sharing a glimpse of his dimples before he jogged to his car and pulled away.

An ache wove through my chest. Andrew had listened. He had remembered. His thoughtfulness stirred the ashes of emotion I thought I'd tamped down. The conflict between the answer I had received then and the fact that I enjoyed every moment we spent together even now knocked against my ribs. He had listened, and I wondered if I had done the same.

Seeing Andrew on Monday made the rest of the week drag. The constant rain that fell over the next two days didn't help speed things up. When we finally got a break from the weeping sky and patches of blue appeared between the rolling gray clouds, Yasmin, one of the women from the playgroup, texted everyone for an impromptu gathering.

"Should we go to the park?" I asked Noah.

"I go park!" he said. He ran to the basket by the front door and pulled out his shoes and plopped down on his bottom. I loaded him into his stroller, and we walked to the park. The elementary school had let out, and the moms with older children joined us at the playground as well.

Cole acted the part of a big brother to Noah. He guided him up the stairs, helped him down the slide, and shielded him from the other children when things grew a bit rambunctious. I sat next to Hope and a woman named Marylou.

"Cole is such a sweet boy," I said. "He's really good with Noah."

Hope laughed and pulled her son's backpack onto her lap. "I wish he treated Becca the same way."

"My Rutherford is the same with Carson," Marylou said. "He's patient with everyone but his little brother." She held up a finger. "But if anyone messes with Carson, Rutherford won't stand for it."

"Big brothers are good like that," I said. I knew Tucker had my back.

Yasmin and Dixie and their kids arrived together. "Were you all cursing the rain as much as I was?" Yasmin asked.

"Yesterday I was ready for bedtime at five thirty," Dixie said with a laugh.

"The sun feels great," I said.

"Thanks for texting us all," Eloise, another mom, told Yasmin.

We scooted over on the bench, and Yasmin sat down. "It's easier when they have someone else to play with," she said. "Otherwise, Ishmael just wants me to push him for an hour on the swing."

"I can totally relate," Hope said. She pulled a pink half sheet from Cole's backpack. She scanned the paper and heaved a sigh, drawing Marylou's and my attention. "More funding cuts. This time it's art." She handed the paper to Marylou.

"These poor kids. First music, now this. They need something besides the core subjects. I never would have survived elementary school without my enrichment classes." Marylou handed the paper back to Hope.

Noah's scream pierced through the air. "Uh oh." I jumped up and walked around the play set to find him sprawled on his belly, both hands wrapped securely around one of Rutherford's legs. Cole squatted nearby, begging Noah to release his hold. "What happened?" I tried to lift Noah, but he refused to budge.

Rutherford tried to pull his leg loose, but Noah screamed louder. "He won't let me go!" Rutherford said.

"He wants to be first," Cole said. He turned angry eyes at Rutherford. "But Rutherford won't let him."

"It's my turn," Rutherford said.

"Noah." I squatted down and ruffled his hair. "You need to let go." When he screamed further defiance, I pried his chubby fingers from Rutherford's leg.

Rutherford ran up the stairs of the play set and looked back from the platform in front of the slide. "Thank you, Miss Kasie." I was still adjusting to being called Miss Kasie. Hope had told me it was a Southern greeting meant to show respect. I smiled at Rutherford, and he turned and catapulted himself down the slide.

"Can I go play, Miss Kasie?" Cole asked.

"Of course. I'll keep an eye on Noah." I lifted Noah to his feet and began to brush the dirt from his sweatshirt. "You can't hang on to Rutherford."

He pointed and bawled. "I go slide."

I grasped his hand in mine. "You can slide after you say sorry to Rutherford."

Noah's tears continued to fall, but I was a theatrics expert and knew he was faking it. He tried to wriggle his little fingers free. "No sorry. No sorry," he repeated.

"Tell Rutherford sorry. Then you can go down the slide," I said.

Noah's bottom lip pouted, and defiance washed across his face.

"Do you want to sit on the bench or go on the slide?" I asked.

"Slide." Noah pointed again at the play structure.

I pressed my finger against his pouty lip. "Then, no more grump monster," I said in a playful voice. When Noah's expression didn't change, I tried again. "No more grump monster." I stuck out my bottom lip and reenacted the game I'd made up a month ago when he'd gotten angry at me for making him eat his peas. When he pouted, I made silly faces and pressed his cheeks until he ended up laughing. It had worked every time since.

Noah tried to hold his frown, but when I scrunched my nose and puckered my lips, he giggled. "Kasie!" he said, though it sounded more like *Kazie*. He shook his head and smiled.

I tickled his cheeks one more time, waiting for him to sober before finally convincing him to apologize. We played tag up and down the slide until it was time to head home for dinner.

We waved goodbye to Yasmin, Marylou, Eloise, Dixie, and their kids, and Hope and I walked toward our street. Noah jumped out of the stroller to walk ahead with Cole and Becca.

"You're good and patient with him," Hope said.

"We're both learning, and I'm grateful for video chat. I call my mom way more often than I should, but it's working out okay," I said.

"Well, you're a natural with children."

I inhaled and thought about the high school theater company in California that had asked if I'd direct their spring show. If I weren't in Texas, I would be in London, so I would have declined either way, but the offer had tempted me. Sharing the techniques and methods I'd studied invigorated me, and children were eager to learn.

"I like kids," I said. "I thought about getting a teaching degree, but I wanted to pack my résumé with something more first. The market is competitive, and teaching would be more secure, but I don't want to pass up a stage opportunity."

"You're doing a good thing for your brother, Kasie. You'll get your time to shine." We reached the Nottinghams' house. Hope called to her kids to head inside and wash up.

"Noah, come help me push the stroller." I waved him over.

"Oh, I almost forgot," Hope said. "Ian and I are celebratin' our anniversary this weekend."

"Congratulations. How many years?" I asked.

"Nine, and I can hardly believe it." She waved a hand. "Anyhow, we're gonna head to San Antonio for the weekend, and Andrew will be here with the kids. I wondered if I could leave your name as backup in case there's an emergency."

I sensed her hesitation in asking me, but she didn't need to worry. I told her I could help out if needed. "Have fun!" I said.

"We will." Hope grabbed her mail from the mailbox and walked to her front door.

Numerous times my finger had hovered over the delete button on Andrew's contact, but I hadn't been able to do it. I had ended our relationship, but I couldn't completely erase him from my life. He had been joy, a bright spot when I had juggled late-night rehearsals and the assignments and tests of my core classes. He knew more about me than anyone who wasn't related by blood. My feelings for him had rooted deep. Despite our parting of ways, his number remained on my phone, perhaps for a distant day when we might meet again. I'd never expected it would arrive so soon.

Friday night Tucker treated us to burgers and shakes in downtown Del Rio. When we pulled back into our driveway, I recognized Andrew's car parked at the Nottinghams'. I mentioned to Tucker that Hope and Ian were gone for their anniversary. "Yeah, Ian told me," Tucker said. "I guess Andrew's watching the kids."

I unbuckled Noah. "I bet they're having a grand old time," I said to my nephew, only a tiny bit jealous that Cole and Becca got to spend a Friday night with Andrew.

Sleep took a long time to arrive that night, and it seemed I had only just drifted into slumber when my phone began to buzz. I reached to my nightstand to hit snooze, but the buzzing didn't stop. The sky beyond my gauzy curtains pulsed inky black. The ringtone stopped, then started again. I pushed up onto my elbow and blinked into awareness. The clock read 2:18 a.m. Far too early for a Saturday morning. "Hello?"

"Kasie, it's me," Andrew's frantic voice said.

I forced myself to push back the covers and sit up. "Is everything okay?" Given the time, I already knew the answer.

"Becca's sick," he said. "She puked all over herself and her bed. I put her in the bathroom and pulled off her sheets, but she puked again all over the floor."

I climbed out of bed and padded to my closet. "I'll come over and help."

"I can clean up the mess. I . . . I'm not sure if I should take her to the doctor." I could hear the worry in Andrew's voice. "I don't want to call Hope if it's just a passing thing 'cause I know she'll worry, but what if it's not just a passing thing and Becca's sick with something more?"

"If it were you, would you go to the doctor?" I put the phone on speaker and pulled on a pair of cotton pants.

Andrew paused before answering. "No. I'd wait to see if it passed."

"Then, don't take her yet. I'll be right over." After hanging up, I dressed comfortably and slipped on a pair of flip-flops. Then I pulled my hair in a short ponytail and left a scribbled note for Tucker on the kitchen counter.

Andrew answered the door before I could knock. He wore joggers and a dark-blue T-shirt. Dark stubble covered his jaw. Even in the dead of night, he looked good. Warm. Inviting. And I had a desperate urge to wrap my arms around his middle and snuggle in tight. Thankfully, he flipped on the porch light and startled some sense into me. "Thanks for coming," he said.

I stepped inside and left my keys on a table near the door. "Where's Becca?"

"In the bathroom, crying for her mom." Andrew looked defeated.

"Aren't pilots supposed to hold their cool in stressful situations?" I teased.

Andrew rubbed a hand across his stubbled cheek. "I think this is worse than an engine malfunction."

I scoffed and walked down the hall. "Is Cole still asleep?" I asked on a whisper.

"All the commotion woke him up. He's in his room playing a game on the iPad," Andrew said.

"At three in the morning?"

"I'm not vying for babysitter of the year. I'm just hoping we all survive the weekend." Andrew stepped into the bathroom doorway. "Becca, look who's here."

The poor girl sat on a blanket on the tiled floor. "I want Mama!" Tears leaked from her eyes, and the smell made me want to wretch. I tried not to breathe too deeply.

"Hey, Becca girl. Mom can't be here right now, so Andrew and I are gonna take care of you." I touched the top of her head as I stepped over her and started some bathwater. "Let's get you cleaned up so you can feel better, okay?"

"I want Mama," she cried again.

"Did you start a load of laundry?" I asked Andrew.

"Not yet," he said.

"Why don't you grab some clean pajamas for Becca, and I'll help her while you get the laundry going."

Andrew and I worked for the next hour, cleaning, disinfecting, and trying to assure Becca she would feel better soon. I urged her to sip some water, but she gulped down half the glass. We hunkered down on the couch, watching a cartoon movie. Cole sat next to Andrew, and I held Becca on my lap with a bowl. Fifteen minutes later when she vomited the water back up, the mess was at least contained.

By five in the morning both kids had fallen back asleep. Becca was curled up in my lap, clutching her favorite blanket, which had thankfully been saved from the puke. Cole had claimed Andrew's right shoulder, and I leaned on Andrew's left shoulder.

My head slipped forward and I jerked awake. Andrew's head lulled against the back of the couch, and a breathy snore escaped his open mouth. The scene resonated with intimacy, and I took a moment to wonder, if different choices had been made, could this have been a glimpse of us? His kissable jaw, only inches away, tempted my lips. The warmth of his body as I leaned in to his side dared me to snuggle closer. I was tempted to carry Becca to her bed and return to the couch to curl into Andrew's arms. Despite the turmoil of the last few hours, being beside him felt right. And that thought made me bolt upright with a startled gasp. Andrew's eyes flashed open.

"Sorry," I whispered and leaned away, determined to put some space between us.

Andrew moaned and looked at his watch. "What a night." He shook his head as if trying to clear it.

"They're both sleeping well now," I said. The poor kids had to be exhausted.

"Wait here. I'll come back for Becca." Andrew shifted his hips and scooped his arms beneath Cole. He carried Cole to his room and then retrieved Becca from my lap.

I stood and shook out my legs, then followed him to her room. Her bed hadn't been remade, so I hurriedly spread a blanket over the mattress. Andrew laid her down, and I tucked another blanket around her and followed him from the room.

He scrubbed a hand across his whiskered cheek, then wrapped his fingers around the back of his neck. "I can't thank you enough."

"You may not be out of the woods yet. Cole might get it." I yawned a huge, mouth-gaping yawn, laughing as I covered my mouth with my hand.

Andrew smiled. His dimples appeared. "Well . . . I know how to reach you," he said.

"Yeah, you do," I said, wondering why my stomach got fluttery thinking of Andrew's name lighting up my phone.

I slept for ninety minutes before Noah's high-pitched scream woke me. I texted Tucker a brief summary of my night, buried deep into my covers, and went back to sleep.

Shortly before noon I crawled out of bed. The house sat quiet. Tucker must have taken Noah out. Exhaustion settled through my limbs, though considering I'd managed over five hours of sleep, I didn't understand why. I sat at the table eating a bowl of Cheerios when Tucker walked through the door with Noah.

"Kasie!" Noah's welcome smile lifted the fog from my brain. He ran to where I sat.

"Hey, sweet boy." I lifted him into my lap and poured some Cheerios from the box onto the tabletop, where Noah snatched them up.

"Feel better?" Tucker asked.

"Yeah." I nodded. "Where'd you guys go?"

"We walked over to the stables and watched the horses." Tucker sat at the table.

"I didn't know there were horses on base." Military life continued to surprise me.

"Lots of bases have stables for the military members to house their horses. Wendy told me about them at church. She boards her horse there," Tucker said. I'd shoved a bite of cereal into my mouth, but Tucker noticed my raised brows. "She runs the nursery."

"The brown-haired woman just older than me?" I asked.

"Yeah," Tucker said. "She suggested I bring Noah by sometime."

I swallowed. "And Wendy was there?"

"No, but an older woman named Louise let Noah pet her horse."

I twisted and looked at Noah. "Did you like the horses?"

"Horses," Noah repeated. He began bouncing in my lap. "Horses."

Tucker laughed. "We'll go see them another time, Nono."

I moved Noah to his high chair and sliced a banana for him to eat while Tucker showered. After Tucker finished and settled Noah down for a nap I sat at the desk in my room, reading through an online theatre forum. The chat revolved around a new workshop premiering in London. I clicked on the posted link, read the details, and let out an audible gasp. A six-month course at the England Academy of Dramatic Arts focused on adaptations of contemporary works through devised movement and stage design. The program sounded divine. I'd always been interested in bringing stories to the stage, and the study of movement and its effect on a production had long been a favorite of mine.

The first session would begin in June, but there was also a smattering of dates trickling into the following year. Mom and Dad would be home a year from now, next April. I scrolled down—May 13 of next year. I hesitated only a moment before clicking the link and opening the application. Each course allowed fifteen students, so my chances were slim. Still, I could manage the required essay and the twenty-five-pound application fee. And if I did get selected . . . giddy hope rippled through me. I could get my foot in the door. Make contacts. Be in London. Sure, it was still a year out, but they would release the accepted names in early summer. If I was offered a slot, I'd have the confirmation that God wanted me in London.

I texted a link for the program to Annabelle. She preferred set design, but maybe she'd want to branch out. The application would take some time, and I needed to update my résumé, but I bookmarked the tab and opened a new document to begin typing my essay.

My phone buzzed with a text, and Andrew's name appeared. I held my phone almost reverently. This morning I had longed for this connection so opposite of everything I had convinced myself of a year ago. My muddled mind couldn't reconcile the fluttering in my heart with the reasoning in my head. I sighed in confusion and read the text.

Andrew: *Did you get some sleep?*

Me: *Yeah. You?*

Andrew: *A little. These kids have built-in alarms.*

Hope had mentioned her kids woke early, like 6:30 a.m. early. Andrew had a long night, and if the kids got up on their regular schedule, that meant he'd gotten very little sleep.

I didn't give my brain time to reason before I texted, *Want me to take the kids for a while so you can sleep?* I could take my laptop and work on my essay at the Nottinghams'.

Andrew didn't text back right away, which in my estimation meant the answer was an obvious *yes* but he felt bad saying so. I closed my laptop and slipped on some shoes.

Tucker sat in front of the TV watching the history channel.

"Hey, I'm going to go next door for a bit," I said. "Let me know if you want to do something together when Noah wakes up."

"Wait. What?" Tucker muted the program and looked over his shoulder. "Did Hope and Ian come back?"

"Not yet," I said. "But Andrew didn't get much sleep, so I thought I'd keep an eye on the kids while he takes a nap."

Tucker's eyes narrowed, and he stared at me as if he knew I questioned whether or not this was a good idea.

"What?" I feigned innocence.

He shook his head. "I hope you know what you're doing."

"Just helping out a neighbor," I said.

Tucker chuckled. "Just any old neighbor."

"Exactly." I offered a smile and a wave. "I'll be back," I said and made a quick exit before Tucker could say anything more.

I crossed the lawn and Cole opened the door. "Hi, Miss Kasie."

Andrew appeared behind him. His short hair was a mess, matted on one side and sticking out in various directions on the other. His harried eyes were a confirmation of a long night with very little sleep.

"I think it's my shift," I said. I refrained from commenting on his appearance.

Andrew rubbed a hand over the matted side of his head. "Kasie. Hi." He stepped back from the door. "Come in."

I dropped my phone and keys onto the table near the door. "How's Becca doing?" I asked.

"I gave her toast and applesauce for breakfast, like you said, and she kept it down." Andrew walked to the table where Becca was coloring a flying unicorn.

"You feeling better, Miss Becca?" I realized how I'd addressed her and chuckled. The sweet Southern habits were rubbing off on me. I ran my fingers through her hair and pulled it back over her shoulder.

She nodded and Cole answered. "Andrew told Mama not to come home yet, and she said she's gonna bring us a surprise."

"Oh!" I grinned. "I like surprises. That will be fun." Cole skipped back to the front room, where a car track was spread across the floor. I turned to Andrew. "You might get better sleep if you go back to your place. We'll be fine."

His face shifted to an adorable combination of disbelief and gratitude. "Really?"

I couldn't help but laugh. "Yes. Go." I waved him toward the door.

He didn't need more encouragement. He went to the guest room, grabbed his wallet and keys, and headed for the door. "You always were an angel, Kasie."

I thought on his comment too many times while Cole and I worked on connecting the car track, making overpasses and jumps. Becca shot the cars out of the launcher to test our engineering skills. I sliced apples to snack on and discovered a list of meals Hope had left for Andrew. At three thirty, I set the oven to low and placed Hope's chicken casserole inside. I hashed out five hundred words on my application essay while the kids watched a show.

We were drawing with chalk on the driveway, enjoying the fresh air, when Andrew returned. He parked on the street to spare our artwork.

"Feel better?" I asked as he climbed out of his car.

"So much better. I owe you." He opened the back door and pulled out a bouquet of spring flowers. His hair was still slightly damp, and he wore jeans and a pressed button-down shirt, but his face remained stubbly and unshaven. "You deserve more than this, but I didn't want to keep you waiting." He held the flowers forward.

The cellophane crinkled as I accepted his offering. "You didn't have to do anything."

“Neither did you.” He shrugged and his dimples appeared. “You rescued me last night and again today. I wanted you to know I’m grateful. Plus, I like you.” His grin made my pulse speed.

“Pretty!” Becca exclaimed.

I lowered the bouquet for her to admire, but I looked at Andrew. Our eyes locked, and as subtle as the fragrance of the flowers, something passed between us. A small acknowledgment of recognition. More than our shared middle-of-the-night experience, a familiar spark of interest burned like the warm embers buried under the cooled ash. Something had shifted. A connection beyond the simplicity of helping a neighbor. But that possibility existed in a different time and a different place, where we could simply be a boy and a girl, aloof from our dreams pulling us in different directions. Standing on a military base on the border of Texas, I was an aunt and a sister, and Andrew was a student pilot on track to meet his goal. Those designations fought a fierce battle in my chest, struggling to mute the pounding of my heart.

CHAPTER 4

Becca's stomach bug hit me hard and fast. At eleven o'clock Saturday night, Tucker found me kneeling over the toilet regretting my second helping of dinner. He brought me a blanket, a water bottle, and a headband to hold my hair away from my face, and then I waved him away.

"You and Noah do not want this," I said. I heard the door click closed, and my stomach clenched again.

The long hours slowly ticked by, and once my stomach had emptied, I crawled back to my room and texted Tucker to only use his bathroom until I could clean the shared bathroom. I hoped Andrew didn't get sick since Hope and Ian wouldn't be home until the following evening. If he did get the stomach bug, there was nothing I could do to help him. I was out of commission.

Tucker took me to my word and steered clear. I texted him a request to drop crackers and a Sprite at my door, and I didn't emerge until after Noah had gone to bed Sunday night.

"Should I take tomorrow off work?" Tucker asked.

"I'll be okay." I sat at the table and bent over to press my cheek against the cool wood. "Becca felt better after twenty-four hours, so by morning I'll be tired, but I don't think I'll be contagious. Noah and I will just have a chill day."

"Are you sure?" Tucker asked. "At church I told Wendy you were sick, and she offered to take Noah tomorrow."

I lifted my head from the table. "Wendy with the horses?" I asked.

Tucker nodded.

"That's nice of her. Does she have kids at home?" I asked.

Tucker hesitated a beat before answering. "She's not married. I mean, she was, but she's divorced. They didn't have any children before they split."

I mumbled an incoherent sound, then laid my head back on the table. I wanted to say more. To ask Tucker if he'd left Noah and gone to Sunday

School after the sermon today. Or had he stayed in the nursery and talked to Wendy? Since Stacy's funeral, his care and love for Noah had never wavered, and he gave a hundred percent at work, but he'd been the antithesis of social. Telling me about a conversation he'd actually had with someone was new. Perhaps Tucker appreciated her attention to Noah, and maybe he purposely avoided Sunday School and all the questions people would ask.

"Anyway, she can take him tomorrow, if you'd like. Noah seems to like her, and I have her number." Tucker set a plate with a scrambled egg in front of me.

"Thanks." I sat upright and took a bite. "I think I'll be okay, but if you want to wait another day to make sure I don't give it to Noah, that might be a good idea."

"I'll give her a call and see if she's still free." He walked to the sliding door and stepped outside before dialing. I ate another bite of eggs and pondered my growing curiosity about my brother and the nursery leader.

When Tucker reappeared at the sliding door, Hope stood beside him in the doorway. "Oh my goodness, Kasie. I am so sorry." Her face scrunched.

"It's not your fault," I said.

"I know it can't be helped, but Andrew told me how great you were with Becca and how you watched the kids, and now Tucker said you're sick." She clapped her hand over her heart. "I swear I'm never gonna leave my kids again."

"A stomach bug is never fun, but I'm already on the upswing." I pointed to my partially empty plate. "Tucker's taking care of me."

"It's a role reversal of the last month," Tucker said.

Hope tsked and shook her head. "Y'all should have demanded our return. You're probably cursing my name."

"You and Ian deserved a weekend away. We survived," I said. Though, I did hope Noah wouldn't get it. "Has Andrew caught it?"

"Not yet." Hope held up crossed fingers. "He said you were a godsend." The compliment sifted through me, and I couldn't decipher the prickly feeling left behind. Hope pegged me with a no-nonsense stare. "I told Tucker I'm bringing dinner tomorrow."

"That's not necessary," I said, though I knew it wouldn't make a difference.

"I told her the same thing," Tucker said.

"Maybe not, but it will make me feel better." Hope turned to leave and called back over her shoulder. "I'm throwing in dessert too."

"Thank you!" I called after her.

Tucker laughed and stepped inside. "Wendy said she'll watch Noah while I'm at work. I also called Ian and he said I could come in late, so I'll drop Noah off at Wendy's house at eight and then head in."

"You got her address?" I asked.

"Duh," Tucker teased. "She lives right off base."

I leaned back and stretched my legs out to rest on the seat of another chair at the table. "Well, could you share her phone number and her address with me? I'd like to know where my nephew is."

"I'll share her contact. All the info's there." Tucker tapped his phone.

My phone dinged a few seconds later. "Wendy Stockman," I said aloud.

Tucker planted his hands on his hips. "Yeah?"

I acted innocent. "She's taking Noah for the day. As his coguardian, I have the right to be curious." I tilted my head to watch my brother. "What else can you tell me about her?"

"Not much." Tucker shrugged. "She works on base as a housing coordinator. She requested the transfer to Texas a year ago to put some distance between herself and her military ex-husband. Her horse is named Honky, and she owns a cat named Fran."

Turned out, Tucker could tell me quite a lot about Ms. Wendy Stockman.

The next day I read and then binged the first half of a mystery series on Netflix. Around noon I called Annabelle.

"No kissing yet, huh?" she teased.

"I don't plan on any kissing," I said.

"Those words might come back to haunt you." She laughed. "Did you get your application in for the England Academy of Dramatic Arts?"

"I'm finishing up the final few things. I know it's a long shot, but I figure it can't hurt," I said.

We talked about Annabelle's current job working with a local high school to build a set for their spring play. "I work with the students, then head straight to *Macbeth* rehearsals."

I asked if she'd read through the script I was working on. "Sure thing," she said. "As long as you keep me posted on all the Andrew drama."

"I'm hoping to keep that to a minimum," I said. We hung up just as Tucker texted he had finished work and was on his way to pick up Noah. I could have managed watching my nephew, but he would have been bored and

I would have been irritable. Beyond some lingering tiredness, my stomach had finally settled, and I felt almost normal. The doorbell rang at five thirty sharp, and I opened the door, expecting to find Hope. Instead Andrew stood on the welcome mat with a basket of food in hand.

I quickly ran my fingers through my unbrushed hair.

"Hey," he said. "Hope forgot she had a PTA meeting tonight, so she asked me to bring this over. I heard you caught Becca's flu." His face scrunched into the cutest expression. "I'm so sorry. You should have told me."

"You had your hands full. Besides, Tucker took Noah and I slept." I shrugged. "I'm mostly better now."

"Still, I could have brought medicine or something," Andrew said.

"Something like dinner?" I teased, eyeing the basket of food he held. "I really am feeling better, but Hope's a good cook and she wouldn't take no for an answer." I stepped back so Andrew could enter.

"Did Noah get sick?" Andrew asked.

"No. At least, not yet. The nursery leader from church took him for the day, so I've been resting and reading, and my appetite is finally back."

"Well, it smells good." He lifted the basket a little higher. "Homemade soup and bread and a salad."

"Sounds delicious." I led Andrew to the dining room table, and he began to lift the containers of food from the basket and set them on the table.

"And cookies, of course." He set a plate of oatmeal cookies next to the food.

My phone buzzed, and I pulled it out to find a text from Tucker. *Wendy made Noah dinner, so we're going to eat with her. Be home after.*

I texted back, *Remember Hope offered to bring us dinner?*

Tucker's reply came quickly. *I can take it to work tomorrow for lunch.*

"Everything okay?" Andrew asked.

Tucker's actions grew my suspicions. "Yeah, I think so," I said.

Curiosity filtered through Andrew eyes. I knew him well enough to know he wanted to ask more, but instead he said, "I'm sorry again that you got sick though. I owe you big time." Andrew picked up his delivery basket.

"Can I cash in on that?" I asked. My heartbeat quickened. I wasn't great at improv, but my mother had always told me I was impulsive.

Andrew cocked his head. "Now?"

I held up my phone, knowing I treaded a fine line. A bold line. But I couldn't resist drawing it. "Tucker won't be home for a while, and I can't eat all of this by myself." I waved my hand over the food Andrew had set out.

Andrew shifted his weight, and his dimples appeared with his grin. "Are you asking me to dinner, Kasie?"

"Forget it," I said, trying to backpedal. "I don't want to overstep or give you the wrong idea." The internal tug-of-war, the back-and-forth—my mind and my heart kept throwing punches, and I didn't know if I was being tough or simply getting beat up.

Andrew reached for my hand and held it between his own. "I'd love to have dinner with you."

"I don't mean anything by it," I said, though my breathless words contradicted my statement. I slipped my hand free.

"I know," Andrew said. "We'll figure it out, Kas. I promise."

"It's just nice not to eat alone," I said. A truth with a caveat. I needed to keep reminding myself that we weren't meant to be together. This easy conversation and happy moment held the possibility of hurt. Texas spread so big and wide, and over the last two months I had felt a bit like the lone star on the state flag. Andrew's smile quelled some of the loneliness. He had been more than a boyfriend. He had been my best friend, and I really needed one right now.

We dished up, and I offered a prayer over the food. When I opened my eyes, Andrew sat with his hands clasped, staring at me.

"What?" I asked, my voice sounding pitchy and off.

Andrew gave a small shrug, then lifted his fork and pulled his napkin onto his lap. "I wonder where we went wrong." He paused and evaluated me before looking at his plate of salad. "Where I went wrong."

We'd talked through this numerous times. Andrew had insisted we could find a way to move forward. He felt we could support each other in our dreams. My argument, pointing to the fact that our dreams were on opposite sides of the globe, had never fully convinced him. In the end I could only tell him I didn't understand but being together didn't feel right.

"We had two different paths," I said.

"But those paths intersected again, and now here we both are," he said.

Here we were, sitting three feet apart instead of thousands of miles away from one another.

"Maybe this was God's plan all along," Andrew said before taking another bite.

My heart clenched and I stared at my soup. "I'm only here because my sister-in-law isn't. She suffered. She died. She left her husband and son way too soon. Do you think her cancer was part of God's plan?" I raised my eyes to Andrew's.

"That's not what I meant, Kasie." His eyes caught mine, pulling me in as if he could read the tender feelings etched into my heart. "You know me better than that."

I took a slow breath. I knew his comments were neither malicious nor presumptuous. He was simply trying to figure out the purpose of our circumstance. I was confused with our situation, too, so I couldn't fault him for feeling the same.

"I don't know why your sister-in-law got sick. We don't know God's ways and why things happen when they do." He pulled his hand back in front of him. "I'm just shocked that I thought I had lost you, yet here we are, sitting together." I didn't know how to feel about the fact that his thoughts echoed mine. "I'm grateful we can do this. We were friends before we were something more. I miss our friendship. I've missed you."

Andrew's words gave me a lot to consider. Why? Why were we both here? Where did coincidence end and Providence begin? I twirled my fork over my salad plate, wondering over the questions that kept resurfacing without a plausible answer.

"Let's eat the soup before it gets cold," Andrew said. His enthusiasm was both forced and sincere. He wanted to be happy, so he made it happen.

I nodded, and after a few minutes of silent bites, Andrew asked, "What funny Noah stories do you have to share?"

Noah made for a much easier topic of conversation. "He tried to kiss the computer a few days ago on a video call with my parents. It was my mom's fault, really. She asked him for a kiss and leaned her cheek near the screen. Noah complied, and I got a lovely drool mark on my screen."

"I bet your Mom loved that," Andrew said.

"She did." I smiled, remembering Mom's delight mixed with tears. It was hard for her to be far away.

"How are your parents doing?" Andrew asked. "I never had a chance to meet them."

We had talked about Andrew meeting my family, before everything had gotten complicated. Mom and Dad had planned to travel from Colorado to California, but a huge snowstorm had derailed their plans. Followed by the breakup and then Stacy's diagnosis, they hadn't ended up coming until the following August, when I graduated.

"They love serving the people, but Dad's been a little too adventurous in sampling the local cuisine and he's gotten food poisoning several times."

"Yuck. The stomach bug and I are not friends."

"Yeah." I laughed. "A little too relatable, huh?" I grabbed a second roll. "He's been told he'll adjust; it just takes time."

We finished eating and cleaned up. I'd forgotten how smoothly we could transition from working side by side in the kitchen to sitting side by side on the couch. Everything familiar and beautiful was a natural transition. I had missed it, and emotion tugged at my heart in all sorts of ways.

My legs were pulled up beneath me on the couch cushion, and Andrew sat a mere three feet away. The evening had been enjoyable. Happiness lifted with hope that we could live peaceably near each other and perhaps even renew our friendship. "Can I ask you a question?" I hesitated only because for all that Andrew knew of my dreams, I knew his as well.

"Sure," he said.

I'd learned that the trainer airplanes Andrew now flew were for pilots training to fly cargo planes, or as the military called them, heavies. Sure, Andrew would get his wings, but not for the airplane he'd dreamt about.

"I thought you wanted to fly fighters," I said.

"Yeah, well . . ." He offered a rueful smile. "Pilot training opened my eyes. I changed my mind." His words surprised me. He'd talked about flying at Mach speeds more times than I could remember. He sighed. "Most everyone comes in wanting to fly fighters, but only a few slots are available, and when the time came . . ." Andrew lifted his shoulder. "It didn't feel right, so I opted for heavies."

Wow. For all the explaining I'd done a year ago, my explanation that "it didn't feel right" had been difficult for Andrew to accept. He'd wanted a more concrete thread to pull, one he could tangibly unravel or snip off so he could convince me we could work. Maybe he better understood now, even if it was at the detriment of what he'd thought he wanted.

"But you seem . . . happy." I tried to think of another word, but *happy* fit the bill.

His eyes softened. "I learned quickly how stressful flying can be," he said. "For me, flying fighters would always have a high level of stress because the inherent mission is combat. Some of the heavies have intense missions, but carrying cargo started sounding more appealing than carrying missiles."

"So you're okay going this route?" I asked.

"I am," Andrew said. I allowed my eyes to scan his face. I believed him. "The missions are varied, and I still want to do well and get my top pick of aircraft, but honestly, if the drop happened tomorrow, I don't know yet which plane I'd pick."

We continued to chat about training and the air force, and almost two hours had passed when Tucker walked in carrying a sleeping Noah. Andrew's demeanor changed in a single breath. He jumped to his feet and stood at attention. "Hello, sir," he said.

Tucker froze. His jaw tightened, and he looked between Andrew and me. I rose slowly and walked to my brother. Since I'd been exhausted and then sick, he'd been going nonstop for three days. "Want me to change him and put him down?" I asked.

"No," he snapped. "I'll do it." He dropped the diaper bag to the floor and glared at Andrew while speaking to me. "Looks like you're feeling better." His sarcasm swept the simple contentment from the room.

His ire stoked mine. "Much better, thank you. Remember how Hope offered to make us dinner? I didn't want to eat alone, so when Andrew brought it over, I asked him to join me." My faux smile dripped sickly sweet. "Did you enjoy dinner with Wendy?"

"It was fine." Tucker huffed, but a hint of guilt flashed through his eyes. "I'm going to get Noah to bed." He walked down the hall to the bedrooms.

I took a calming breath, then turned to Andrew with an apology on my lips. He spoke first. "I should get going," he said. His posture remained tense, but his shoulders fell. He walked to the door, and I followed him outside.

"Sorry about Tucker," I said, shoving my hands into my back pockets. "I think he's really tired."

"Eh, well, I probably crossed a line." Andrew pulled his keys from his pocket and unlocked his car.

"What do you mean? I invited you to stay." I felt like I'd missed something imperative.

We walked to where he had parked. "I'm a student. Tuck's an instructor. Ian tries to steer clear so there's no bias, but everyone knows we're related and there's still mumblings of preferential treatment. Bottom line is I shouldn't be hanging out at an instructor's house." He opened the car door.

I stood close, wanting to understand. "My brother wasn't even home. This has nothing to do with him. I'm the one who invited you."

"People don't care about the details. Besides, it's all semantics. I belong on the student side of base. Not here." From the firm set of his eyes, I knew his opinions would not be swayed. At least tonight.

I took a step back and stood on the grass. "Well, for what it's worth, I enjoyed tonight," I said before realizing the implication. "You know, catching up and stuff," I quickly tacked on. My heart sped. It had been a great evening.

"I did too." A small smile touched his lips. "Thanks, Kasie. It was nice to remember our friendship and all the good stuff and forget reality for a little while." He climbed into his car and shut the door before I could ask what he meant about forgetting reality.

Tucker could not escape so easily. He owed me some answers. While Andrew's taillights grew smaller, my frustration grew larger. I found Tucker in the kitchen, pouring a glass of juice. As much as I wanted to yell at him, I reined in my temper. "Did Noah go down okay?" I reached to the cabinet in front of him and got a glass. He filled it with juice too.

"Yeah. Wendy said they played all day, so he was tired." Tucker returned the juice to the refrigerator and sat down at the table.

I joined him, setting my glass in front of me and turning the base slowly around and around. "Is there a reason Andrew shouldn't be here?" I asked.

"There are several." Tucker planted his elbows on the table and scrubbed his hands over his hair. I waited, rotating my glass in another tidy little circle. Tucker would talk eventually. He dropped his arms to the table and looked at me. "What are you doing, Kas?"

"We had dinner. That's it," I said quickly, though I realized I felt lighter than I had in a long time.

"You two had your chance. It didn't work, and your heart broke. Why waste your time if it won't go anywhere?" Tucker asked.

"Andrew is focused on training. I'm here for you and Noah. Nothing has changed." I sighed and confessed. "It was nice to talk to him, Tucker."

Tucker's jaw tightened. "I don't want to see my baby sister get hurt. That doesn't make me the bad guy."

"I don't expect anything from Andrew. We went our separate ways, and that won't change because we had a meal together." Though, as Andrew had pointed out, our paths had led us back together. "What's going on, Tucker? You kind of acted like a jerk. I haven't seen you like that since Jason Jacobs tried to frame you for the marijuana the principal found in his locker."

Tucker's gaze focused like it was set on target lock. He sat unblinking, contemplating, until he said, "Beyond the past you two have, Andrew's a student. I'm an instructor."

"And I'm a nonmilitary civilian who happens to be living on base." I wrapped both hands tightly around my glass.

"In officer housing." Tucker stared at the ceiling over my head and sighed. "Kas, I want you to be comfortable here; I do. But here on base, rank matters."

Despite the many stereotypes of military members, I'd never seen Tucker hoity-toity, all full of himself. "'Rank matters'?" I squeezed my glass tighter. "So it's fine if we hang out with the major next door because he ranks higher than you, but if someone ranking lower than you wants to be friends, you get to play the superiority card?"

Anger laced the lines in Tucker's forehead. "You've been on base a handful of weeks. You don't get it. Pilot training is different. Our job is to throw everything we've got at these students." His hands flew to the side.

Things were becoming clear. "To wash them out," I filled in.

"No." Tucker placed his hands flat on the table and leaned forward. His voice dropped to barely a whisper. "To make sure that when they fly in combat, they survive. Do you have any idea what that's like? To differentiate between an enemy and an ally? Their maneuvers and emergency procedures have to become second nature. They have to know their boldface checklists backward and forward. They need to prove they can work under pressure, understand the importance of the mission, and multitask when they lose an engine or a crewmember. They're not training to be airline pilots who fly to the Caribbean. These airmen are training to fight in war, and if I do my job and push them to the limit, they have a better chance of success. We push so they can survive." He took one deep breath, then another. He sat straight and folded his arms across his chest. "Andrew needs to focus on training. Sorry, Kas, but you really have no idea what he's going through right now."

Tucker's words rattled me. "What do you mean?" I asked. I didn't doubt the training was important, but maybe I had failed to see the larger picture.

"Some people are meant to fly. Others are better off on the ground." Tucker snatched his glass and stood. "It doesn't matter what airframe they're in—they will get shot at. They will have maintenance emergencies. Lives will depend on them and their training. Andrew's focus needs to be on training, not flirting with you."

I pushed back from the table and followed Tucker to the sink. "I know it's dangerous, Tucker. That's inherent if you're in the military, but are you saying Andrew is in trouble?"

Tucker rinsed his cup and set it on the counter. He faced me and crossed his arms, leaning back against the countertop. "I can't tell you anything. You know that."

"But you are hinting at something." I looked up at my brother, using my best please-tell-me expression.

"The class has already lost six members. The group's been thinned, and they've made it through track select, but passing the first two phases doesn't put them in the clear. They still have to graduate from phase three, and a few of the students are struggling. At this point, distractions can be detrimental. I can't tell you anything more." Tucker flipped off the kitchen light. "I'm tired, and I've gotta work early tomorrow. Good night, Kas."

"Good night," I mumbled and moped back to my seat at the table.

I sat in the dark and sipped my juice. The tree in the yard blocked the view of the sky, but I still glanced upward, thinking of the picture Tucker had painted. Combat. War. Enemies. What had felt so distant in my small corner of giant Texas could be the reality for these pilots. Chasing dreams was important. Despite everything, I cared for Andrew. I wanted him to find the success he'd worked so hard to achieve. Tucker was right. Andrew shouldn't spend time thinking about me or encouraging my love of theatre. No matter that tonight had been so great, so easy, so full of peace and calm, it now felt like the remnants of a drenched campfire—messy, doused, and hopeless. I'd acted on my heart and not used my head, and my impulsive invitation had backfired. I would text Andrew in the morning with a reminder of our separate paths. I would take a step back and encourage him in his training. He'd come too far to fail. My attentions would go to Noah. After all, that cute two-year-old was the boy I'd come to Texas for.

CHAPTER 5

Sleep only riddled my dreams with variations of texts to Andrew. How would I tell him that we needed to draw clearer lines, especially when I was so grateful that last night the lines had blurred? I hadn't realized the gaping hole that had come with my move to the Lone Star State. I had Tucker, and Hope had been great. My parents were always willing to talk, and so was Annabelle, but Andrew had filled my soul like none of them could. Whether from our connected past or the ties of friendship still weaving through our relationship, I couldn't say. I only knew that the few hours I'd spent with Andrew had been a balm to my soul. And now I needed to tell him I was fine without him, even if it wasn't true.

I settled on simplicity. *Thanks for eating with me last night. It was nice to catch up, but let's remember that we're still headed separate ways. Wishing you all the best in training.*

I read it at least five times before hitting Send. Then I left my phone on silent while I got ready for the day.

Noah and I went for a walk after breakfast, and by the time we returned, I still didn't have a response from Andrew. Maybe that was good. Maybe.

After Noah's nap we ventured to a community park in Del Rio and stopped at the grocery store on the way home. I strapped Noah in his high chair for a snack while I unloaded groceries, and after putting the milk in the refrigerator, my phone vibrated in my pocket.

Andrew: *Nice try, Kasie. Last night only confirmed that we're good together. I loved every minute with you. I'm ready to fight.*

He even included an emoji of a boxing glove. I knew I should grumble or take a firmer stance, but I couldn't deny the exuberant bubbles lifting my heart.

March 27 I sat playing blocks with Noah on the floor. He'd taken a long nap and was well rested. I stacked a tower high, and he giggled and shouted, "Boom!" as he knocked it down.

The doorbell rang, and I answered the door to a lovely woman in a flight suit. Her curly hair was pulled back in a tight bun, and she held a round chocolate-frosted cake. "Are you Kasie?" she asked.

I nodded and glanced at her nametag: Paula Desoto.

"Andrew asked me to bring this to you." She sported a knowing smile. "He tried to get it delivered sooner, but they wouldn't let the delivery guy through the gate." She extended the cake toward me. Across the top of the cake were the words *Happy Half Birthday*.

"Half birthday?" I said with a laugh, both amused and impressed that he'd remembered.

"Sounds like he was adamant about getting it to you. I don't even know the guy," Paula said, handing over the cake.

"Then, how did you get wrangled in?" I lifted the cake in question.

Paula shrugged. "I graduated from the academy with Harper. She's in his class and reached out to see if I could help." She glanced at her watch. "I've gotta run."

"Thank you," I said.

She turned toward her car, then called over her shoulder, "And happy half birthday!"

Noah had toddled over to stand beside me. One of his arms wrapped around my leg, and we waved goodbye as Paula drove away.

"Well," I said to Noah. "Do you want a piece of cake? It's from Andrew." I set the cake on the table and maneuvered Noah into his high chair, all while vocalizing my disbelief. If only Noah could help me make sense of all things Andrew. "My half birthday!" I exclaimed while making a goofy face at Noah. "Do you believe it? I haven't even talked to the guy for almost two weeks. Right when I think I've moved out of the danger zone, he drops another surprise."

Noah managed to get more frosting on his face than he got into his mouth. I laughed with him and enjoyed the cake, but after I took my last bite and swallowed a drink of milk, I looked at the wording at the top of the cake. It now read, *Happy Half Birt*. Andrew had always been thoughtful, but this . . .

I'd navigated the past few weeks of church carefully, making sure I exchanged only brief hellos or goodbyes with Andrew. Hope had tried several times to strike up a lengthier conversation, but I had dodged thus far. Despite my efforts to avoid him, he'd still found a way in.

I pulled out my phone, took a picture of Noah's messy face, and texted Andrew, *Thank you for the cake. Noah loved it.*

Forty-five minutes later I got a response. *I'm glad Noah enjoyed it, but I didn't get it for him. I wanted you to know that although I'm busy, I'm thinking of you—always.*

Slow and steady, I could feel my heart beat in my chest. It seemed silly, like a cheesy rom-com with sound effects framing a scene, but there it was. And I could not deny it.

I had dismissed Andrew's words as a fleeting assertion, something he'd thought was a good idea in the moment but would later realize our lives had shifted too much to see through to the end. I should have known better than to doubt him.

My heart was beating again, solid and strong. The rhythmic beat sounded like a drum. A call to action. One I felt drawn toward, a pull strong and constant. I only wondered, if I marched forward, if I entered the battle zone, would I come off conqueror, or would my heart be torn to pieces and left in a foxhole?

After dinner Tucker played with Noah and I retreated to my room to work on my script. I read over the last scene I'd written and started working through the dialog of the next scene when my phone lit with a call from Andrew. I'd always been a sucker for guilt. He'd been kind, and I didn't want to be rude, so I answered.

"Hey, Kasie. I wanted to say sorry I couldn't wish you a happy half birthday in person."

"I can't believe you even know when my half birthday is," I said.

"How could I forget? Celebrating your half birthday is one of my favorite memories," he said.

Andrew had always been nostalgic when it came to our relationship timeline. And I didn't know why I hadn't thought of it before, but at the mention of our celebrating my half birthday, I knew exactly what Andrew was referring to. March 27, two years ago, had been our first kiss.

We'd been spending a lot of time together. Study dates, walks, and even a few more formal dates. That evening Andrew had surprised me with tickets to a showing of *Come from Away* in Los Angeles. I'd tried to get tickets, but the available seats had been out of my price range.

"I know you really wanted to go," Andrew had said.

The show had proved incredible, and I'd been euphoric, gushing my thanks and reveling in all of Andrew's thoughtfulness as we drove back toward campus. Back at our complex, we sat together in the quad.

"It means so much that you would do this for me," I'd told Andrew.

He had pulled my hand into his and scooted close on the bench we shared. "I really like you, Kasie," he said. "You're easy to talk to, with the perfect amount of spontaneity and grit."

I'd teased him about those descriptors, but he'd said it was important to balance work and fun. "And you perfectly balance me," he said.

My heart had been near to bursting. I adored his frankness, his decisive ideals, and his ability to make me feel like sunshine. With a gentle tug on my hand, he had pulled me closer. One hand moved to my waist and with the other hand he had brushed my hair back, trailing his fingers along my cheek. Then slowly, ever so slowly, he had closed the distance between us. He had given me every chance to pull away. Every chance to press on the brakes and step back. But I hadn't wanted to. I'd wanted to wrap myself in all things Andrew. All of his warmth, his charm, his smile. So I'd moved in unison with him.

Even now I could remember the sensation of his lips meeting mine. Bursts of radiance had pulsed from somewhere deep in my gut, buoyant and clear. That kiss had confirmed my adoration for him.

"I remember that day," I told him.

"Kasie." Andrew's voice mellowed. "I want you to know I still care for you. I'll do all I can to convince you of that. A chocolate cake is just the start."

I didn't have a response to his words so I whispered good night and we ended the call.

Why did things that had once been so easy feel so . . . difficult? I kneeled at my bedside that night, begging God to grant me understanding. I didn't feel like talking to Andrew was wrong; it simply felt dangerous. I didn't trust myself to be able to remember the *why* of our breakup. I knew those hazel eyes and dimpled cheeks had magical magnetic powers. Add to that Andrew's good heart—I knew I didn't have the strength to walk away again. A year ago my prayers about our future had left me feeling all kinds of commotion. My stomach wouldn't settle, I'd tossed through the nights, and I couldn't focus on my schoolwork. Turmoil had reigned, which meant our relationship was wrong. Right? A flirtatious conversation and Andrew's kindness in sending cake needed to be compartmentalized. I'd made a decision, and I hoped God would remind me why.

April and Texas couldn't agree on a weather pattern. Rainstorms raged, followed by a galloping heat wave. The Friday after Easter, Hope invited our playgroup to her house for Popsicles and water play. The kids ran between the small plastic pool in the yard and the bubble-blowing sprinkler Hope had set up. Noah giggled for thirty minutes straight. I would have to get him a bubble sprinkler of his own.

Hope, Yasmin, Alyssa, Dixie, Marylou, Eloise, and I all sat in the slim patio shade. Alyssa was the only woman with one child. The others had two or more and were talking about an upcoming talent show.

"The elementary school hosts one every year to celebrate the students," Hope said.

"Ishmael wants to play the *Star Wars* theme on the piano," Yasmin said. "I wanted him to play something more refined, but my husband reminded me he's a nine-year-old in fourth grade, so *Star Wars* it is."

"Clara plans to dance. Thank goodness she remembers her tap routine from when we lived in Oklahoma." Alyssa batted away a bee. "And her costume still fits, so we're going with it."

"Cole said they aren't auditioning and anyone who wants to participate can. He's got me a bit worried," Hope said.

"Uh oh. What does he want to do?" Marylou asked.

"Has Rutherford not told you about it?" Hope asked, and Marylou shook her head. "They want to do a comedy skit with the two of them and Frankie Alvarez."

"Oh dear," Marylou said with a laugh.

"That could be fun," Dixie said.

"Those boys think they're hilarious, but half the time I don't even understand what they're saying," Hope said. Becca ran up, and Hope wiped the water from her eyes. "There ya are, darlin'." Becca ran back to the sprinkler and waved her arms as she ran under the falling droplets. Noah toddled beside her and mimicked her movements. Hope sighed. "Cole is determined to be a comedian. I've heard more knock-knock jokes in the past two weeks than I have in my entire life."

"I could help the boys," I said. The women all looked at me. "Managing a stage is kind of my specialty."

Hope widened her eyes. "You've seen these boys' antics. They won't be winning any prized pupil awards."

I smiled. "I could use a good challenge." My words rang true. Excitement fluttered in my chest at the idea.

"They will definitely be a challenge," Marylou said.

"I'm serious. It'll give Noah and me a project. Plus, I could use this." Caring for a child was not for the weary—Noah constantly moved and needed and tested—but I missed many parts of my pre-Texas life. I had been busy in an entirely different way. Wrangling three boys on a stage would serve as a good outlet.

Hope grinned and shook her head. "That's awfully sweet of you, Kasie. I won't pass up your offer if you're sure."

"Let's give it a go," I said.

"Rutherford will be so excited," Marylou said.

A little thrill pinged through me, and I began thinking through past performances and sketches for something that might work for three boys to win over a crowd.

Once Tucker got home, I passed off Noah duty and holed up in my room to complete the final steps of my application to the England Academy of Dramatic Arts. I called Annabelle with some final questions. She'd submitted her application last week and helped me clarify some of the credits I should highlight on my résumé.

"Thanks Annabelle. I think I'm all ready to submit," I said.

She squealed. "Can you imagine if we got into the program together?"

"That would be amazing."

I told her about my volunteering gig to help the boys at the talent show, and she reminded me of an online forum that offered free use of its materials. "Thanks for the reminder. It's a bit tricky to find something that fits their age and ability," I said.

"What's the Andrew update?" Annabelle asked.

She and I had talked and texted nearly every week. She knew everything up until the half-birthday dilemma. Recounting my conversation with Andrew elicited plenty of dramatic *ohh*s and *ahh*s.

"I hope you're writing all of this down in a diary or something. It'll make for a great script one day," she said.

I laughed. "Yeah, the story that goes on and on and on."

"Don't you wonder why that is?" she asked.

"What do you mean?"

"You keep circling back to each other. Isn't that kismet or fate or something? Like the universe is trying to tell you to figure it out?"

"Stupid universe," I said.

Annabelle laughed. "Maybe you just need to stop fighting it."

"Maybe," I said, wishing the universe and God would have a conversation and get on the same page, 'cause right now they were pulling me in opposite directions.

CHAPTER 6

I MET FRANKIE AND HIS mom, Emmaline, the following Friday. They were not a military family and owned a Mexican restaurant off base. Since Emmaline didn't have base access, we met at the municipal park, and Hope took charge of Noah so I could work with the three elementary school boys.

We sat around a picnic table, and I said, "Hey, guys. Why don't you tell me what you want to do for the talent show."

"We wanna tell jokes," Cole said.

"Why did the cookie go to the hospital?" Frankie said to no one in particular. "Because he felt crummy." All three boys giggled.

"Knock, knock," Rutherford said with wide eyes.

The other two boys replied in unison, "Who's there?"

"Who," Rutherford said.

"Who, who?" came the expected response.

Rutherford grinned wide. "Is there an owl in the house?"

For the next three minutes every classic knock-knock joke bounced around the table, and the boys laughed and laughed. Their laughter proved to be more entertaining than the jokes. I watched, silently calculating each of their strengths.

When the jokes began to slow, I added one of my own. "How do you make a Kleenex dance?" I smiled and looked at each of the boys.

"Turn on some music," Cole said.

I shook my head. "You put a little boogie in it."

They busted into laughter.

"Good one, Miss Kasie," Cole said.

"It's one of my favorites. Now, let's plan something amazing for the talent show." I gave them the elementary version of what I do, how I help transform a stage and pull the audience into the action. "You guys have some funny jokes, but do you only want to tell jokes, or do you want to perform a skit?" They pegged me with looks of confusion. "Have you guys ever seen Studio C?"

Frankie snorted a giggle. "It's funny."

"It is funny, but not because they're telling jokes. Instead, they act out a funny story. It's called a comedy sketch." I made sure each of the boys understood, then pulled out my phone and had them watch an example from YouTube. They laughed and repeated some of the punch lines. I set my phone down. "What do you say? Do you want to do something like this for the talent show?"

"Yeah!" Cole said, pounding his hands on the metal table. The other boys copied him, and it took me a moment to convince them to stop.

"Okay. What do you guys think of this?" I presented the idea I'd prepared: a series of puns and misunderstandings on a science project. We moved from the table to the grass, where I explained the parts to the boys and had them walk through an extremely rough semblance of the scene.

An hour passed quickly, but we had two weeks to perfect the sketch and the boys were eager to please. "I'll give your moms your parts, and you'll need to practice at home."

"Okay," Rutherford said. "Can we go to the slide now?"

I shooed them toward the play structure, and they ran while I walked.

Hope held Noah on her hip. "Poor guy took a little tumble," she said.

Noah's eyes glistened with tears. When he saw me, he reached out. My heart warmed as I took him in my arms and he sniffled into my shirt. "You're okay," I whispered into his hair and cuddled him close.

Hope leaned near so both Noah and I could hear her. "I told my kids we could have Popsicles when we get home. Do you think Noah would want one?"

I pulled back so I could see Noah's face. "What do you think? Does a Popsicle sound good?"

Noah smiled. "Popsicle," he said, dropping half the pronunciation.

I drove us back to the base and walked Noah over to the Nottinghams'. Cole ran out the front door and handed him a blue Popsicle. "Mama said she'd be out in a minute."

I helped Noah with the wrapper, then followed the kids to the side yard. Becca and Cole ran on the grass between our two houses, and when I sat down on the grass, Noah plopped into my lap.

A few minutes later Hope appeared. "Sorry. I was having words with Ian." She sat next to me in the grass.

"That doesn't sound fun," I said.

Hope sighed. "Andrew's mama called. Said she felt something was wrong with her boy and wanted an update. I guess they keep playin' phone tag. I couldn't tell her much 'cause I haven't seen Andrew lately." She turned abruptly. "Have you?"

"Only at church," I said, not mentioning how I still worked to avoid him.

"Hmm, I figured as much," Hope said.

Our renewed friendship was tender, like a dandelion weed. One puff and the fragile pappus might catch in the wind and blow away. I didn't want to go back to drifting uncertainty. We had a tenuous connection, and rooting anything deeper could only lead to heartache. Best to keep moving and not let Andrew catch up.

Hope's phone buzzed, and she flipped it over to check the screen. "Andrew hooked a ride last week, and now the commander's got his eye on him."

My heart jolted. "Hooked? That's not good, right?" I asked.

Hope's brow furrowed, and she shook her head. "It's basically failing a test. A big test, 'cause it's in the airplane. If they hook, they get two more chances. If things don't go well, they wash out."

"Done!" Noah turned and held up his empty Popsicle stick. His lips were stained blue, along with several fingers. I grabbed the end of his T-shirt and wiped first his face and then his fingers.

"Now, go play," I said, lifting him to his feet. He scooted off toward Becca, and I turned back to Hope. "So the commander gets involved? Does he want them to pass, or is he aiming to further thin the class?"

"Lieutenant Colonel Haggar is the nicest man. His call sign is Spitfire 'cause he can sport a sharp tongue, but he gives everyone a fair shake. He wants them all to succeed, but if a student doesn't cut it, he'll tell them straight up." Hope glanced at her phone again. She scoffed and shot off a text.

Worry pooled in my gut. "Will Andrew be okay?" I asked.

"Ian says it's fifty-fifty. That's why he got an earful." Hope smiled impishly and shrugged. "I know he's just doing his job and Andrew shouldn't get any favors, but there's gotta be some way Ian can help him out. Andrew has two more flights to prove himself."

"That sounds like a lot of pressure," I said.

Hope's phone buzzed again, and she looked at the incoming text. "The first of those flights is happening right now, and Tuck's the IP."

Tucker didn't make it home for dinner, and he still hadn't arrived by the time Noah settled into bed for the night. I tried to distract myself with a TV show, but nothing could quiet the worry bounding through my brain. The headlights of Tucker's car flashed in the window as he pulled into the carport.

I jumped up and waited. "Hey," I said the moment he stepped through the door.

He looked at me sideways and dropped his flight bag near the couch.

"Long day?" I asked.

"Long debrief." Tucker bent over and began unlacing his boots.

"Does that mean the student did well or . . . not so well?"

Tucker glanced up and gave me a knowing look. He shook his head and said nothing while he finished taking off his boots. "Is there something for dinner, or should I grab a bowl of cereal?"

I skipped ahead of him. "There're leftovers. I can heat up a plate."

Tucker used the restroom and then came into the kitchen and dropped into a seat at the table as the microwave dinged. I set a plate with rice, chicken, and veggies in front of him.

"Thanks." Tucker scooped up a bite, and I poured him a glass of juice before sitting in the chair beside him.

"So." I feigned a wide smile and rested my chin on my palm. "Did you have a rough flight?" Tucker stopped chewing for a beat and leveled me with a stare. "Geez, no need for the killer look. It's just a question." I dropped my arm to the table and sat up.

"You know who I was flying with." Tucker took a drink. "Did he tell you?"

"No!" I shot back. I tried to glare at Tucker, but his permeating stare far surpassed mine. I broke eye contact. "Ian told Hope, and I heard it from her," I said softly.

Tucker took another bite. After he swallowed, he asked, "How did Noah do today?"

I'd forgotten Tucker hadn't been home since six a.m.

"Good. We went to the park so I could work with Cole and his friends on the talent show. Noah fell and scraped his elbow, but he's fine. We had Popsicles, and he wanted me to read the same story three times before he went to bed."

Tucker scraped his bowl clean and leaned back in his chair. "The one about the teddy bear?"

"Yeah," I said. Noah loved the rhyming words.

"It's his current favorite." Tucker inhaled deeply. "Thank you, Kasie, again. I don't know how I would do this without you."

I poked Tucker in the side. "You wouldn't." I aimed for him again, but he grabbed my finger.

"I know." Tucker held my wrist and patted the top of my hand like my grandma used to do.

I tilted my head and blinked a few times. "So are you going to tell me about Andrew's flight?"

Tucker's smile slipped. "I can't. You know that." He stood and carried his plate and glass to the sink.

I jumped up and followed behind him. "Hope said he hooked one ride and had two chances to get back on track." I touched Tucker's arm.

Tucker sighed and shut off the water. "I need you to let it go, Kas."

I pulled my hand away. "Then, just tell me if you passed him."

"All I can say is it's been a rough day," Tucker said. "And not just for me."

That night I knelt beside my bed and prayed. My life had been blessed. I knew that. And while I'd experienced trials, including the loss of my sister-in-law and foregoing a year abroad to live in Del Rio, I trusted patience would prevail. God would make a path for me. I'd been blessed with comfort and peace and the knowledge that future doors would open and allow me to pursue my chosen career. But somewhere on the other side of the base, Andrew had to be wondering what his future held. I prayed he would feel the Lord's comfort and trust in His goodness.

Tucker would be the first to admit God's plan did not always parallel the path we plotted for ourselves. I wished he could tell me more. What happened? What were Andrew's chances of passing his next test? Why did all those years of dreaming come down to one last flight? One last chance to prove he could cut it?

When I entered the kitchen the next morning, Tucker had Noah strapped in his high chair. He placed a bowl of oatmeal in front of Noah. "There you go," he said, scooping the first bite into Noah's mouth before handing him the spoon.

"Did you get some rest?" I asked my brother.

"Not much, but I'm good." He got some oatmeal for himself and sat next to Noah, then pointed toward the stove. "There's enough for you."

How could he sit and calmly eat a bowl of oatmeal when, the day before, he'd crushed Andrew's dreams? My pulse pounded with my volatile emotions. I knew I didn't understand the intricacies of Tucker's job, but if Andrew had flown and landed the plane, why couldn't Tucker have cut him some slack? Instead he'd left Andrew with only one more chance. And why was I so fixated on Andrew's training, wondering if he was beating himself up or blaming my brother for his failed flight? I set high expectations for myself, and I knew how when I fell short I spiraled in self-doubt, fearing that I could never regain my footing. But eventually I would get my feet under me. I would dig deep and find my strength and determination. Now the turmoil churning through me as I thought of Andrew filtered like ice through my veins. I stood watching from the sidelines, and there was nothing I could do beyond wave my pompoms and shout encouraging words.

I needed a distraction. "I'm going to find some props for the boys' skit. I'll be gone for a few hours." I filled a glass with water and drank it all.

"Are you going to eat first?" Tucker asked, pinching his lips together and wiggling his nose to make Noah laugh.

"I'm not hungry," I said.

Tucker stood and gathered his and Noah's bowls. "No need to rush back," he said. "We'll probably walk to the stables."

"Will Wendy be there?"

"I think so." When Tucker didn't meet my gaze, I knew he planned to see her. I didn't know how I felt about it or why I thought my feelings mattered. I only knew I was angry with my brother, no matter how unfair my feelings were.

After I showered, I pulled out my tub of costumes and looked for items that might work for the boys' skit. Most everything I owned would be too large, but I found a few fun hats and wigs and made a list of props I hoped to find, like a magnifying glass and a Sherlock-esque hat. I figured Hope and I could make or modify the rest. I drove across base, where Del Rio had a Walmart, a Ross, and a small-scale department store. The city was not known for versatile shopping, but thanks to my status as Noah's coguardian, I had access to the Base Exchange, or BX. It wasn't huge, but I hadn't shopped in an actual retail store for three months, so I would compromise.

A poster advertising an air show hung in the glass door. I showed my ID card to the store employee and began wandering the aisles. I found the first prop but would need to order the hat online. Mom said I could spoil her grandson in her absence and she would reimburse me, so I decided to browse for Noah. I piled a pair of gray shorts, a cute military-kid tee, and another shirt with dinosaurs into my handheld basket before heading to the shoe section.

"Kasie?"

I returned the orange sports sandals I'd been holding to their shelf and turned to find Andrew walking toward me. His hazel eyes were dull, his smile forced.

"Hi," I said, trying to plunk a bunch of cheer into my tone and force a smile.

"I don't think those shoes will fit you." Andrew jutted his chin toward the infant sandals I'd been holding.

I appreciated his attempt at humor, but I knew his quirks and his tone well enough to recognize how he truly felt. "If they had them in purple, I think I could make them work," I said, trying to play along.

"Are you here with your brother?" Andrew asked.

I shook my head. "He has Noah. They don't get much time together during the week, so they play on the weekends, and I get some time to myself." Andrew gave a small nod, and I wondered if he was as angry with Tucker as I was. "I hope you get some downtime this weekend too. I hear training is . . . hard." I fidgeted with the handles of the shopping basket.

Andrew stared silently across the tops of the shelves of shoes. His voice was soft. "I bet you've heard more than that."

My heart ached for him. "Hope mentioned something yesterday. I heard it was rough, but I didn't get much info from Tucker." I leaned forward, wanting to offer support but not knowing how. "I . . . I'm sorry."

He offered a mirthless chuckle, and the veins in his neck pulled tight as he leaned his head back and sighed. I missed his dimples. We stood there, the awkward tension building with each tick of the clock. I shifted the basket to my other hand and opened my mouth to offer some lame excuse about needing to be on my way, but Andrew spoke first. "Did you say your brother has Noah all day?"

"Yeah."

Andrew swallowed, then turned to face me. "Are you up for an adventure?" His eyes lit with his question.

Alarm bells sounded in my gut. We'd shared all kinds of adventures only to have our happily-ever-after ending cut short. "What kind of adventure?" I asked.

"A trip to San Antonio?" One side of Andrew's lips tugged up, and a single dimple appeared. "Have you been yet?"

"I haven't. But we'd be getting a late start," I said. The city was over two hours away, and it was almost noon.

"Which is why it would be an adventure." Andrew's eyes never left my face. His expression proved hard to read. If I'd experienced the rough week he'd had, I would want to spend a day away. Forgetting. "I could show you the Alamo and the River Walk."

"Okay," I said, ignoring the pulsing siren of reason. Instead I latched on to a gossamer thread of excitement and the hope that spending the day together might help Andrew find his smile. "Let's go."

I texted Tucker not to expect me home until late and shared my plans so he wouldn't worry. Then I added two water bottles to my basket and checked out while Andrew grabbed a few more snacks for the car.

He followed me the two miles to my house, and I parked, not bothering to head inside before jumping into the passenger seat of Andrew's car.

I handed him a water bottle, then tipped mine forward. "Here's to an adventure," I said. Andrew smiled and touched his water bottle to mine in a toast.

Popping tunes streamed through the car speakers. Even if Andrew's mood wasn't upbeat, his music was. We drove east on highway 90, snacking on popcorn, dried fruit, and chocolate pretzels. Not the healthiest lunch, but I felt oddly content. It seemed the universe had once again placed Andrew and me on the same parallel, and it felt comfortable, everything opposite of my previous prayers about my relationship with Andrew. It was like God had granted his blessing for us to find each other, to comfort one another, today.

"I hear you're helping Cole with the talent show," Andrew said.

"I'm teaching the boys how to get laughed at in the right way," I said.

"That's important," Andrew said.

I glanced at him. "Are you going to make it to the performance?"

"If I can. You might not know this"—he smirked—"but I'm training to become a hotshot pilot, and it's not going so well. I might need to hunker down and study that day. Or I might"—he blew out a breath—"not even be around then."

Whoa. That turned heavy fast. My stomach knotted, and I stared out the windshield, offering a silent prayer that I would know what to do.

"Sorry. Our adventure barely started, and I'm already a downer." Andrew checked his blind spot and switched lanes.

I rolled up the top of the popcorn bag and set in on the floor behind the driver's seat. "I don't know what to say here."

"'You got this!'" He held up a fist. "Or how about, 'Shake it off!'" Abundant sarcasm laced each of his words. "'The third time's a charm.'" He scoffed at his self-mockery. "I wish it could be so easy," he said to himself as he returned his second hand to the steering wheel. "I was dumb to think phase three would be easier than the others."

Our adventure had turned too somber too quickly. "I'm sorry about my brother," I said.

"Tuck?" Andrew glanced at me, his brows scrunched together. "Oh, 'cause he was my IP?"

"I heard he flew with you yesterday." Then all the thoughts I'd reasoned around poured out. "His wife's death changed him. He used to be pretty mellow, but now it's like he constantly feels the need to be in control. He felt helpless during her disease, but there was nothing he could do. I'm sorry his control-freak side couldn't cut you some slack when you needed it." I'd probably said too much. I hadn't meant to throw Tucker under the bus, but I didn't understand. I clamped my lips shut.

A beat passed, then another. "I don't blame your brother. It wasn't his fault," Andrew said. His fingers tightened around the steering wheel. "It was all me." Then he laughed, a single chuckle at first, then another, and before thirty seconds had passed, he was laughing hard enough that I wondered if I should suggest he pull over. He did move to the slow lane. He wiped at his eyes and blew out a breath. "Sorry," he said. "It's just so stupid." He drummed on the steering wheel with his palm. "It was all my fault." Andrew shook his head. "I oversped the flaps."

I knew the flaps on the wings of the aircraft had something to do with speed, but I couldn't explain anything other than their location. Andrew clenched his jaw. Frustration washed across his features.

"I made a rookie mistake. No matter what else I did right, your brother had no wiggle room. When you overspeed the flaps, it's an automatic fail. That's on me, not Tuck," he said.

Pieces began to fall into place: Tucker's frustration when he got home as well as his reluctance to talk about it. Appropriate or not, if Andrew had passed, Tucker would have shared the news without a second thought. I was grateful to be wrong about my brother. I owed him an apology.

"Oh," I said lamely. "So that was why you hooked? I mean—you don't have to tell me. I know I'm being nosy," I said.

"Kas." Andrew breathed out my name like a blissful sigh. "I want to tell you. I want to share all of it. And the truth is I wanted to call you last night. I wanted to share with you because I knew you would understand. You get me. You always have."

I opened my mouth to tell Andrew that he'd misunderstood. I had asked out of curiosity, as a measure of politeness. But if I said that, I would be lying. He was right. I did care. I thought I had moved on. I had tucked all my emotions away in box, and it was mixed and messy, like my basket of costumes. And now I found myself rifling through the chaos, searching for the one floppy hat I knew was buried somewhere within. The one costume piece I loved that would make my ensemble complete. I forced myself to stare at the flat road and tried to breath evenly. I fiddled with the air conditioning vents, not sure how to deal with my epiphany. My feelings for Andrew hadn't faded in the least.

"Can I ask you a question?" I asked.

Andrew glanced at me. "Sure."

"I know I'm observing from the outside, but if I understand correctly, you get another flight, right?"

"One more. It'll probably be on Tuesday with the squadron commander."

"And on your flight with Tucker, the reason you failed"—I flinched a little as I said the word—"was because of the flaps?"

"He gave me two other minor downgrades, but if I hadn't oversped the flaps, I would have passed." Andrew's knuckles paled as he again gripped the steering wheel.

I reached across the space between us and placed my hand on his forearm. "I'm not an expert, but the solution seems rather simple."

Andrew's eyebrows raised in question.

My cheeks heated. I didn't think he would be offended, but enough time had passed, enough awkwardness, that I couldn't be sure. "Fly exactly like you did yesterday, and don't overspeed the flaps."

Andrew chuckled, as I had hoped he would. He let go of the steering wheel with his right hand and wrapped his fingers around my own. Then he lifted my hand to his lips and gave my knuckles a quick kiss before releasing his hold. I'd expected him to laugh, but the kiss I did not expect. I rested my hand on my leg, trying to quell the warm eruption of butterflies in my chest.

He turned to me with a full, double-dimpled grin. "Now, what do you want to see in San Antonio?"

San Antonio? I couldn't even process touring the city right now.

To Andrew, the simple gesture of kissing my hand was exactly that, simple. But to me it meant something. He skipped merrily through life, assuming that if we were good people and did the right thing, things would work out. He believed if we were happy together, we should stay together, regardless of how our aspirations differed. The Lord would provide a way for us both to find a path to happiness, and if it felt right for us to be together, we should continue on that vein and trust in God. I had trusted God. My relationship with Andrew had ended. And now I found myself facing a delicious temptation: like the dessert I knew I shouldn't eat, Andrew was the guy I knew I shouldn't date.

Like me, his faith came first, but now, despite his faith, Andrew's goal teetered precariously like a bug on the windshield. Where did that put our relationship? Could he prioritize me and the things that were important to me? After my faith, relationships were everything to me. That, too, was the reason I lived in Texas, to be with my brother. The small things Andrew had done—the sweet texts, taking me to my favorite restaurants, the walks and stolen kisses—had led me to believe we might have a shot, a chance to be together. But I had been wrong. The path that opened up had only led me to a vast pit of disappointment and heartache.

The one relationship I could count on was my own relationship with God. I made a daily effort to recognize His hand in my life. That recognition had helped me through the hard times. I trusted in His plan for me, and when I had prayed about my future with Andrew, I had felt all kinds of turmoil. To me, that meant I'd needed to let go, to move on. And I thought I had. But now, sitting here beside him, my heart beat all sorts of crazy rhythms, and I wondered how, if something were wrong, it could feel so right. I believed God was not a God of confusion, but my human mind was every bit confused.

I determined today would be about lifting Andrew, helping him through the melancholy of hooking his flight. I would open my heart and trust God to inspire me.

"You're my tour guide. Where do you recommend we go?" I asked.

Andrew pressed his lips together and feigned deep contemplation. "The Alamo's cool 'cause of the history, but I'm sure you'll make it there, so let's start at Brackenridge Park."

"Brackenridge Park it is," I said. "What is there to see?"

The tone lightened, and Andrew began to smile and joke. "There's a tea garden and some food trucks. I think we might even find a wishing fountain," he said with a wink. It was nice to see his mood lift, but I wished I could be immune to his charm. I knew his modus operandi, yet my stupid heart still fluttered at his flirtatious words.

We parked and ate the yummiest tacos from a street vendor. Then we rented electric scooters and rode to Brackenridge Park. At the park we ditched the scooters and wandered on foot over the bridges and trails at the Japanese Tea Garden. We explored the Botanical Garden, but we had only about an hour before they closed at five.

"We'll have to come again when we have more time," I said, not thinking about the implication of my words.

"I'd like that," Andrew said. We exited the park. "Guess I was wrong about the wishing fountains. You'll just have to tell me what you'd wish for."

Skateboards sounded behind us on the walk, and Andrew looked over his shoulder. Before I could move, he grabbed my hand and pulled me behind him as three teenagers cruised by close enough that their sleeves brushed Andrew's arms. They would have brushed my side if Andrew hadn't pulled me away.

"Sheesh," I said, my fingers still threaded through his.

He watched the trio of skaters turn and carve their boards close to a family walking ahead of us. "Are you okay?" he asked. "Do you still have your wallet and purse?"

My free hand went to my purse strap draped across my chest. "They're here," I said. We continued walking, our hands still intertwined.

Andrew squeezed my fingers. "Remind you of living in Southern California?" he asked.

"I definitely developed street smarts living there. Remember the time you took me to the Pantages to see *Come from Away*?" I smiled at the memory.

"You were always spoiling me, and I wanted to spoil you," Andrew said. A man walked by pushing an ice-cream cart. The bells on his cart jingled a happy tune, and Andrew stopped him. "Choose one," he said before asking for a fat ice-cream sandwich for himself. I pointed to the chocolate-covered ice cream, and the man handed me both orders while Andrew fished out his wallet to pay.

"Thanks for spoiling me again," I said, taking a bite of my ice cream.

We continued walking along the river, side by side, eating our treats.

"How do your parents feel about your military commitment?" I asked. I had met Aaron and Rhonda Stoll once when they'd come visit Andrew on a long weekend. They had been kind and gracious, asking about my major and my family. We'd enjoyed dinner and a night of board games together.

"They've been supportive," Andrew said. "My grandpa served in the army, and he's super excited."

"Do they worry you could be stationed far away?" We turned off the main walkway to weave back to where his car was parked.

"They're at a stage in life where they can travel, so I think they're actually hoping I get stationed somewhere overseas so they can come visit."

"There are bases all over the world. Where do you want to go?" I asked.

"I'd love to go overseas. Asia, Europe, even Alaska." He shoved his hands into his pockets and turned to me with a grin. "Maybe I can get stationed in England and we could be there together."

"Andrew . . ." I said his name with a warning, but any finality was missing from my voice. I had never considered being in England with him. When I'd envisioned my time there, I'd pictured taking the tube in London and him being . . . somewhere else. I wasn't surprised by his words. He had warned me.

"You'll make it there, Kasie, with or without me. There's no doubt in my mind."

We returned to the car, and Andrew held the door. I thanked him, and he walked around the car but paused, doing something with his phone before he climbed in.

"Mind if we make one more stop?" he asked.

"What are you thinking?" I didn't mind. It was just after 6:30 p.m., and we still had the drive home, but I could always nap after church tomorrow.

"It's a surprise." Andrew buckled his seat belt and followed the GPS on his phone. About twenty minutes later we pulled up to a comedy club. My heart pinched. Attending stand-up and amateur night at a club near the college had been one of our regular dates.

He grinned. "You up for some laughter?"

"Always." I opened the car door and got out. A cool breeze whipped past, and I shivered. I ran my hands up and down my arms, anxious to get inside. I turned to look for Andrew when he stepped up beside me and set a zippered sweatshirt on my shoulders.

"This should help," he said.

I should have returned it to him. I should have told him I'd be fine once we got inside. Instead, I found myself saying, "Thank you." I grasped the edges of the hoodie and pulled it tightly around me.

Andrew placed a hand on my back, and we walked into the club.

I did warm inside the building, but I didn't remove the sweatshirt. It smelled of mint and man. It smelled like Andrew. The crisp scent relaxed me, and the warm fabric cozied around me like a fluffy blanket as we sat at a small bistro table.

Nostalgia hit like a high surf crashing against the solid rock jetties. Sitting beside Andrew, his face bathed in the ambient lights, his lips pushed up in joy with a smile just for me, I yearned to scoot my chair nearer, to breath in and embrace every feeling I'd held for him. I inhaled and let the wave hit me. I'd always thought drowning would be painful; instead I felt free.

CHAPTER 7

A balding male comedian performed, followed by a hilarious middle-aged woman with a bright-purple pixie cut. She had us laughing until my stomach hurt. Ten o'clock came and went. When the purple-haired woman took a final bow, I stood with the majority of the audience to applaud. I turned to comment to Andrew and realized he had not stood with me. He sat back in his chair, with one leg crossed over the other, staring at me. His dimples were on full display, punctuating his smile like a secret message in parentheses. It was a beautiful sight. My hands slowed and my breathing stalled.

Andrew stood and reached for my hand, then leaned near. "Are you ready to go?"

I pressed my lips together and nodded, hypnotized by all the goodness that was him. In that moment, I would have gone anywhere he asked. My hand remained tethered to his as we weaved around the tables. We walked to the car, and he opened my door, giving my fingers a gentle squeeze before letting go.

I sat in the car, dumbfounded. Andrew climbed in and started the ignition, and before long we were back on highway 90, headed west. My fingers played with the zipper of Andrew's sweatshirt that I still wore. I couldn't deny my attraction to him. His allure had never wavered, but I also believed in self-preservation. My heart had hardly recovered from our breakup. Patched together with duct tape and string, I had just begun to allow myself to feel once again, and all of those feelings swirled within my breast. I may be euphoric now, but had I just set myself up for a complete shattering of my heart?

Andrew turned on some music, a playlist of top one hundred pop songs, and then took my hand again. "Thank you for today. It was exactly what I needed," he said.

I liked my hand in his, but . . . I thought carefully about what I wanted to say.

Andrew glanced at me and spoke again. "Did you have fun?"

"I did," I said and slipped my hand free. Andrew extended his fingers and then clenched them into a fist. "But I went because you deserved some time away. A break from training."

Andrew shifted and placed both hands on the steering wheel. He tightened his fingers, then released a long breath. "I can't be sorry. I had a great time, and I told you I was going to fight to show you how right we are."

I pushed my hands into the pockets of his sweatshirt. Despite the late hour, my brain shifted into overdrive trying to reconcile the energy pinging through the car with the boundaries I had determined for our relationship. Boundaries that after spending one day with Andrew now lay scattered around my feet. But he was right: I couldn't be sorry. Tomorrow, maybe, but not in this moment.

We drove the next forty minutes in silence. Music floated through the speakers, but I didn't really hear it. We sped through the empty black vastness of nighttime with only the illumination of the headlights to guide us. It felt like a fitting analogy for our relationship. The white stripes directed our path, and if we veered, we'd be in trouble. I would be in trouble. Andrew's focus should be on his training. My focus was helping Tucker for a year, then getting to London. Neither left time to re-explore a relationship, yet . . .

Andrew reached forward and shut off the radio. "You know how crazy it is that we both ended up here?" His statement teetered like a question and settled between us. I *did* know, but I stayed silent. "I've thought about you a lot since we parted ways. I've missed you."

I had missed him too. Only after Andrew had reappeared in my life had I realized how often I had thought of him. My bad days were brightened with memories of our time together. My happy days were not quite as full as when I had ended them wrapped in his arms. Wistfulness rained over me like a bath of sunlight. We had been good together, right up until it had come time for the hard decisions. I had walked away assuming I would somehow get over him, but for as much as I had missed his dimples and his warm embrace, I knew he still had a hold of my heart.

He rubbed a hand along his jaw before gripping the steering wheel again. "When we ran into each other again, I felt like God might be giving me—giving us—a second chance. When I looked up and you were there . . ." He blew out a breath. "I felt fireworks. Explosive joy." He paused for a beat. "What did you think in that moment?"

I paused, wanting to get the words right. "I honestly can't say. I think I was numb from the shock." I gave a small smile. "I never heard anything about your commissioning, so in the back of my head, I guess maybe I knew it was possible, but with all the bases around the country, I never thought we would end up at the same one."

Our experiences were the same in one respect though. When Andrew had walked in holding Cole's hand, flutters of joy had winged around my middle.

"You know I never wanted to break up," he reminded me.

I fiddled again with the zipper pull on the hoodie. "And you know why we did."

His finger tapped rhythmically on the steering wheel. "I know you believe it was the right thing to do at the time, but here we are." The tapping stopped. "Can't we try again? Keep it simple?"

We passed a road sign indicating Del Rio was thirty-four miles away. "You're in training. I'm helping Tucker. The timing seems worse now than it did before." I said the words, and I believed the words, but at Andrew's suggestion that we try again, fizzles of temptation snapped inside me, making me want to consider his suggestion. Like trying to light a fire with flint and steel, there were sparks knocking together, but I didn't think anything would—or could—actually ignite. "This doesn't feel simple," I continued. "I don't know how or why we ended up in Texas at the same base. I mean, logically I know why, but . . ." I let my words die away.

"I don't know what would happen, Kasie, but I can't get the idea out of my head that you and I being here together is more than a random coincidence. I believe your answer before was to break up, but maybe God has a different answer this time." His finger resumed tapping the steering wheel, and he nodded as he stared at the road. "We really can keep this simple. Just think about it, okay?"

I let his proposal settle. "Okay," I said, "I'll think about it." Because I wasn't quite brave enough to tell him the same idea had been teasing my thoughts.

Tucker was sound asleep by the time Andrew dropped me off.

I fell into bed, waking all too soon when my alarm announced I needed to get up and get ready for church. Thank goodness Sundays were a day of rest. I didn't bother making my bed. It would be easier to climb back under my covers when we got home.

We scrambled out the door. Tucker didn't utter a peep about my time with Andrew, though I did feel him watching me throughout the service. He took Noah to nursery, and I sat by Hope during Sunday School. Andrew sat three chairs down beside Ian and did nothing more than wave before the lesson began.

After listening to a hearty discussion on the concept of grace, Hope and I chatted and wandered out to the hall. "Cole is so excited to recite his lines for you. He's been practicing them nonstop," she said. Andrew walked up, and Hope looked between the two of us. "How about you join us for dinner, Kasie? Cole can show off, and Andrew will be there."

"Actually, I'll have to pass today," Andrew said. "I played yesterday, so I need to study today." He gave me a knowing grin.

Becca ran up and grabbed Hope's hand. "Hey, sugar," Hope said to her daughter before looking between Andrew and me. "We'll get together again soon. All of us." I know Hope meant well, but the weight of her words stalled the conversation.

I hoped a change of subject would chase away the awkwardness. "I'll make a treat for the boys for our next practice, so prepare Cole. He needs to be ready to impress," I said.

"Sure thing." Hope turned to Andrew. "We're praying for you," she said while she gave him a squeeze.

"I'll take all the prayers I can get," he said.

"I'll pray for you, Andrew," Becca said sweetly.

Hope looked down at her daughter. "What a great idea. You know your prayers go straight to God." She winked at Becca. "Should we go find your daddy and your brother and head home?"

Becca nodded.

"Have a nice day, Kasie." Hope pointed at Andrew. "Now, you go study hard." She left me alone with Andrew, but luckily, he filled the silence.

"Are you going to fit in a nap today?" he asked.

"Aren't you?" We began walking together.

"Not sure if I'll have time. But I'm also not sure I can keep my eyes open," Andrew said. We reached the door, and he pulled it open.

"Sorry to take all your study time yesterday. I didn't mean to distract you," I said. We came to a stop in front of Tucker's car.

Andrew chuckled and his dimples appeared. "It was my idea. And I needed it," he said.

Tucker and Noah were talking to Wendy, making their way slowly toward us. Wendy's brown hair was pulled back in a twist, and she was short enough that she had to tilt her chin upward to look at Tucker. She smiled and shook her head at something he said. When he saw me, he clicked his key fob to unlock the door.

Andrew reached forward and opened the passenger door for me.

"Well, Tuesday, after you ace your flight, we can celebrate," I said. I stepped near and found myself unable to resist the magnetic pull of his dimples. I leaned forward and kissed the dimple on his left cheek. "For good luck." Warmth filled my face.

He stood as if he were stunned. "Best distraction ever," he said.

"I'm just wishing you luck." I climbed into my seat, and even though I knew my actions pushed our boundaries beyond the limits I had set, I couldn't help but smile.

Simple. Keep it simple. I repeated the mantra over and over for the next two days. Andrew didn't need to call me. He needed to study. His next flight determined his future. I understood it in every fiber of my being, but those fibers seemed to malfunction around my emotional nerve connections. I wanted to know how Andrew felt. How was his studying going? Did he need a break? Snacks? Sleep? Did he think of me as often as I thought of him? I was dangerously falling back into everything Andrew.

Early Monday morning my mom called. "Hey, Kasie. You've been on my mind. How are things?"

"How do you have the perfect sixth sense, even when you're in Mexico?" I asked.

Mom laughed. "Moms just know. It's a gift inherent with the title. Is something going on?"

"You go first," I said. I balanced the phone against my ear as I strapped Noah into his high chair and pulled out the Play-Doh. Mom told me about the orphanage she and Dad were assigned to work at. Dad was fixing leaky faucets and patching walls, and Mom was perfecting her Spanish skills while working with the school-aged children.

"Next week a dentist from the States is coming down with his staff to volunteer their services. There are many good people in the world," she said.

"Like you and Dad?" I teased.

"We're trying to do our part, and I think we're making a difference, but there's a lot to do." Mom's humility often led her to sell herself short. "Now, tell me what's going on with you. Tucker told me you spent the other day with Andrew."

Tucker! But if he hadn't told Mom, I would have. I wasn't trying to keep it a secret. "We both needed a day away," I said. "We went to San Antonio."

"Was it a nice break? Did you have fun?" Mom's voice was laced with consolation, like she knew exactly how I felt.

"Yeah," I said and blew out a breath. "I did. I just . . . I just don't know what to do about this whole situation. It's crazy." My conundrum seemed to cycle on repeat. "What should I do? How should I feel?"

"None of that matters," Mom said.

"What do you mean?" I asked.

"What matters is how you *do* feel. What are the feelings sitting on your heart?" Mom had a way of explaining things better than I could.

I snorted. "Talk about a loaded question. My heart is what I can't figure out." I sighed. "Did Tucker tell you Andrew has had some trouble in training? He flies tomorrow with the commander, and if he doesn't pass, he'll be booted from the program."

"You know your brother doesn't share details. He only mentioned you went on a date."

"It wasn't exactly a date," I said at the same time I realized it totally qualified as a date.

Mom laughed. "Your brother just doesn't want to see you get hurt. We all remember how sad you were when you ended things before. Have faith that God is in charge, and if you have a hard time doing that, you can lean on my faith."

I loved my mother, and I told her so. "I'm just confused," I told her. "I wonder if I got it wrong the first time. I'm starting to doubt myself."

"You know what you felt, Kasie. Be patient with yourself as you wait for new answers. I trust you," Mom said. "You'll figure this out."

I said goodbye and hung up. And while nothing had changed, I felt better, hopeful that the answers would soon come. I prayed that Andrew would do well on his flight, and I prayed to understand what God would have me do.

By Monday evening Tucker told me if I lapped the house one more time, the soles would be worn off my shoes. "The process is thorough. If he washes out, it's not meant to be," he said. "I don't know why you're so worked up."

I glared at my brother sitting still and calm on the couch. "I remember Stacy calling Mom several times, worried about a flight or a test you had to take."

"You're not Andrew's spouse, Kas. You're his . . ." He waved his hand through the air. "I don't know—what?—ex-girlfriend?" Talk about taking simplicity to the extreme.

My chest hurt. "That doesn't mean I want him to fail," I said. "And I would have told Mom, you know. About our trip to San Antonio. I hadn't had a chance to talk to her."

"I thought she'd want to know." Tucker's face softened and his shoulders fell. "What *is* going on between you and Andrew?" he asked.

I stared out the window and inhaled deeply. "I'm not sure," I admitted.

"What do you want to happen?" Tucker asked. I turned to face him. His inquisitive look reminded me of my mom, full of sincerity. "I remember you guys were pretty serious."

Andrew had never met my family before coming to Texas, but my family knew all about him, mostly because anytime I wasn't in class or working or involved in something with theatre, I was with Andrew. He had represented a big chunk of me. When things had ended, I'd tried to fill the gap by overexerting myself with anything and everything theatre, but despite running myself ragged, I never could replenish the space he had once filled.

"You broke up with him," Tucker pressed. "There had to be a reason."

My sad smile confirmed Tucker's words. "It felt right at the time," I said. "Or maybe it's more accurate to say it felt wrong. When I prayed about our future, all I felt was confusion." I moved to sit on the love seat across from him.

"And now?"

"Now I'm not so sure."

Tucker leaned his head back on the couch. "I guess God throws us curve balls to keep us on our toes."

"Sorry," I said. "I know this isn't a big deal compared to everything you've faced." Considering Tucker had lost his wife, my worries ranked as trivial. "You don't need to worry about me."

"Our trials are individual to us, Kas. I'm trying to learn whatever it is I'm supposed to learn from mine, and you need to learn whatever you're supposed to learn from yours." Tucker chucked a throw pillow at my head. "Besides, I do worry about you. It's my job as your big brother, and it lets me think of someone besides myself. God gives us trials for a reason."

"Is that how you feel? Do you really think God is involved?" I knew my faith in the divine centered on God and His love. I believed He loved us enough to allow Christ to atone for us. But the trials . . . that became more complicated. Why did we have to face such hard things? If we were doing all that we could, trying to be good, trying to do right, why couldn't that be enough to ensure a peaceful journey? Tucker had committed his life to his country, to his family, to God. It wasn't fair that he had to lose his wife. "With everything Stacy suffered, and now having to raise Noah on your own, do you still believe it all?" I asked.

Tucker sat up and leaned forward, resting his arms on his knees. He met my eyes with surety. "I do."

His conviction felt right. Solid. Unwavering.

"Kas, God loves us. Which is why He allows trials. I'm not saying I understand it, but with everything I've been through, I can't deny feeling His arms around me. I know I'm not very open and I don't share my emotions with others, but I pour my heart out to God. I still don't know why Stacy had to die, but my faith hasn't wavered. I wouldn't be able to move forward if it weren't for the peace and comfort He's given me." Tucker's words rang sincere. Sacred, even. He stood and then pulled me to my feet. He wrapped me in a hug, and moisture pricked my eyes. "I know it's tough being here," Tucker said. "I know having Andrew show up wasn't part of the plan, but . . ." He pulled back and pointed skyward. "It's His plan. Not ours. Take some time to figure out what feels right. What makes you happy. What God wants for you."

"Thanks, Tucker. You kinda sound like Mom," I said, squeezing him tightly around his middle, grateful for his vulnerability to help me understand. "I love you."

"Love you too, Kas," he said and ruffled my hair.

I headed to my room that night and sent Andrew a *Good luck* text. His future depended on his flight the next day. Then I knelt and prayed. I asked God for clarity. I asked for assurance that He heard me. And I prayed for Andrew. I prayed that he would recall all he needed to, that the checklists and protocols he'd studied would come naturally and that he would receive a fair assessment. I pleaded with God to guide Andrew because the one thing I wasn't conflicted about was the fact that I wanted him to be able to soar.

CHAPTER 8

Andrew never responded to my *Good luck* text on Monday night, so by Tuesday my nerves were completely off-kilter.

I'd learned to identify the three different training planes flying around the base. Whenever a T-1 roared overhead, I wondered whether it was Andrew's plane and whether, while he ran a million other protocols and procedures, he also remembered to watch his airspeed when he lowered the flaps. Like every other day on base, there were a lot of planes flying today, and my patience was frayed.

Several times I pulled out my phone, determined to text Tucker. I could ask what time Andrew's flight began or, more specifically, if he'd passed. I returned my phone to my pocket because I wanted to hear the details directly from Andrew—good or bad—though I really, really hoped it would be good. Noah got extra practice on saying prayers, as I'd been offering them hourly. No matter what happened between Andrew and me, I wanted this for him. He deserved to achieve his dream.

I ended up calling Annabelle and dishing all my anxieties to her.

"That's heavy stuff," she said after I told her about Andrew's failed check ride.

"My heart ached so badly for him," I said. "We spent the next day together in San Antonio, and then at church I gave him a good-luck kiss."

"Whoa, whoa, whoa. Back up, girlfriend. We jumped from messing up a flight to kissing. You need to fill in the blanks."

So I told her all of it. How I'd been swept up in emotion when I'd offered the good-luck kiss and how my nerves were fried today. Annabelle said she'd say a little prayer for Andrew and send good vibes. Considering that religion was not Annabelle's thing, her offer touched my heart.

Hope had arranged to bring Frankie and Rutherford to her house after school. Rehearsal would be a good distraction. I whipped up a batch of cookies, and when Noah woke from his nap, I got him a quick snack, grabbed the bags of cookies I'd made for the boys and Becca, and walked Noah over to the Nottinghams' house.

"Miss Kasie!" Cole swung the door wide. "Ready to hear my lines?"

"Most definitely!" The moment I released Noah's hand, he ran into the house, heading directly for the toy kitchen set up against the far wall.

I followed Cole into the main room, where Frankie and Rutherford sat on the floor eating sliced apples and watching a cartoon. "Miss Kasie's here." Cole skipped to the couch, grabbed the remote, and turned off the television.

Rutherford and Frankie protested until I held up the cookies and told them they each got their own bag if we had a good rehearsal. Becca entertained Noah, and Hope helped me work with the boys to block their scene. They'd all done a fabulous job memorizing their lines, so we worked on entrances and exits, comedic timing, and pronunciation. When one boy made the other two giggle, I knew we were close.

I help up my hand for a high five. "Excellent job, gentlemen."

"Do you think we're funny, Miss Kasie?" Rutherford asked.

"You are definitely funny." I gave each boy his bag of cookies. "We'll run through it for a couple more weeks. Then the week of the show we'll practice on Monday, have dress rehearsal Thursday, and the final performance on Friday."

"I'll talk to Marylou and Emmaline and let you know where would be best to meet for the next practice," Hope said.

"Sounds good." I paused. Rehearsal had been a good distraction, but Andrew's flight and its outcome soared around the back of my mind. "Any word from Ian?"

I didn't mention Andrew's name, but Hope knew why I'd asked. She shook her head. "Nothing yet."

"Fingers crossed it goes well," I mumbled awkwardly. I'd text Tucker when I got home. I couldn't wait any longer. I wiggled the last bag of cookies in the air. "Becca, these are for you." She grinned, and I set them on the dining room table. "Thanks for playing with Noah." Then I picked up Noah's shoes from near the door and walked to where he sat playing with Becca's drawing pad. "Ready to go home? Daddy should be home soon." I began putting his shoes on, but he wasn't having it. He kicked his foot free from my grasp.

"No go home!" he said. He planted his hands on the ground, pushed himself up to standing, and tried to run away.

I caught his wrist and reminded him what a nice time he'd had but that now we needed to head back to our house. Noah dropped to the ground, kicking and turning on the waterworks.

Becca came over with concern in her eyes, and Hope smiled. "It's okay, Becca. He's had a good time, so he's just sad to go home."

I pinched Noah's shoes between my fingers and hauled him into my arms. "Let's go, big man."

"Cole," Hope called. "Open the door for Miss Kasie, please."

Cole shoved the last of a cookie into his mouth and jumped out of his seat at the table. "Bye, Noah," he said with a smile, waving at my tantrum-throwing nephew.

I lugged Noah out the door, careful not to bump his head, and started the trek across the lawn. "You leave quite an impression," I said to Noah. My arms grew weak as he continued to wriggle. "What do you say to an early bedtime tonight?"

"No!" Noah shouted louder. "No bed!"

I laughed. I might have been the theatre major, but this little kid had theatrics in his genes.

"Rough day?"

The familiar voice had me raising my head with lightning speed. I looked up to see Andrew standing at our front door. My heart skipped a beat, quickly absorbing everything from his cocky smile to the bouquet of white daisies in his hand. He still wore his flight suit, his flight cap on his head, looking every bit the hotshot pilot.

I shifted Noah to the opposite hip and turned my chin to keep my hair out of Noah's reach. "Hi," I said, my voice breathless.

Andrew looked at the flowers in his hand. He twisted the bouquet, shared his dimples, and nodded. "Let's just say I remembered my flaps."

My heart sped. I wanted to clap, to shout, to run and jump into his arms. I settled for an unrestrained smile.

"These are for you." He held the flowers up. "I'm crediting your good-luck kiss for the success."

Noah kept squirming, so I set him down near the spigot by the front door. He loved playing with the hose, and he reached for the nob to try to turn the water on. It would distract him for a few minutes.

I dropped Noah's shoes on the stoop, then turned and accepted the flowers from Andrew. "You didn't have to buy flowers," I said, secretly giddy that this was the second bouquet he'd gifted me.

"I wanted to."

"Congratulations," I said, my heart hammering in my chest. "I'm really happy for you." I fingered the petals and sniffed the clutch of daisies. The scent wasn't strong, a trace of just enough grassy sweetness to tickle my nose.

Tucker pulled into the carport, and we made eye contact as he passed. He parked, shut off the ignition, and got out of the car while I squatted down and messed up Noah's hair. "Look, buddy. Daddy's home." We had made it a tradition to run and greet Tucker when he got home. I grabbed Noah's hand, and together we called to Tucker. "Daddy!"

Andrew stepped away from the door and stood on the lawn. Tucker squatted low, and Noah jumped into his arms. Tucker lifted him up, tickling his belly, and said, "Hi, Nono." Then Tucker walked to where Andrew stood. Andrew saluted, and my brother reciprocated, then held out his hand. "I heard you rocked it."

"I'm just glad it's done." Andrew shook Tucker's hand, his smile wide.

Tucker looked over his shoulder at me. "I've got Noah and me covered for dinner." He turned his attention back to his son, scrunching up his face and making growling noises as they walked into the house.

Andrew laughed at Tucker's not-so-subtle hint. "Wanna go grab dinner?" he asked me.

"I'd love to," I said, meaning every word. "But first, I need to put these in water, and you probably want to change." The cellophane crinkled as I held up the daises.

"Thirty minutes?" Andrew asked.

I nodded, and we parted ways to get ready.

I texted Annabelle the good news, freshened up my hair and makeup, and changed into a flowy cotton top with my jeans and a pair of heeled sandals. Andrew returned in khaki pants, a green collared shirt, and casual tennis shoes. He looked good and smelled like minty yumminess, fresh soap, and warm masculinity. We pulled off base, and I suggested the Mexican restaurant Frankie's parents owned, explaining the connection once we were seated.

The waiter brought out water glasses and chips and salsa.

"So . . ." I clapped my hands together. "Tell me about your flight."

"It's honestly a bit of a blur." Andrew shook his head. His smile hadn't faded since he first greeted me near the door. "I didn't sleep great last night, so my nerves were crazy this morning. I prayed, which helped me settle a bit. In the pre-brief, Lieutenant Colonel Haggar told me his goal was for me to pass and stay in the program. His encouragement made a huge difference.

Before, I thought the IPs were all about washing us out, but that's not the case . . . for most of them, at least."

"So you did it," I said.

"I did it." Andrew held up his water glass, and I lifted mine to his in a toast. "Which means I get to order dessert," he said.

"You could even order dessert first." I grinned and opened my menu. My eyes skimmed the options, but my exuberance kept spilling from my mouth. "You're awesome, you know that? I can't even imagine how stressed I would be. You had so much pressure, but you did it!"

"Thanks Kasie. Your support means the world to me."

I looked over the top of the menu and met Andrew's eyes. They tinted green to match his shirt, and they pulled me in and wrapped me up, cozy and complete, and I never wanted to leave.

We had been close before breaking up. I could even say I loved him. But this feeling, this wholeness, was new, like an epiphany that the world outside could be falling apart but I would be okay—because I was here with Andrew looking at me like his entire orbit centered on my existence.

I didn't have words. And neither did he. We simply absorbed one another until the waiter returned.

The food hit the spot, and I felt guilty for so thoroughly enjoying the break from Tucker and Noah. I generally considered being with them to be a privilege more than a duty, but I hadn't realized how much I'd needed the *me* time. And then throw Andrew into the mix, insisting I choose a dessert to share—fried ice cream for the win—and looking at me with the conviction that he was going to fight for us, for our future, as hard as he fought to keep his slot in pilot training. His smile tilted with a confidence I'd not seen from him before. It was empowering and endearing, and when a comment from him sped my heart or a twitch of his lips made words tangle in my throat, I wondered if re-exploring a relationship with him might not be as simple as I thought.

We finished off dessert, Andrew insisting I take the last bite. "How's the skit going?" he asked. "Cole's recited his lines to me at least three times."

"I'm glad he's excited. I worry about Rutherford getting stage fright, but not Cole."

"That kid cracks me up." Andrew chuckled. "I'm glad you have a way to use your talent, even if it's not quite like you pictured."

"Definitely different from where I thought I might be. I don't think teaching is the route I want to take, but it has been fun." The truth of my statement had hit me several times over the past two weeks. "And I'm still working on one of my scripts."

"I'm rooting for you too, Kasie," Andrew said.

I wondered if I should tell him about the program in London. I shook the thought away as soon as it came. I'd only just applied and my chances of getting accepted were slim. No point in talking about something that hadn't yet been decided.

Andrew paid for dinner, and we walked out to the car. He glanced at his watch. "It feels later than seven thirty."

"Probably because you didn't sleep last night."

We buckled our seat belts, and Andrew plugged the key into the ignition but didn't start the car. He twisted his hips and leaned against his door. "I don't want to take you home yet," he said. Heat pooled in my middle because I knew exactly what he meant. "I passed my flight today, but I can't let down my guard. Tomorrow we start a new round of academics, and then we have simulators and start night flying. I don't know when I'll get to see you again." His brow softened, and my heart tripped, my emotions still bold and solid as I admired the curve of his cheeks, the angle of his lips. "Are you up for a drive?" he asked. "Or a movie? I'm not sure what else there is to do around here. Bowling?"

I wanted to wrap up in his arms, even though I knew it would be a direct contradiction of everything I had told him. A contradiction to the answer I had so surely received all those months ago. "No bowling, and you look too exhausted to drive far. Besides, we got our miles in going to San Antonio." I scrambled for a compromise. "Maybe we can walk and burn off the fried ice cream." Walking seemed like a safe option. Standing, moving, no cuddling involved.

We drove back to base and parked near Andrew's dorm-style room. The evening had cooled enough that we wouldn't get sticky, but a tinge of humidity still hung in the air. The sun blazed strong on the horizon, lighting the vast, cloudless sky. It wouldn't get dark for another hour. A few airmen passed, some heading toward the gym, others back to their apartments. Andrew and I wandered slowly, not saying much. We never decided on a direction, but our feet kept moving forward, step after step. We walked down the sidewalk and turned the corner. When we reached a road crossing, Andrew reached down and grabbed my hand. I looked at our clasped fingers, then at his knowing grin.

"This is simple, right?" he asked. It wasn't a cuddle, but it did feel nice and a little less scary, so I nodded.

Our joined hands swung between us. We made our way toward the flight line, walking past the squadron buildings on the street that paralleled the runway. Andrew pointed to the building where he had classes, then another. "And there's the hangar, where maintenance crews work on the planes," he said. We walked another half mile with our backs to the sun until we reached a place where we could see the tarmac clearly. Lights flashed as two of the fighter trainers taxied. Andrew released my hand, shifting so he could get the best view of the planes taking off.

"Are you still sure this is what you want to do for the rest of your life?" I asked.

"I love it." He chuckled. "Most of it, anyway." He sighed. "Honestly, it's so, so, tough, and this last week I wasn't sure if flying would even be an option for me anymore." His eyes remained on the runway.

"But it is," I said. "You got through today, and you get to do it again tomorrow."

"Yeah. Funny thing is, I'm excited to fly heavies. I thought it might bother me not to fly fighters, but I'm honestly okay with it. There are some cool mission options in heavies and simply being up there in the sky—that's really the dream. To fly, no matter the plane." Andrew motioned me over to his side as the engines began to scream. He pointed through the chain link fence. "Here they go."

The planes gained momentum as they rolled down the tarmac. In one fluid movement the nose of the aircraft angled upward and the wheels left the ground. "Gear up," Andrew whispered under his breath a moment before the landing gear folded into the underside of the aircraft. He sighed. "Such an amazing sensation. It never gets old."

"Which means you chose the right profession," I said.

He stepped away from the fence and faced me, reached forward, and took my hands. His eyes softened. "And thanks to you, I get to keep flying."

"I had nothing to do with it," I said. "You're the one who climbed into the cockpit and mastered the ridiculous number of checklists you have."

Andrew's thumbs brushed across the backs of my hands. "I told you I'm crediting your good-luck kiss."

Butterflies fluttered through my stomach, and I shrugged playfully. "I *am* a good kisser."

Simple was unraveling rather quickly.

A slow smile spread across Andrew's face. He stepped forward at the same time he pulled my body closer to his. The initial humor in his eyes shifted, like the quick strike of a matchstick against its box, igniting the yearning we both felt. The kisses we'd shared while dating ranked at the top of my list. The desire to taste a real kiss, to remember the deliciousness of our connection, drew us both in, closer and closer, until only a mere breath separated us.

"Maybe it's not so simple," Andrew said before his lips pressed into mine. I'd been fighting the attraction I had always felt for him, and our mouths moved together, mine anxious to explore all I'd tried to forget. His arms wrapped around my back, his hands pulling me firmly to him. His warm lips. His euphoric presence. I slipped my arms around his neck, brushing the sharp ends of his cropped hair with my fingertips.

Engines sounded on the runway behind us, growing louder, matching the thrumming of my heart. The sound faded away, our kiss slowed, and Andrew held me close. His lips lingered near mine, his breath quick. He turned his head and leaned to whisper near my ear. "I'm still in training. I'm going to need a lot of luck."

Oh, how I wanted to wish him luck every day. Andrew dropped his arms from my back and took my hand, and we walked to Tucker's house. My hand fit nicely in his. Silence prevailed, which made my brain cycle around this new opportunity with Andrew—similar yet different.

We turned up the walkway leading to the front door. "Thanks for celebrating with me," Andrew said.

"I'm happy you passed."

"Happy enough that you'd be willing to give us a second chance?" he asked with a reserved but dimpled smile.

His words stirred something inside of me. "I'm praying about it," I said.

Andrew kissed my cheek, then dropped my hand. "That's all I need to hear."

I waited for a minute before heading inside, wondering why the decision to stay together had once felt so wrong and why it now felt so right.

CHAPTER 9

Our Friday rehearsal at the city park was rough. The boys giggled and attempted to ad-lib all sorts of ridiculous additions into the script. I tried to explain how the best comedy was timed to perfection and did not include throwing random jokes about bodily functions into a scene, but they insisted they knew better than me.

"What do you think?" I asked Hope. "I'm not getting anywhere."

"It's hot, and they've had a long week of school. Fridays are often rough. Probably better to tackle it another day."

Becca ran up and held out her hands for the water bottle Hope held.

"We only have three more weeks to rehearse. We're running out of time."

I watched Becca run back to where Noah stood pushing an empty swing.

"The show must go on. Isn't that what you theatre types say?" Hope offered a sympathetic smile.

I laughed. "That or break a leg." We walked to the play set. "Do you want to swing?" I asked Noah.

He raised his arms. "Swing!"

I lifted him up and pulled his feet through the leg holes on the child swing so he could sit down. Then I pulled the swing forward and let go.

"One at a time on the slide," Hope called to the older boys. She walked to the side of the swing set and faced me. "Ian said you and Andrew have been seeing each other more often."

Seeing each other? Simple? To me it all felt jumbled. I'd been praying, as I told Andrew I would. I had yet to be hit with a definitive answer but felt surprisingly at peace while considering the possibility. It was the exact opposite of the way I'd felt before. Now, after the intense kiss we'd shared, I wondered if there might be a way we could join hands and soar together.

But the thought that immediately followed pressed on my faith: why would I get an answer now that was opposite to what I'd felt before? Our goals had not changed, so why did I feel peace now when considering a future with Andrew?

Hope still waited for my response. "We're keeping it simple," I said.

Her smirk told me she didn't believe me. Becca ran over again, and Hope lifted her into an empty swing and gently pushed her.

Noah kicked his feet, and I kept his momentum going. "I don't want things to end up like they did before," I said.

Hope pushed Becca in her swing. "And how did they end up before?" she asked.

I let her question settle on my brain. *Sad*, I thought to myself. Noah swung forward, and I tickled his legs. He giggled before he swung away. "They just sort of ended," I told Hope.

"But why?" she pressed. "Did he call things off?"

"No." Noah kicked his legs as he swung forward again. "I did." I tickled him again. "His future was set in stone, so I could follow him, or I could not."

"You didn't want to try a long-distance relationship?" Hope asked. Becca started twisting sideways in her swing. "Be careful, darlin'," Hope told her.

"I had plans to go to London. It would have been a super-long-distance relationship. I prayed about us, and it didn't feel right."

Noah tried to twist like Becca, but his grunts and wiggles proved vain.

Becca's swing slowed, and Hope lifted her down. "Well, now you live—what—a mile and half away from each other? It's hardly long distance."

I knew where Hope's thoughts wandered. "Andrew's committed to Uncle Sam now, and I . . ." I didn't know what I was anymore. I wouldn't be with Noah and Tucker forever, but lately the thought of London hadn't pulled and pressed me like it had before.

Hope walked near and slipped her arm through mine. "Maybe this is your second chance," she said.

Her words settled over me, and the thought of trying again with Andrew felt solid and tangible and doable.

"That's what Andrew wants," I said. "And I'm praying about it."

If Andrew and I were going to try again, I wanted to be all in. I needed 100 percent confirmation from God, and then I would give 150 percent to my relationship with Andrew.

Hope leaned forward and gave me a hug. "Then, you'll figure it out." Her words echoed those of my mom, and I couldn't decide where that landed on the scale of random chance to inspired. "Are you planning to go to the air show?" she asked. "The Thunderbirds will be performing."

I appreciated her change in topic. "I saw a poster at the BX." I lifted Noah from the swing, and he ran to the slide.

"The IP spouses are gonna do a booth to raise money—snow cones, I think," Hope said.

"What do they use the money for?" I asked, following Noah with my eyes but still listening to Hope.

"They do baby gifts for newborns, or flowers if someone has a death in the family. Or they send a little something when someone new arrives or when someone gets their next assignment and PCSs to a new base. Things like that." Hope called for her children to go down the slide one last time before they left. "Anyway, you should come help in the booth. Get to know more people. We can sign up for the same shift."

"I'll check with Tucker to see what the plan is for Noah, but it could be fun," I said.

I picked up hamburgers for Noah, Tucker, and me on our way home from the park and pulled into the empty driveway. If Tucker was still at work, the students were there also. I had practiced great restraint not to text Andrew during the day. The class was falling behind schedule and wouldn't be ready to begin their night flying the next week. The IPs had threatened that the airmen would have to come in over the weekend if they didn't get caught up, so they'd pulled some long days. Andrew had texted a few times, but I hadn't seen him again.

Noah and I washed up and ate our dinner. The park and heat had worn Noah out, so he fell asleep as soon as I laid him in his bed. I resigned myself to a quiet Friday night with Netflix.

Not long after 10:15, or 22:15, as Tucker would say, my brother walked through the door. I paused the movie I was streaming. "Long day?" I asked.

Tucker groaned.

"Do you have to go in tomorrow?" I asked.

"Thank heavens, no." He dumped his backpack by the door and began unlacing his boots.

"I bought hamburgers. Yours is in the fridge. Should I warm it up for you?"

"Nah, I'll eat it cold." Tucker peeled off his boots and shuffled to the kitchen.

My phone buzzed with a text from Andrew. *Finally home.*

I texted back, *Tucker said it was a long one.*

Andrew: *Soooooooooo long. And more studying tomorrow.*

Me: *Heading to bed?*

Andrew: *After I eat. Talk tomorrow?*

Me: *Yeah. Sweet dreams.*

Andrew: *You too.*

I picked up the remote and hit play on my movie. Tucker plopped onto the couch holding his burger. "I'm so glad we don't have to go in tomorrow." He ate half his hamburger in a single bite.

"Do you have any plans?" I asked.

He swallowed, then answered. "Sleep. Play with Noah. More sleep." He took another bite. "What are you doing?" he asked with a mouthful of food.

I shrugged. "I'm not sure yet." I had hoped Andrew would want to do something, but he'd had an exhausting week.

Tucker headed to bed, and I finished my movie and fell asleep with the hope that Andrew would call in the morning so we could have another impromptu adventure.

I woke to Noah's shrill scream. The clock read 7:17, and I wondered if Tucker had been up long. When I wandered to the kitchen, Tucker stood flipping pancakes on the griddle.

"I'm gonna go for a walk," I said. Andrew was probably still asleep.

"No pancakes?" Tucker asked.

"I'll eat when I get back, as long as you don't eat them all," I teased.

At the bottom of the driveway I stretched my calves and thighs and then started my power walk. I headed toward the perimeter fence beyond the officer housing and circled near the nine-hole golf course. The day began to warm, and the heat forced me to turn back home. I walked along the main road to the crosswalk and headed back, slowing my pace at the Nottinghams' house. Hope was outside watering her flowers. "Hey there," I called from the street.

She turned off the water and walked down her driveway to say hello. "I didn't expect to see you today."

"How come?" I asked, wiping the sweat from my brow.

She grimaced. "Nothing. I'm being presumptuous."

"About . . . ?" I prodded.

Hope laughed awkwardly. "Ian told me Andrew went to Ciudad today. I assumed . . ."

Ciudad Acuña was the town across the Mexican border. "I'm not sure what he's up to." I smiled and shrugged, but my gut clenched. "He mentioned needing to study." But if Hope was correct, he wasn't hitting the books.

She changed the subject. "Cole is excited for the next rehearsal."

"I'm hopeful it'll all turn out," I said, following her lead.

"It'll be delightful. You can't go wrong with kids," she said. We chatted a bit more before she waved goodbye and headed back inside, and I returned home full of questions and doubts all circling one prospective air force pilot.

Our simplicity mantra was well and good. We'd established we liked one another. Our kisses had always been good, but the electricity of our recent kiss had confirmed our attraction, and each time I had replayed it in my head, giddy joy sparked outward from my heart. I knew Andrew had felt it too, which made my phone's silence all the more confusing.

Not long after lunch, Tucker walked in with Noah asleep on his shoulder. I hurried to the bedroom and arranged the blankets so Tucker could settle Noah in his bed. Then my brother walked back into the living room and untied his shoes. "I don't know where he gets his energy."

"If I got a two-hour nap every day, I might function with the same spunk." I folded the blanket on the couch and straightened the decorative pillows. "What did you guys do?"

"We were at the stables. Wendy let Noah sit in the saddle, and I held onto him while she led the horse around the pen." Tucker walked to the kitchen and fished through the refrigerator, finally pulling out a stick of cheese. He peeled open the wrapper and took a bite as he walked back toward the couch. He swallowed, then asked, "Do you have a plan for dinner tonight?"

"Nothing in particular." I had hoped I might be with Andrew, but I'd not yet heard from him and assumed he was still in Mexico. It hit sort of like a sucker punch, but I didn't want to be clingy or demanding. And, in reality, I had yet to tell him whether I was willing to try again. Ugh! I ran a hand through my hair, then kneeled on the floor to pick up Noah's toys. Tucker downed the rest of his cheese. "I have stuff for tacos or spaghetti. Or we could make pizzas on the naan bread I bought." I tossed Noah's collection of cars into their designated basket.

"Do we have toppings for a salad?" Tucker asked.

"A basic one. I have lettuce, tomato, and cucumber. Does that work?"

"Yeah." Tucker abruptly sat on the couch near me and rubbed his hands over his knees. "I invited Wendy over for dinner." He glanced at his watch. "I told her five thirty."

What? Where? Huh? None of my single-word questions actually surfaced.

Tucker wouldn't meet my gaze. His eyes danced around the room, and his left leg started bouncing. "She was super patient with Noah, and because she spent time letting him ride Honky, she didn't get all the training done she wanted. I thought it would be a nice way to say thank-you."

"So she's coming here?" I pointed to the carpet.

"Yes, Kasie," Tucker said, as if the answer was obvious. He stood and walked to the refrigerator, looked inside, then walked back. "But I don't want it to fall on you. I think the pizza thing would be super easy, and I can prep the salad." He shoved his hands into his back pockets, looking all kinds of vulnerable. "Do you think that's okay?"

I pulled my legs beneath me.

Tucker sighed. "It's weird, huh?" He sat back on the couch and finally looked at me.

"A bit," I admitted with a small smile. "But . . . I'm sure Noah liked the horse, and it was nice of her."

"I don't know what I'm doing, Kas." Tucker closed his eyes and rubbed a hand across his forehead.

"Are you . . . happy?" I asked.

Tucker raised his head. Exhaustion pulled at his features. His mouth turned down. Moisture began to pool in his eyes. "I miss Stacy, Kas." He dropped his head, and his shoulders shook as emotion took over.

I moved from the floor and sat next to Tucker. I rubbed his back. He had sobbed at Stacy's funeral but not since. Dad had taken care of him while Mom and I tag-teamed Noah and the guests. I hated seeing my brother in pain, but in a way, I felt the release was good for him. He'd been pushing strong for a long time, being brave for Noah, being responsible in his military duties and as a provider. I knew him well enough to know he wouldn't break, but a few cracks to allow him to feel, to mourn . . . maybe they weren't such a bad thing. I kept my hand moving in slow circles across his shoulders.

His sobs slowed. "I shouldn't have asked Wendy to come. I don't mean anything by it. I just thought it would be nice. A way to say thank-you."

I dropped my hand. "How about this?" I nudged his shoulder playfully with mine. "Let's order pizza. Then it's casual and easy. No expectations. This is all about Noah. He'll even provide the entertainment."

Tucker straightened and blew out a breath. He lifted his shoulder and used the sleeve of his T-shirt to wipe the tears from his eyes. "Is that okay?" he asked.

"Definitely." I playfully slapped his back a few times. "I'll order the pizza, and you can go shower." Tucker turned to me with a question on his face. I lifted one shoulder. "You smell like a barn."

Wendy arrived with a package of pudding cups in hand. Perfect. Tucker hemmed and hawed for the first couple of minutes, but when Wendy got down on the floor to tinker with the toy xylophone with Noah, the anvil seemed to lift from Tucker's shoulders. He laughed along with Noah's giggle, and when the pizza arrived ten minutes later, he plopped it onto the table along with a stack of paper plates and napkins. We had also prepared a salad. I pulled it and a bottle of dressing from the refrigerator, and we sat around the table to enjoy the casual meal.

"Tucker said you've been in Del Rio for a year?" I asked Wendy. I hadn't interacted much with Wendy beyond friendly waves and smiles in nursery. I really didn't know much about her, but she had bright, happy green eyes.

"Yep. Transferred out after the divorce became final."

"Where did you move from?" I asked.

"Oh, not far. I lived in Arkansas."

"Texas and Arkansas. I don't notice a Southern accent," I said.

Wendy grinned. "I was born and raised in Washington state."

"You said your dad retired from Boeing?" Tucker asked.

"Yeah. He worked as an engineer there, mostly designing jet engines. There's a slew of military retirees working various jobs on-site. One of his buddies set me up on a blind date. That's how I met Lane." Wendy took a bite and wiped the pizza sauce from her lips with a napkin. "The ex," she clarified.

I broke off a chunk of crust and passed it to Noah. "Do you mind if I ask how long you were married?"

Wendy took a drink of water, then held up three fingers. She covered her mouth while she swallowed. "We met five years ago and were married for three." Longing washed over Wendy's features. "I wanted to start a family, but Lane wanted to wait. I see it's a good thing now since it didn't work out. Divorce is messy, and it's hard enough on adults. I wouldn't wish it on children."

Her married timeline mirrored Tucker's, though in his story, Noah proved a ginormous blessing.

Tucker's pizza consumption slowed, as if he'd had the same thought.

"And now you're in Del Rio by choice?" I asked. A laugh burst from Wendy, and it was contagious. "Sorry," I said, covering my mouth.

She waved her hand. "No, it's okay. I get it. Totally." She leaned back in her chair and looked at me. "Sort of by choice. I worked on one of the bases in San Antonio, and it's hard to get a transfer within the system. I applied, and for three months nothing came available. Then"—she rapped her hands on the table in a drum roll—"Del Rio!" She said it with the voice of an announcer.

Noah giggled and tossed his soggy pizza crust across the table.

Tucker picked up Noah's crust and placed it on his plate. "Don't throw food, Nono."

Noah kicked his legs, then picked up his sippy cup for a long drink.

Wendy's smile remained in place. "Del Rio wasn't my choice, but I didn't have many options. I could have applied for different jobs, or I could have returned to Washington, but one thing I learned from my failed marriage was that I needed to have a direction. I needed to figure out what I wanted. I needed to know my priorities and expectations, both for myself and for a future partner. Del Rio gives me the space and time to ponder." She glanced at Tucker, her expression unchanging. "I'm still figuring it out."

I decided then that I liked her. Not for Tucker but for me. Her explanation reflected my thoughts. Del Rio did provide an opportunity for quiet that wouldn't have come from living in a bustling city like London.

"Did you grow up with horses?" Tucker asked.

Wendy told us how ever since she was little, she'd wanted to have a horse of her own. "We didn't have the space to board a horse in our suburban house, but my mom did what she could to make my dream come true. She drove me to lessons every week for years.

"Another bonus of living in Del Rio; it's fairly cheap," she explained. "I bought Honky with my divorce settlement. Lane is tightfisted—always has been—so it made him furious."

"Onky!" Noah shouted, bouncing in his seat.

We all laughed.

Tucker cleared the food, I washed Noah's hands and face, and Wendy wiped off the table. We visited for another hour, playing clapping games and ring-around-a-rosy with Noah. One little boy had a big hold on three adults, and none of us minded. His joy in the simple things amplified with his laugh. Interaction with Noah lifted my heart.

Wendy left around eight. I snuggled Noah in my arms, then lifted him up to Tucker. "I think it turned out to be a nice evening," I told my brother.

"It did. Thanks, Kas," Tucker said. A sincere smile touched his lips. "You're a great wingman . . . or wingwoman."

My heart smiled along with my lips. "Anytime, Tucker. Anytime."

CHAPTER 10

On Sunday I walked into church with a jumble of emotions ricocheting through my chest. I wanted to see Andrew. I wanted to talk to Andrew. I wanted to keep it simple at the same time that I wanted more. I feared pushing too hard. I feared appearing too lax. Needless to say, I couldn't stay focused on the sermon.

Tucker said he'd take Noah to nursery, so I hurried to Sunday School. I figured if I sat down first, I could watch where Andrew sat and gauge his intentions, so I found a seat and watched the room fill slowly. When an elderly woman and her husband sat on my left, I subtly set my purse on the seat to my right. The teacher took his place at the front of the room, and Hope slipped through the doorway. I waved at her, willing to give her the seat I'd saved for Andrew, but she held up two fingers. She found two seats together, and Ian came in shortly after. No sign of Andrew. I moved my purse under my chair, and a few minutes later the woman who led the choir sat down beside me. The hour passed, and Andrew never appeared.

After class I met Tucker and Noah at the nursery and watched Wendy interact with the children. She was patient and good. One day I hoped she'd get her family. I waved hello, then walked outside with my boys. Tucker secured Noah in his car seat, and the little guy's eyes immediately began to droop as Tucker pulled out of the parking lot.

"Too bad Andrew missed the service today," Tucker said.

I didn't want to think about it. I didn't like the mix of annoyance and sorrow the thought stirred. I eyed my brother. "Why's that?"

"I know you wanted to see him." Tucker kept his eyes on the road, making it tough for me to read his expression. He chuckled. "Am I wrong?"

"No," I said and turned to look out the window.

"You look nice today," he said.

I had taken extra time to straighten my hair and do my makeup.

"The Nottinghams are barbecuing tonight and invited us to join them," Tucker said. "I figured we could cut up the watermelon you bought and then we wouldn't have to cook." He glanced at me, and I raised my brows in question. Tucker, planning an outing? "I told them Noah and I would come, and Ian made sure to tell me you're invited as well," he said.

"I can come." I always enjoyed Hope and Ian and their children. Tucker didn't mention whether Andrew would be there, and while I really wanted to ask, I didn't, though it took a lot of restraint. Another affirmation that I was falling for Andrew—again.

Before it was time to leave again for the barbecue, I scooped watermelon balls into a bowl, then cut a cute zigzag pattern around the rind and dumped the fruit back inside the green shell. Tucker wrangled Noah, and I carried the watermelon to the Nottinghams' backyard. Ian stood at the grill, and Hope waved.

"I don't have an extra table to set the food on, so we can dish up inside," Hope said. She pointed to the watermelon I held. "You're so good. I would have just cut wedges and thrown them into a bowl. Do you wanna set the watermelon on the dining room table?"

"Sure thing." I pulled open the sliding-glass door and saw Andrew snatching some chips from the spread. "Busted," I said. Not the first word to cross my mind, but I wanted to be reasonable not reactionary.

Andrew's face lit when he saw me. "You caught me." He popped another chip into his mouth and chewed with his dimpled grin. I set the watermelon on the table, and before I knew it, Andrew had moved beside me and scooped me into a hug. "I've missed you," he whispered softly near my ear. As quickly as he released his hold, I wanted to feel it again. "You look nice today," he said, walking to where four folding chairs were leaning against the wall. He picked up two chairs in each hand and motioned with his chin for me to follow him outside.

We worked together to set the chairs around the patio table. Reactionary or not, my patience broke. "What did you do yesterday?" I asked.

Andrew grimaced. "I ended up in Mexico," he said.

Hope clapped her hands and asked everyone to gather for a blessing over the food.

Andrew leaned near and whispered, "I'll explain later."

Becca offered a sweet prayer, and Hope ushered us inside to dish up. I ended up in the seat next to Andrew. Hope and Ian sat together, and Tucker worked to keep Noah from toppling off his chair. Becca and Cole sat at a small plastic picnic table.

Ian's barbecue ribs were divine. I listened to the conversation but didn't internalize much. *Mexico?* My rationale kept trying to knock some sense into my emotions. I had no reason to be upset, other than my imagined justification that I possessed a claim on Andrew's time.

"Don't forget to cross-check your airspeed," Ian said. "Too many students run into trouble because they make it more complicated than it needs to be."

Tucker held a piece of watermelon on a fork for Noah, but he directed his gaze at Andrew. "How did you spend your Saturday?" he asked.

Andrew glanced at me and swallowed. His sudden somberness wiped his dimples away. "I'd rather not say, sir."

Tucker dropped his eyes and shook his head.

"Why not?" I asked.

Andrew fidgeted in his seat. He looked at Ian, more like pleaded with Ian, to have his back. "It might get some of my classmates in trouble."

Ian frowned and Tucker's eyes narrowed. "Is everyone safe?" Ian asked.

Andrew nodded.

"Any DUIs?" Ian asked.

"No," Andrew answered. "Just some stupidity."

"Then, I don't have to know." Ian wiped his fingers on his napkin.

So Andrew had been with his friends yesterday. Anger assailed me. Anger at myself. Why did I feel jealous and left out? I didn't want to be *that girl*, the one who complained or demanded. But I also wanted more than heart-stopping kisses without strings attached. Was that a fair expectation when I had been the one to end our relationship? Or was the truth that I didn't have a right to have any expectations because I hadn't told Andrew the direction I wanted to go?

Tucker surprised me when he spoke. "Have you guys met Wendy Stockman? She works in the nursery at church."

"Oh yes," Hope said with extra cheeriness. "Kasie told me she owns horses."

"One horse named Honky," Tucker explained. "I guess the saddle club is hosting a fundraiser in two weeks. They'll have a bake sale, a petting zoo, and some food trucks, and you can pay two dollars for a pony ride." He speared another watermelon ball with his fork and handed it to Noah. "They're raising money to replace the cooling fans for the barns."

"We should take Becca and Cole," Ian said.

The conversation shifted to funny stories about animals, and I wondered if that had been Tucker's intent. I kept my mouth full of food so I wouldn't have to comment, still battling my anger—along with my justification for it.

After eating, Andrew helped Hope clear the table. Ian made up a silly game for the kids with their set of toy golf clubs, and Tucker and I joined in the fun. Hope served strawberry shortcake for dessert, and afterward we worked together to haul everything back inside the house. Tucker and I waved goodbye, and Andrew followed us out the front door.

He quickened his step and touched my shoulder. "Kasie, do you want to go for a walk?"

Tucker held Noah on his hip. "I can get Noah to bed."

My brother's offer put me on the spot. "I'm not sure," I told Andrew. The not knowing made it hard to think.

"Please," he said, pleading with his eyes as much as his words. "We should talk."

He was right, and I was curious. I kissed Noah good night before walking with Andrew to the street. Our pace started slow. Andrew made some random comment about the food we'd eaten, then went quiet. His silence stoked my emotion, the pinching behind my ribs intensifying. I wanted to tell him everything I'd been wondering. I wanted to explain the roller coaster of emotion he'd ignited within me. I wanted to tell him how many times I'd replayed our electrifying kiss in my head and how it brought a happy smile to my face. Every. Single. Time. But my heart stuttered in confusion.

We reached the end of the pavement, an abrupt curb with half a mile of dirt and scrub brush before the base perimeter fence appeared. The chain link and barbed wire was barely visible in the dimming dusk. A streetlight stood nearby, but we stopped beyond its halo of illumination.

"You're mad at me," Andrew said, addressing the awkwardness drifting on the air between us.

I blinked my emotions into check and looked at him. "I'm not sure *mad* is the right word." I tossed a few descriptors around in my head. "I think *sad* is a better fit. Or maybe . . . *hurt*." It felt silly to claim Andrew had hurt me, but the tightness squeezing my chest testified that he had. "I hoped to hear from you yesterday, but I guess . . ."

"I'm sorry, Kasie. I really am." Andrew shoved his hands into his pockets and blew out a breath. "Pluto got into some trouble."

"What do you mean?" I asked.

"He . . . he's a real hothead sometimes." Andrew exhaled again and held my eyes before shifting his gaze to over my shoulder. "After work on Friday a few of the guys and Harper had the sudden notion to go to Mexico. They drank way too much there, and the border authorities tossed them into a cell to sober up. They were released early Saturday morning, but when they returned to their car, it had been towed. They went back to the police station and started arguing, so the police threw them back in jail. That's when they called me to come help them out."

"You could have let me know."

Andrew winced. "The first call came at three thirty in the morning. I figured you would want to sleep."

"Well, once you got back . . . ?"

Andrew reached forward and took my hand. "The police made things difficult. They wouldn't let me use my phone inside the police station, and they insisted we fill out all sorts of paperwork, which Harper had to translate because it was all in Spanish." His thumb rubbed across my knuckles. "It took four hours for the police to agree they were sober enough to leave again." I looked at our clasped hands while Andrew continued his explanation. "But then we couldn't leave because we had to track down where the car had been towed. Pluto couldn't withdraw enough from the ATM, so we had to call the bank, and by that time, my phone had died."

I pulled my fingers free from Andrew's grasp and placed a finger on his lips. "I get it," I said. I moved my hands to his face and my thumbs brushed across his cheeks. "I'm sorry."

Andrew's hands settled on my hips. "I didn't get home till two this morning. I would much rather have spent the day with you."

"I'm sorry," I said again. "I got jealous of your time." I dropped my arms to his shoulders.

"Jealous?" A grin spread across his face. "I like the sound of that." He tugged me close, and before I knew it, his arms wrapped around my back and he cradled my head in one hand. "Have you had a chance to decide whether you're willing to let me win you over?" he whispered near my ear.

A weight lifted and I felt like I could finally take a deep breath. "It's only been a week, Andrew. I told you I'd pray about it, and I am praying. You're going to have to be patient with me."

"I can do that." He pressed his cheek to my temple and blew out a long breath before loosening his hold. "It's gonna be a long week. We start night flying tomorrow, and I can't screw up."

"Don't overspeed the flaps," I joked with a halfhearted smile.

Andrew grinned. "Noted," he said. "I'm not sure how much time I'll have to see you, but feel free to be jealous of my time, and know that I'll be thinking of you often."

His magnetizing pull held me in place while my thumping heart pounded. Andrew moved his hands to my shoulders. He ran his fingers down the length of my arms and latched them with mine. He met my gaze with a direct stare, his chest rising and falling. "Before . . . I should have fought harder." My pulse accelerated even more. "This time I'm going to do better. I won't take you, take this"—he squeezed my fingers—"for granted. I plan to let you know exactly where you fall on my priorities list."

CHAPTER 11

The night passed with restless dreams. But my fatigue the following morning was nothing compared to what would come throughout the week. I finally understood why everyone dreaded night flying. Monday teased us into thinking it wouldn't be too bad. Tucker, Noah, and I went to the swimming pool before naptime, and afterward, when both boys laid down to sleep, I prepped a yummy dinner and had my favorite chocolate pie chilling in the refrigerator by the time they woke up. Tucker's shift started at six thirty Monday night, so we ate early and waved goodbye from the front door as he pulled away. Noah and I snuggled and read books until he went down for the night, and I binged a Netflix show.

Tucker rolled in just after eight the next morning. He ate three bowls of cereal and fell into bed. I hadn't realized how loud Noah talked and how a two-year-old could truly screech when I refused to give in to something he wanted. With Tucker trying to sleep, any noise amplified, and I knew he had only a short window before he had to return to work. I also knew the inherent danger of flying with student pilots. I wanted Tucker to get every minute of rest possible so he could be alert and safe.

I wiggled Noah's toes into his sandals and plopped him into the stroller. Hope and Becca planned to join us at the pool, along with one of Becca's friends. The heat hit early and fast, but the pool was only a mile away, so I justified walking. Noah splashed happily in the kid pool, and when we moved to the shallow end of the large pool, he jumped bravely into my arms. I sure loved that boy.

He lasted until half past noon before his eyes grew heavy and his temper grew short. Hope spread a picnic lunch out on the pool towels for Becca. When she offered a cracker to Noah, he grabbed it and threw it toward the swimming pool. Thankfully, his weak toss didn't land the food in the pool, but we needed to head home. He kicked and squirmed while I buckled him into the stroller, but he fell fast asleep before I crossed the main street to the instructor housing.

When I reached the corner of our street, a breathless voice called, "Kasie!"

I stopped and turned to see Andrew jogging toward me. I tried not to stare too long at his well-defined legs. "Shouldn't you be home sleeping?" I pulled the stroller back and forth, hoping the constant motion would keep Noah asleep.

Andrew stopped a few feet away. Ignoring his chest as it rose and fell with his labored breath proved difficult. I met his eyes, and he gave me a wide, dimpled grin. "I couldn't sleep. Thought I'd wear myself out and try again," he said.

"I've been praying you'll have a good week. And a safe week. Go get some sleep." I nudged my chin in the direction of his dorm and began pushing the stroller again.

"Kasie?" Andrew set his hands on his hips, further accentuating his shapely arms and torso, and blew out a frustrated breath. It seemed as though he wanted to say something more, but he only said, "I'll see you later." Accentuated with a wink.

I smiled. "Sweet dreams," I said and turned the stroller down the street and walked home.

While Noah slept, I checked in with Annabelle. *Macbeth* opened on Friday.

"How are tech rehearsals going?" I asked her.

"You know how it is. The first one is always the worst. Tonight will be better. I love creating the sets, but it's been fun to be back on stage." She told me about her costume and how the fog machine had busted. "Hopefully they get that replaced so the three witches are a little more creepy."

"I wish I could be there," I said.

"Well, if you can't personally come to support my drama, you should tell me all of yours." Her voice was far too jubilant. "Any more news on the Andrew front?"

"I told you he passed his check ride."

"Yep, and that you were going out to celebrate. How did that go?"

My face warmed as I recalled our kiss. "Can a kiss be tender and explosive at the same time?"

Annabelle squealed through the phone. "You really celebrated!"

"I guess that's fair," I said. "We've hung out since, but no more kissing."

"I knew fate had it in for you. But, Kasie . . ." Annabelle's voice was laced with concern. "What happens if you get into the drama program?"

"That's a long-shot *if.*" I had wondered the same thing myself, but I didn't want to get worked up over something that hadn't happened.

Annabelle agreed, but before we hung up she told me she didn't think it was such a long shot. "Don't dismiss yourself. You've got an impressive list of credits from college. I think you'll hear something soon."

My mind and my battered heart were crammed full. Worrying about something a year away wouldn't do me any good.

I worked on my script until I couldn't hold my eyes open. It was nearing completion, and excitement pulsed through me as I imagined how the final scene might be blocked. I jotted some notes down, then scrolled over to a web app to make a quick invitation for the talent show so the boys could pass them out to their friends. I also posted the invite on my social media pages. It couldn't compare with a performance at the Globe, but I wasn't ashamed of my current project. That night, as I brushed my teeth, I swiped through the comments on my pages and noticed Andrew had responded to my post about the talent show: *I can't wait.*

By the time the weekend rolled around, Tucker was spent, and the lack of sleep had taken a toll. I planned to watch Noah on Saturday and let my brother sleep in, but at seven o'clock Saturday morning, Tucker stumbled into the kitchen, where Noah and I were eating waffles. "Good morning," he said with drooping eyelids and a scruffy face.

"Are you sleepwalking?" I asked.

Tucker rubbed the back of his hand across his eyes. "Nope." He twisted his hips, stretching out his back. "Gotta get up and moving to get back on a regular schedule."

"If you say so," I said.

"I've flown enough overnight missions to know you can't just stay in bed. Pushing through is best."

My phone chimed with a text from Andrew. *Would you like to come with me to Lake Amistad?* Before I could type a reply, he called. He told me a group from his class wanted to rent a boat at the lake to relax after the long week. "I thought you might want to meet some other people our age. The catch is we need to leave in twenty minutes," he said. "You up for it?"

"I don't know, Andrew." A day at the lake sounded divine in theory, but I wasn't ready yet to commit to one hundred percent Andrew.

I could hear his exhale through the phone. "I'm trying to be patient, Kasie. I really am. I won't push. You can come meet some other people and just enjoy being out on the water."

His gesture came from a genuine place. It *would* be nice to expand my social circle. "Will there be other nonmilitary people there?" I asked.

"Yeah, some of the spouses. Jenga's bringing his wife, and I think Brash's wife and son are both coming."

"And you're sure it's okay if I'm there?" Hesitation fought against the idea of a day at the lake. Cool water sounded refreshing.

"I promise."

"Okay," I said. "But two rules."

"Shoot," Andrew said.

"First, I'm driving because you're tired."

"I won't say no to that."

"And second, no talking about us. Let's go as friends and have a good time."

"I'll do my best."

"Andrew," I warned.

"I can't help it if you're gorgeous and I'm sleepy so I might want to put my head on your shoulder. But I promise I'll do my best to resist," he said. "It's all I can promise right now."

He couldn't see me, but I shook my head anyway. "I guess that'll have to do."

I gathered a bag of everything I'd need. I wore my black tankini under a knee-length teal ruffled skirt and a white T-shirt and tossed a towel, sunscreen, and a hat into a rainbow-colored tote. Andrew said he'd prep food.

I told Tucker my plans, and soon Andrew and I were headed north. We followed the signs to Lake Amistad and made our way to the marina. Rocky slopes covered with scattered green bushes, cacti, and loose shale inclined upward from the shoreline. One covered pavilion sat among a handful of picnic tables on leveled slabs. Three men worked together to launch a motorized boat near the decent-sized marina. We had our choice of parking, and we climbed out of the car and grabbed our bags.

Waves lapped gently against the hardened ground, offering the promise of coolness despite the pressing sun.

"Not really comparable to the beaches in California," Andrew said. He held a canvas bag stuffed with picnic treats in his hand.

"No, but the water will feel great," I said, anxious to jump in and swim.

We walked down toward the marina, where a group of guys and gals waved as we neared the docks.

"Hey, everyone," Andrew said. He placed a hand on my back. "This is Kasie."

I got a collective hello. One man had his head shaved, revealing a smooth brown scalp. He stepped forward and gave Andrew a fist bump. Then he turned to me. "Did you fly in for the weekend?"

My surprise at the question must have shown. "No, I live on the base."

"Huh?" the man said with a dimpled smile. "You keeping secrets, Stoll?"

"Kasie and I know each other from college and recently ran into each other again. Nothing secret about it," Andrew said.

The man shrugged. "Whatever you say, man."

Andrew playfully rolled his eyes. "Kasie, this is Pluto," he said before introducing the others. "Martin, Lulu, Cal, Harper, and Ricky." Martin was a short, solid man with a strong jawline, large muscles, and brown skin. Lulu had pinned her short, blonde hair back with a couple of bobby pins, revealing a white freckled forehead and wide blue eyes. Harper wore a tank top and swim shorts, showcasing her toned arms and bronze skin. Cal radiated a mellow surfer vibe in board shorts, flip-flops, and a logo T-shirt that matched the trucker hat on his head. Ricky had a happy grin, full brown cheeks, and thick black lashes.

"Thanks for letting me tag along," I said.

Andrew offered his hand to a cute curvy woman with strawberry-blonde hair. "You must be Martin's wife. I haven't met you yet."

"I'm Sophie," she said.

We both shook her hand, and then she waved at someone behind us. I turned to see a lovely dark-skinned woman walking beside a tall, sturdy Black man. In his arms the man held a giggling toddler, who reached forward and tried to swipe the brim of his mom's floppy mustard-colored hat. She nuzzled her nose against the toddler's cheek and shared a radiant smile.

"This is Brash, Janie, and adorable little Mitchell," Sophie told me as they joined the group.

I smiled and waved. "Hi, I'm Kasie."

"Friend of Stoll's?" Brash asked.

"They went to college together," Cal said before I could respond.

"Cool." Brash handed Mitchell to Janie, then rubbed his hands together. "Are we all here? I'm itching to get out on the water."

"We're all here," Andrew said.

Before long we were cruising at twenty miles per hour on a rented pontoon. Mitchell stood on the bench and held on to the railing, mesmerized by the ripples on the water. His excited rapture entertained the adults. Cal and Martin asked about my education and how I knew Andrew. I simplified our history and told them we had lived in the same apartment complex and had hung out a few times. When they asked how we'd met up in Texas, things became a bit more complicated.

"My brother is an instructor pilot—"

"Here?" Ricky asked. "At Laughlin?" He turned to Andrew with large eyes and a look asking, *Why didn't you explain that earlier?*

"Who's your brother?" Lulu asked.

"Tucker Foster," I said.

Brash snapped his fingers. "I totally see it now. You look a lot alike."

"Wow," Cal said, leaning back and draping his arms across the top of the seat cushions.

Andrew delicately explained Stacy's passing and how I'd come to Texas to take care of Noah.

"That's amazing you'd move here to help," Lulu said.

"We're a close family, and the timing worked out," I said.

"And Stoll's here to keep you company." Martin grinned and reached for his wife's hand.

"Neither of us realized we'd both be here, but it's been nice to see a familiar face," Andrew said. I appreciated his efforts to explain our relationship to the others.

Cal steered us into an open bay and anchored the boat. We divvied out snacks and chatted and ate until the heat made the lake too enticing to resist. After swimming and splashing for over an hour, we climbed back into the pontoon.

Sophie passed out cookies. "Are we still on for next Saturday?" she asked.

"What's Saturday?" I whispered to Andrew.

"They've been planning a trip to San Antonio," he said.

"I'm in." Harper stretched her legs and lounged back in her seat.

Cal grabbed a cookie and pointed it at Harper. "Have you been to New Braunfels yet? It's worth the drive."

"The farmers' market won't be running," Lulu said.

"Which means we can find parking," Ricky said with a chuckle.

"True," Brash said. Mitchell had fallen asleep on the bench beside him. "And we have to eat at the Gristmill."

"Can we get a sitter?" Janie asked.

"Of course." Brash gave her a sweet kiss on the cheek.

Cal placed his palm on his chest. "It's my turn to drive."

"You're coming too, right, Stoll?" Lulu asked.

"Yeah, I'm in." Andrew grabbed two water bottles and handed me one.

I accepted it from him and took a long drink before standing and moving with practiced balance out from under the shaded canopy to the rear of the boat before Andrew could invite me to New Braunfels. He shouldn't invite me, in light of the whole *I need to keep my distance and allow him to focus on flying* thing. I figured if I left the conversation, he could make his plans without feeling any pressure.

He interpreted it differently. "Hey, you okay?" he asked, coming to stand beside me.

"Yeah." I motioned with my water bottle to the blue lake. "This has been great."

Andrew's eyes swept over my face. "You sure?" He turned and leaned back against the railing. "I kind of thrust you into the middle of everyone. They can be a bit rowdy."

"They've been kind, and it sounds like you're all close. I think it's great you have that camaraderie." I took a drink. "I'm sure going through this together gives you all a special bond too. It's good you have a chance to hang out away from base."

Andrew began to nod. "Ah, well, they like to keep busy and find a way to take a break from UPT. You should come with us to New Braunfels. It's a cool town with a bunch of German history."

I pinched my lips together. "That's probably not the best idea," I said. "And Tucker's committed us to a fundraiser at the barn next weekend." I turned and leaned against the railing beside him.

"Kasie." When Andrew said my name, it became hard to remember why it was a bad idea to be in his company. "I told you I want to keep crossing paths." He touched my arm. "I want this to work. I'll show you we can work."

There was no hesitation in his touch, and his fingers were warm on my skin. I turned back around to face the water, breaking the connection. "Remember rule number two?" I asked.

"I only promised to try my best" Andrew's voice was soft beside me.

I knew if I looked at him, things would change. I would see the sincerity in his eyes, the plea framing his brow. The soft pull of his lips would draw me in.

I watched the sunlight glitter on the surface of the lake instead. The shoreline looked so near and also so far. The pontoon suddenly felt suffocating. The reality of standing beside Andrew a thousand miles away from the joyful memories we shared collided with the aching parts of my heart.

He touched me again. I wondered if he knew how much power his touch had to sway me. "I'm not going to push you. I don't need an answer now. I only ask that when you pray, you do so with an open heart. Don't close the door on the possibility, thinking that this"—he motioned between us—"has to be complicated. It doesn't. We can take it one step at a time, keep it simple. Please?" he asked. "Give us a chance."

"Simple, huh?" I laughed. I couldn't help it. Because the problem was rooted in the fact that I already felt all kinds of confused.

CHAPTER 12

Tucker and I had a hard time connecting with Mom and Dad for our weekly Sunday video chat. The connection kept cutting out on their end, so we defaulted to a phone call. Noah held the phone for a bit, but he was more interested in running away and making Tucker chase him than talking to Grandma.

We met on Wednesday for our skit rehearsal and Noah decided to cling to my leg the entire hour. He was irritable through the afternoon and earned himself a prompt bedtime of 7:00 pm.

Tucker got home around nine. He changed into comfy clothes and plopped at the table with a plate of warmed-up leftovers. "How are you doing?" I asked.

"Right now I'm tired," Tucker said, pulling his plate close to him.

"We've been here three months. Are you thinking this assignment was the right thing?" I asked. Lately I'd been focused on myself. Praying about Andrew, writing my script, and working on the talent show had consumed my thoughts. I realized I hadn't checked in with Tucker for a few weeks.

His chewing slowed, his eyes narrowing as he contemplated my question. He nodded his head and swallowed. "I do," he said. "I really wanted to focus on the important things, and for me, that's Noah. My hours are much better here than they were in Arkansas." He took another bite.

"I'm glad," I told him.

"I do feel bad about dragging you here."

"It's not like I was kicking and screaming. I volunteered to come. Don't forget that."

"Well, I don't feel as bad as I once did," he said. A playful glint touched his eyes, and he scooped up his final bite.

"Why's that?" I asked.

Tucker stood and took his plate to the sink. He rinsed it and placed it in the dishwasher and dried his hands. "I can't tell you," he said.

I pushed up from my seat. "Why not?"

"Cause in high school you told me not to get involved in your dating life."

"You're talking about Andrew?"

Tucker shrugged. "He's growing on me."

I liked that my brother liked Andrew. My smile was hard to contain. "He's growing on me, too."

When I emerged Saturday morning at 7 a.m., Tucker was dressed and feeding Noah. "I thought for sure he'd sleep in since he hasn't been napping well," I said, taking a seat at the table.

"Today's the fundraiser at the stables, remember?"

That clarified a lot. "Oh yeah. But doesn't it run for a while? Do you need to go now?"

Tucker pulled out a chair and dropped into it. "I want to go support the cause." More like he wanted to go to support Wendy, but that was a good cause too.

"So do I, but I like to offer my support when I've gotten all of my beauty sleep." I stood and grabbed a plate and utensils and set them down on the table.

"More!" Noah demanded. I broke off a portion of waffle and handed it to him to dip into his bowl of syrup.

"I know weekends are your time to catch up on sleep." I pushed the waffles toward Tucker. "So eat up and go back to bed. I can watch Noah for a couple of hours this morning."

My brother shook his head, then stared at his plate for several seconds before picking up his fork and cutting a bite. "Nah. I think I'd rather go now, then sleep when Noah sleeps." He shoved a huge piece into his mouth, and then he pointed his fork at me. "If you don't want to go to the stables, I'll take Noah, and you can get a break." He turned to his son. "Hey, Nono, want to go see the horses?" At the mention of the word *horses*, Noah forgot about the food in his hand. "Do you want to ride one?" Tucker asked.

"Horse," Noah said.

"Well, now you have to go before sleeping," I said with a laugh. "And I want to go. It's something different to do. Besides, I like Wendy, and I need to meet Honky."

Thirty minutes later we were on our way. Tucker parked, and my phone chirped with an incoming text. *What are you up to today?* I smiled at my phone.

"Andrew?" Tucker asked.

"Yeah," I said and typed a reply. *Aren't you headed to New Braunfels?*

Andrew: *Change of plans.*

My fingers stilled as I thought about my response. Did he cancel? Were the others still going? Questions hurtled through my thoughts till I shook my head, willing them to clear. Andrew had said we could go slow. He'd said to keep it simple. I typed a new text.

Me: *Well, if you're up for a pony ride, Tucker, Noah, and I are at the base stables for a fundraiser.*

Andrew: *Count me in. I'll be there soon.*

Three food trucks lined the road, and various signage directed visitors to the different activities. A pen of chickens and another with goats had been set up around the perimeter of the buildings. I pointed out all the animals and activities to Noah, and Tucker went to purchase tickets for the attractions. A long string of tickets flapped in his hand when he walked back a few minutes later.

"Looks like you're planning on a lot of pony rides," I teased.

"I thought it would be fun to watch Andrew get bounced around a few times," Tucker said with a half smile. Then he shrugged. "We don't have to use them all. Just doing my part to support the fundraiser."

Tucker held Noah's hand and handed two tickets to the teen managing the chicken pen. The teen gave Tucker a small paper sack of feed.

"Are you gonna feed the chickens, Noah?" I asked.

Noah tried to pull Tucker to the gate. "Hold on, Nono," Tucker said. "I'm coming." Tucker looked back at me. "You coming too?"

"Nope. This looks like a good father-son opportunity. I'll take pictures for Mom."

The attendant opened the gate, and Noah tugged with all his might for Tucker to follow. Once the gate closed, Noah released Tucker's hand and went straight for the nearest chicken. The fowl darted and flapped its wings. Noah frowned and tried again, but Tucker grabbed his hand, bent down, and pointed to the birds while explaining something to Noah. Tucker dumped some feed into Noah's hand, and Noah chucked it all at a group of chickens. It took a few more attempts and patience from Tucker, but Noah soon became an expert chicken feeder, scattering bits of grain across the ground. I snapped some shots of the two of them together.

"Hey there," Wendy said. She stood beside me and crossed her arms. "I used to love this sort of thing when I was a kid." She watched Noah reach forward to try to pet a chicken. Tucker squatted to Noah's level and poured more grain into his hands. "Tucker's a good father," she said.

"He is," I said. "He'd do anything for Noah."

"Like move to Del Rio, Texas," Wendy said with a laugh. "I essentially had a choice to come here. He didn't really. At least, not if he wanted to avoid deployments. Here he can fly and be a good dad who gets most weekends off." I appreciated Wendy for seeing that side of Tucker. His somberness and then his efforts to mask his somberness sometimes veiled how big of a heart he truly had.

"He's had a rough year," I said.

"He told me, you know—about Stacy. The night we had dinner after I watched Noah." She turned to face me, as if she needed to gauge my reaction. I don't know exactly what my face revealed. I didn't mind that Tucker had had dinner with her. My frustration that night had been fueled by my brother's forgetfulness of Hope and her efforts, not Tucker eating dinner with Wendy.

"I appreciate you watching Noah that day. I was still feeling off, so the break was nice," I said. "So was the extra sleep."

Tucker handed Noah the paper sack, and Noah dumped all the remaining grain out near his feet. The chickens came clucking over, and Noah danced in giddy excitement.

"Did Tucker tell you anything we talked about then?" Wendy asked.

"Uh . . . he never mentioned anything specific." I racked my brain trying to recall whether I had missed something.

"Men," Wendy said with a sigh. "I realized offering to watch his kid and then having them over to eat probably appeared a bit forward. I wanted Tucker to know I did it for Noah more than anything." She paused for a bit, considering. "No, that's not true. It was for me. Tucker's not the only one who's had a rough year." She gave a mirthless chuckle, and her breath hitched. "For as long as I can remember, I couldn't wait to have children. When Lane and I first married, he said we could start our family after a year. Then it became two, and whenever I brought it up, he pushed me off again and again. When I finally realized he was simply stalling, I looked closer at our relationship and noticed the red flags. The next year we were divorced, and while I'm grateful we didn't have to put a child through all the yuck, I worry that maybe I won't get a chance to be a mom."

Wendy's words clarified a lot. Her divorce had not only cut ties with her husband but hindered the possibility of her being a mom. No wonder she volunteered to help in the nursery. She carried a sincerity with her. She was authentic. Real. And it made me hope to be her friend, someone she could share all the weighty realness with. Because I got it. I understood plans changed. Life shifted. And sometimes the load felt impossible to bear.

"I don't know why I'm telling you all of this," Wendy said. "I guess I thought you should know."

"Thank you," I said. "Hearing your words and your experience makes me feel a little less alone in dealing with all the crazy life throws at me."

A large smile spread across her face. "All the crazy," she said, and I knew she could relate.

Tucker and Noah exited the chicken pen and walked toward us.

"What are you two talking about?" Tucker asked.

"Men," I said.

"And boys," Wendy added, bending down to ask Noah about the chickens.

"Great," Tucker mumbled.

Wendy wasn't giving rides on Honky for the fundraiser. She trusted him one-on-one, but with the larger crowd, she didn't want to risk the horse acting up. She led us over to an older man with ashy gray hair, brown skin, and wrinkles of wisdom. He held a lead rope for a black pony with a long white blaze on his nose. "This is Norma," the man said, pointing to the pony. "She's as patient as a sunflower and as steady as a rock."

"Can Noah here get a ride?" Wendy asked.

"Anything for you, Miss Wendy," the man said with a friendly wink.

"Thank you, Mr. Perez," Wendy said.

Tucker handed Mr. Perez a ticket and lifted Noah into the saddle. "Dada," Noah whined, reaching his arms out for Tucker to hold him. He began to wiggle and started slipping sideways off the saddle. Tucker moved closer to the pony and wrapped an arm around Noah's waist while keeping him in place.

"What's wrong, Nono?" Tucker asked. Noah's bottom lip pushed forward, and he began to cry. "It's okay. Don't you want to ride the pony?"

Noah's volume increased, and he practically launched himself from the saddle into Tucker's arms. Bewilderment filled Tucker's face, and he turned to Wendy and me. "Is he scared? He loves riding Honky, who's way bigger than Norma. I don't understand."

Mr. Perez patted Norma between her ears. "Sometimes something unexpected and unfamiliar simply throws us off," he said.

Wendy stepped forward and rubbed a hand up and down Norma's neck. "Noah didn't jump right onto Honky's back. He took some time to get to know him." She peeked over Tucker's shoulder and caught Noah's eye. "Do you want to try to ride Norma?" she asked Noah. "She's a nice pony."

Noah squeezed Tucker tighter and sucked in ragged breaths.

"I think that's a no," Tucker said.

"Well, if you want to try again, swing on by." Mr. Perez shortened his hold on the reins and turned to a family with two young kids waiting at the gate. "Do you want to go for a ride?" he asked. He invited the young girl and boy to come forward and pet Norma.

Our group moved to the outside of the fence so the others could enjoy their turn. We started walking toward a nearby table, where a banner advertising an animal rescue hung from an E-Z UP. Containers were spread across the top of the table, and two women and a man held different animals for visitors to pet. Tucker held Noah on his hip and pointed to a container with a hamster. Noah leaned forward to get a closer look, so Tucker squatted down and set Noah on his knee so he was eye level with the hamster. Wendy stood a few feet back with a content smile, watching my nephew.

Tucker stood and moved to another container. "And there's a tarantula," he told Noah.

One of the women, who looked to be in her forties, with dyed blonde hair and perfectly styled bangs, took the lid off the tarantula box.

"This is Al," she said sliding her hand under the belly of the hairy spider and lifting him out. I leaned back for self-preservation, but Noah had no inhibitions. He reached a pudgy finger forward. "Do you want to pet him?" the woman asked, looking at Tucker for approval.

"We can pet the spider?" Tucker asked her.

The woman rotated her hand so the tarantula's abdomen pointed toward us and its head faced her. She pointed to the speckled hair on the fat part of the body. "You can help your son run his finger along Al's back, right here. As long as he is gentle and doesn't poke or pinch, Al probably won't move."

"'Probably'?" I repeated. I took another step back and wondered if tarantulas could jump.

Tucker placed his large hand around Noah's small one and together they petted Al, if petting is what one did to a tarantula. "Kas, get a picture," Tucker said.

A few clicks later I caught Noah's laughing smile on camera. "Mom will love these," I said.

"Aww, it's cute," Andrew said from behind me. "Are you going to pet it next?"

I guess *pet* was the right word. "Nope," I said slipping my phone back into my pocket. "You know how I feel about spiders."

Andrew chuckled. "Yes, I do."

I'd had to call him once in college to come to my rescue because a spider had posted itself near my bedroom doorframe, and I'd refused to walk past it to leave my room.

"Have you met Wendy?" I asked Andrew. "She helps in the nursery at church."

He stepped up and offered his hand, introduced himself, and explained that he was in training.

"And where are you from originally?" Wendy asked.

"San Jose, California, is home," Andrew said.

Noah started to wiggle, and Tucker set him down. The worker lifted the hand cradling Al a little higher and looked at me. "You can hold him if you'd like," she said.

I shook my head with a vehement no, but Andrew stepped up next to Tucker. "Are you and Noah done?"

Tucker held both of Noah's hands while he tried to squirm away. "Have at it," Tucker said. "I'm going to take Noah to see the goats."

"Okay," I said.

When I looked at Wendy, she nudged her chin toward Andrew, her eyes filled with questions. Questions I couldn't answer because I had to figure them out myself. A tight-lipped smile was all I could manage, but the look on Wendy's face communicated that she would be revisiting the conversation, even if we hadn't actually had a real conversation to begin with. She turned to follow Tucker and Noah, and I realized I sort of wanted to talk to her about my situation, my mixed answers, and the fondness I felt for Andrew.

After they'd walked away, the woman instructed Andrew on how to slide his fingers slowly beneath Al's belly. The spider simply lifted his legs and transferred from the worker's hand to Andrew's. "It's a bit ticklish. All the hair," Andrew said.

"Run your finger along his abdomen. It's soft," the woman said. Andrew did, and the worker shared a few facts about Al. "Tarantulas are heavy spiders. There are fourteen identified species in Texas. They prefer to live in burrows rather than webs but will leave a few strings of silk across the entrance of their burrows to detect prey. Luckily, bites from the Texas species aren't serious."

"Aren't serious, as in they can't kill you?" I asked.

"No," the woman said with a laugh. "That doesn't mean a bite wouldn't hurt, but their bites aren't deadly."

"To humans, anyway," I said under my breath.

"You'd know before they strike because when they're disturbed, they rise up on their hind legs and stretch out their front legs to intimidate the threat. That's how we know Al is calm right now and we can hold him," she said.

The tarantula shifted the tiniest bit, and I stepped back again. "Come on, Kasie." Andrew tried to sound encouraging. "See how mellow he is? You can hold him."

I shook my head. "Nope. I have absolutely no desire to hold Al," I said.

"Think of how cool this is. Not many people get to say they've held a tarantula," Andrew said.

"I'm okay with not being one of those people," I said, then wondered whether I really was. Not because of peer pressure—Andrew wasn't forcing anything—but because an opportunity stood before me, one few people had. What would I do with it?

The worker smiled. "You don't have to hold him. Al won't be offended."

Andrew chuckled and stroked Al's abdomen again. "Do you want to touch him?"

I bit my lip. My heart pounded, and I suddenly felt hot. I kinda did want to touch the spider, maybe even hold it. Nerves danced in my stomach. It seemed silly to feel to conflicted over a spider. A huge, hairy tarantula, but still.

"It's your call. Only do it if you want to," Andrew said.

I inhaled a deep breath, hoping the oxygen in my lungs would bolster a little courage. I didn't know why spiders were an aversion. I was like ten thousand times bigger than the furry thing, but for some reason, my arms and legs stilled like petrified wood. No, I could do this! For me. To prove to myself that I could overcome something hard. Slowly, slowly, I raised my right arm, extending my forefinger, but Andrew still stood three feet away.

He raised his brows. "You want to touch him?"

I nodded, blew out a breath, and mumbled, "Yeah."

Andrew stepped closer, his finger continually stroking Al's abdomen. "Al's such a calm, happy spider," he said. I remained frozen. No matter that I had determined to touch Al, my limbs were not obeying my internal commands. Andrew seemed to sense my hesitation. "You got this, Kasie." He maneuvered Al to my outstretched hand. "Here you go." He slid his hand with Al slowly forward until my finger brushed along the hair of Al's back. The spider's soft fur danced under my fingertip. All the muscles in my body tensed.

"You did it, Kasie," Andrew said softly. His dimples appeared.

"I . . . I'll try to hold him," I said. I don't know why the words surfaced, perhaps because I felt brave and wanted to prove I was capable of more.

Andrew's grin grew wider. "Here." He rotated his hand slowly, and I extended my fingers and palm as I had watched him do a minute before.

I gasped, and my chest clenched when Al lifted his front legs to transfer to my palm.

"He's just getting himself situated," the worker said.

I held my breath, and Andrew slipped his hand free. Al sat in my palm. Still. Silent.

"Wow," Andrew whispered.

I stood mute, slowly exhaling. "Okay, you can have him back now." I waited, not blinking, while the worker moved her hand onto mine to take Al back. My hand fell back to my side, my palm still tingling with prickles.

Andrew chatted with the worker for a moment while I reveled in my accomplishment. Andrew said thanks, then turned and lifted my hand. He stroked his thumb over the place the tarantula had sat only a moment before. "You're amazing. You know that?" he said.

My triumphant smile came naturally. "I am pretty awesome," I teased.

"Yes, you are." Andrew flipped my hand around and slipped his fingers through mine, and a warm, secure sensation, opposite of facing my arachnophobia, thrummed through me as we walked to meet Tucker and Noah at the goat pen.

Holding Al had required me to do something hard. It seemed silly—Al was just a spider, after all. A large, hairy one with visible fangs, but still. As Andrew and I stood hand in hand and he chatted with Wendy, asking the familiar get-to-know-you questions, it hit me. I had held the spider. I could own that. I had faced a huge phobia, and while I wouldn't rush to repeat the experience, maybe I could at least calmly call for help during my next encounter with an eight-legged arachnid instead of shrieking and fleeing to a corner of the room. Like Mr. Perez had said, sometimes the unfamiliar threw us off. But that didn't mean I had to run away. Noah had ridden the horse, but the pony was different. I had dated Andrew in college, but now we had another opportunity in a shifted situation. Maybe it didn't need to be so scary. I had done something hard for no particular reason, except to try to overcome a fear, which meant I could conquer other fears.

I looked at Andrew's happy smile while he visited with Wendy. The familiar contours of his face, his gentle hand in mine, the possibility of *us*—another fear. I didn't want to pull back or take a step forward only to chicken out. Because if I was in, I wanted to be all in. Commitment meant exactly that, and I squeezed Andrew's hand and decided to wait for the opportune time to let him know I was ready to face my fears.

CHAPTER 13

"It's time for my shift with the ponies," Wendy said after Noah had had his fill at the goat pen.

Before she disappeared, I texted her my number. "We should get lunch sometime," I said. She agreed and walked off with a wave.

Tucker tried to convince Noah to return to the pony rides, but my nephew wouldn't relent. Instead of a pony ride, he got a shark painted on his lower arm, played in the bounce house, and worked with Tucker to do a few of the carnival-style games. We ran into the Nottinghams and chatted for a moment before their kids got anxious to check out the booths. Naptime hit, and Noah got grumpy, so Tucker took him home hoping they both might get some sleep, and I stayed behind to spend some time with Andrew.

The funnel cakes from the food truck tasted delicious, but they didn't offer much sustenance. Andrew and I circled the festivities one more time, then decided to drive into Del Rio to get something to eat.

Italian food won out. My hesitation to order the shrimp fettucine proved futile. Del Rio may be far from the coast, but my meal was yummy. We dined in between the busy hours, and the sun still shone brightly by the time we returned to Andrew's car.

"I have an idea," he said, "unless you have something you need to get home for."

"I don't have anything pressing," I said. His contagious smile convinced me I had all the time in the world. He held my door, and I got in the car as I asked, "Are we doing another San Antonio run? I'm sure you're tired."

"Not San Antonio, but kind of San Antonio," Andrew said. He ran around to the driver's seat.

"What's that supposed to mean?" I asked.

"No spoilers." He shook his head.

We pulled out of the parking lot, and at the next stop sign he winked at me before turning right. Happiness swirled around me. Forward motion felt right. It kept me grounded. I planned to keep moving forward, one pace at a time. Sometimes those steps were large. More often, they were tiny, incremental gains, but they were still progression.

We hit highway 90. I didn't know what lay between Del Rio and San Antonio—a few gas stations and restaurants, but I couldn't remember much else. Thirty minutes later Andrew pulled off in Brackettville, Texas, a small town off the main road. We drove past the sparse buildings and headed north, where the road grew narrow with tar-patched repairs and wild grass growing too close to the asphalt. Andrew sat happily humming under his breath and never doubting our destination. I, on the other hand, wondered where in the vast, vacant desert he was taking me. A fitting metaphor. I even snuck a peek at the gas gauge. If we dipped below half, I would require an explanation or ask him to turn around.

Signage appeared up ahead. Orange with white letters grew larger until I could read Alamo Village.

"The Alamo?" I asked.

"This is where the John Wayne *Alamo* movie was filmed. The set is a full-size version of the real deal." Andrew turned left and drove through the entrance. "It might not be open much longer because the owners have passed away and they don't have a new investor. But since we didn't see the real deal, we can start here." He pulled into a lot with maybe a dozen other cars.

The movie set of *The Alamo* compound proved impressive. Wood beams, rock with fat stripes of mortar, stone columns, and detailed carvings around the heavy doors made to match the original building in San Antonio, and this one I could touch. We could take our time exploring.

"You up for it?" Andrew asked. A touch of hesitation laced his voice.

"Yeah, let's check it out," I said, opening my door and hopping out.

And explore we did. A short video related some of the history of the set and the absurd number of bricks it had taken to make the outlying buildings to represent San Antonio's existence over 180 years ago.

"Can you believe they made a million and a half bricks on-site?" Andrew asked as we left the theater and walked outside.

"And built a runway," I said.

"That's how I knew about this place. Our training flights take us nearby, and we can see the runway from the air. One of my IPs told me about it."

We wandered around the outside, then took our time in the inner courtyard of the Alamo. A few of the San Antonio buildings were boarded up, and some were basic facades. But one held a museum with various props and costumes from the movie, and another housed a small gift shop. I bought a sticker more relatable to my current situation than the movie: a smiling cactus in the middle of the desert.

Andrew grabbed two ice-cream sandwiches from the deep freezer, and after paying for them, he handed me one, and we walked outside.

"Let's take a picture." I held up my phone to take a selfie in front of the stables. Andrew leaned close and shared his dimples, and I snapped the shot. "You look good," I said, leaning over to kiss his cheek. Andrew turned the opposite cheek toward me and tapped it with his finger. I kissed that one too.

"My turn," Andrew said. I offered one cheek, then the other. Andrew's kisses were gentle and soft. I offered my lips, and he answered with another delicate kiss on the corner of my mouth.

We found a bench under the shade of one of the few trees and sat down to enjoy our ice cream. The sun headed steadily toward the horizon, and the sky began to tint orange and pink.

"Good day?" Andrew asked.

"Good day," I said, taking another bite of ice cream. The tiniest breeze touched the branches overhead, and a leaf fluttered down, landing in the silence between us.

"What's on your mind?" Andrew asked.

"Texas," I answered. It wasn't a purposeful avoidance of his question, but it had been a nice day, and I didn't want to muck things up.

"What about it?" he pressed.

I shoved the end of the ice-cream sandwich into my mouth and thought on my answer. Being all in meant admitting the hard things. I wiped my hand across my mouth and swallowed. "It's not England," I said. Greenery, trees, tall buildings, parks, and history had once encompassed my vision of my future, yet I sat staring at cacti, endless horizons, tumbleweeds, and the dust coating my shoes. "There is beauty in Texas," I said. "The sunsets are screen-saver worthy, and . . ." I paused. "There's legit Mexican food." Another beat passed. "Noah's here, and Tucker." I reached over and touched Andrew's arm. "And you."

Andrew leaned over and kissed my cheek again. "But there's no Globe Theatre. No street performers. No high tea or English pasties," he said.

"I'm not partial to English pasties," I said, leaning close and leaning my head on his shoulder.

"Phew," Andrew said with a light laugh. He wrapped an arm around my back and tilted his head to rest against mine. His shoulder rose and fell with his breath. "I know this isn't want you wanted. I'm so torn because I wish you could be riding the tube and viewing a new performance every night, but I'm also really glad you're sitting beside me on this obscure bench in the middle of nowhere."

"Right now, I'm happy to be here too." I snuggled a little closer, unable to explain this moment. Everything on the outside seemed wrong, from the man I sat beside to the sparse landscape spread before me. Inside, though, everything seemed right, like hunkering down in a pounding rainstorm and enjoying the rhythmic melody while waiting it out.

Sitting beside Andrew again after being apart renewed my previous feelings and swelled new ones. But the question remained: Was this right? for him? for me? for us? I had been praying multiple times a day, asking God to grant me some sort of assurance that following this course was the right thing to do. No random rainbows had appeared. No unicorns either. But I also hadn't felt the squirming uncertainty I had back when Andrew and I had dated before. For me, that meant I should push forward.

Andrew planted a kiss on the top of my head. He said nothing more. He didn't need to. For all the prickly cacti on the horizon, it had turned out to be a perfect Saturday, even if I wasn't in Hyde Park.

Sunday service the next day passed just as peacefully, but no lightbulb-illuminated answers arrived then either. Beyond extra-long prayers, I turned to my scriptures, and a passage in Proverbs 3 hit me. "Trust in the Lord with all thine heart; and lean not unto thine own understanding. In all thy ways acknowledge him, and he shall direct thy paths." My understanding felt like circling a roundabout. Around and around, moving but not hitting on anything definitive.

Was I acknowledging the Lord? Was I allowing Him to direct me? I set my Bible aside and kneeled beside my bed. Bowing my head, I prayed for humility to accept whatever path God had in store for me along with the clarity to see what that path might be.

"Kas!" Tucker called from somewhere in the duplex.

I finished my prayer and wandered out of my room. Tucker walked toward me, waving his phone. "Mom and Dad just did a video call with Noah and want to talk to you." He handed his phone to me.

"Hey, Mom. Hey, Dad." I flipped the screen around and walked back into my room to sit on my bed.

"Kasie!" Dad said happily. "It's been too long since I've seen my little girl."

"You look good, Dad," I said. He wore a big smile, and his hair had grown long, hanging over his ears and brushing his collar. "You too, Mom." She wore her hair pulled back, and her face was makeup free.

"Thank you, hon. How have you been?" Mom asked.

I gave them an update on the elementary variety show. "I also finished the script I'm writing," I said. "And Noah is getting better at communicating. The other day he told me he wanted a *slup*." My parents' faces mimicked my confusion when I'd first heard it. I laughed. "He meant a straw. Whenever he has a straw in a drink, he slurps the end of the drink, and I tell him not to slurp, so he called the straw a slup."

Mom's smile widened. "Oh, I love that age," she said.

"We use straws all the time here," Dad said. "I'm going to adopt the word *slup*."

I told a few more Noah stories. Tucker and Noah had already shared their experiences with the goats, chickens, and bounce house, so I talked about my heroic tarantula feat.

"Andrew joined you, too, right?" Dad asked. He obviously had insider information.

"He did," I said. "We spent time at the fundraiser and then grabbed some food before heading out to a place called Alamo Village. It's the film set for the *Alamo* movie John Wayne starred in."

"That sounds fun," Dad said.

"Yeah, they've actually filmed a lot of movies featuring the Alamo there, but it was built originally for the John Wayne film." I arranged a section of comforter so I could balance Tucker's phone in the blanket and didn't have to continue holding it.

"And how are things with Andrew?" Mom asked. Her soft eyes and patient stare warmed my heart.

"I think I need to give us a go." I looked at my parents through the screen and hoped my future marriage would match the strength and surety of their relationship.

"That's how you'll know for sure," Dad said.

"I know, but we *have* tried before. I still don't understand all of it, but I realize I can't walk away without knowing for sure." I placed a hand over my heart. "So I'm gonna try again."

Mom's smile pushed her cheeks upward, hiding most of her wrinkles. "I think you're making a wise choice."

"Really?" I asked, desperate for her endorsement.

"I do," she said. "You're happy. I can see it. And I'm glad for it."

"Yes," Dad echoed. "Happiness is all we want for you, sunshine." His nickname for me plucked a tender heartstring.

"I love you both," I said.

"We love you too," Mom said.

"Now, go figure out whether you love that Andrew fellow," Dad said.

"I plan to," I said. But deep in my soul, I already knew the answer.

CHAPTER 14

Dress rehearsal on Thursday scored a solid five stars. In their excitement to deliver the laughs, the boys rushed a bit and forgot a few lines, but I was extremely pleased with their performance and the confidence they had gained through the process.

Hope did not have such great success with Noah. "He really was fine," she assured me when I picked him up from her house.

But Little Becca set the record straight. "Noah broke my tea set." She held up two broken halves of a miniature plate. "And he cried a lot."

I inhaled and squeezed Noah tightly to keep him from wriggling out of my arms. "I'm sorry, Becca. I'll get you another tea set."

She grinned. "Okay. Can it be purple?"

"Of course."

Noah's attitude did not improve. He must have said no fifty times before I became resigned to the fact that he wasn't going to stop screaming and I needed to set him in his crib and walk away. I hoped the tantrums wouldn't continue. I had talked to Mom two days ago, so I knew she and Dad were on a cenote tour today and weren't available, but I needed a dose of adult conversation. Annabelle's number went straight to voicemail. Tucker was working a late shift and wouldn't be home until ten, so calling Andrew wasn't an option. Hope would answer my call, but she'd put up with my little tantrumming nephew for the last few hours; she deserved solace. Still, I needed to talk to someone who wouldn't scream back at me, and I would prefer to have a conversation consisting of adult vocabulary.

Before I could think for too long on it, I pulled up Wendy's number and dialed.

"Hey, Kasie," she answered cheerfully.

"Hi. I hope it's not too late," I said. It was only 8:15 in the evening, but some people were particular about phone calls.

I couldn't be sure, but it sounded like Wendy snort-laughed. "Not. At. All. I'm a night owl, and I actually don't need much sleep."

"What would that be like?" I joked. "I don't feel like I'm sleeping much, but not by choice. I think it's part of the deal when a toddler is involved."

"Eh," Wendy hedged. "I'd bet teenage years are harder."

"I think my volunteer shift ends by then," I said. I lifted the phone from my ear to listen for Noah. His cries had stopped, so I hoped he had given up and surrendered to sleep.

"Or you'll be raising your own little humans."

"Maybe." I grabbed my guilty pleasure—a pint of Ben and Jerry's Tonight Dough—from where I'd set it on the counter, along with a spoon.

I could pretty much predict Wendy's next question. "I know this is a big jump," she said. "No pressure, but what's the story with you and Andrew?"

I plopped onto the couch and opted for speakerphone so I could eat my ice cream at the same time I filled Wendy in on the backstory between Andrew and me. When I got to the part about running into each other at Laughlin, I didn't have to ask her opinion.

Her voice gushed through the phone. "That's the most fated love story I've heard outside of a movie theater. Maybe you'll have those little humans sooner rather than later."

"I follow the nursery rhyme. 'First comes love, then comes marriage, *then* comes the baby in the baby carriage.'"

Wendy laughed. "Oh, I understand. And how far along are we on the first part?"

Love. A big, full-of-emotion, tidal wave of a word.

Before I could answer, Wendy spoke again. "I don't have to wonder where Andrew stands, but you weren't so easy to read."

"Really?" I didn't know which part of her statement my question pertained to but was content to let her interpret.

"He was all smiles. His feelings were pretty obvious."

"But . . ." I paused, not sure how invasive my next question might sound. "Can I ask you something personal? I mean, you don't have to answer."

"Sure," Wendy said, and when I didn't continue, she took a guess. "If it's about my divorce, I'm not shy about it. It was a rough time, and I'm glad I'm on the other side of it now, but if my experience can help someone else, I'm all for talking about it."

I took Wendy at her word and asked the question. "Did you pray about marrying your ex-husband?"

"I did."

"But you ended up divorced."

"Yep."

"How do you reconcile the two experiences?" I asked.

Wendy remained silent for a moment. "I'm not sure," she said. "Maybe both answers were right."

I had hoped for more insight, not further confusion. "The paradox feels so extreme. How could they both be right?"

"Are we still talking about my divorce?" Understanding laced Wendy's question.

"I can't deny that breaking up with Andrew was the right thing before. It felt off and wrong. But now we're both here, we're both still single, we're both still attracted to one another."

Wendy's chuckle resonated with more irony than humor. "I get it. On my wedding day I thought nothing would ever separate Lane and me. We would have a family, make memories, grow old. It all felt so right. When he looked at me, I knew he loved me. We wanted the same things. But then something changed, and we didn't. I don't think I changed, but maybe I should have."

"What do you mean?" I asked.

"Maybe Lane needed me to be flexible. Maybe he needed to wait longer to have children than I wanted to wait. Maybe . . . I don't know. Maybe he fell out of love with me." Her voice was choked with emotion. "He made bad choices. He turned away from me instead of toward me. Maybe we could have worked through it together, but that only happens if you open up to each other and share your struggles. All I know is something did change, and it ended our marriage. But that doesn't mean the answer God gave me about marrying Lane was wrong. And I know I'm not blameless in the divorce. Both he and I needed to recenter, and instead he ran away and I was left floundering. In the end, wanting something wasn't enough, and I don't blame God for our mistakes."

"Thank you for sharing with me. I know my situation isn't the same, but it helps to hear your thoughts and experiences." Her explanation helped me see a different perspective. Prayers and answers to prayers could change. God expected us to put in the work and then turn to Him. He also wanted us to trust Him. "I know it's different this time with Andrew. It feels right where before it didn't."

"I would have fought, Kasie. I wanted to. I would have fought for my marriage if Lane had been willing. This is where your story is different. Andrew knows he needs to fight, and it sounds like he's willing."

"So he's like my knight in shining armor?" I smiled at the thought.

"All suited up and ready to win your heart," Wendy said.

"That sounds like an ideal ending."

Stage fright was real. I'd learned techniques to channel my jitters into positive excitement before a performance, but Cole, Rutherford, and Frankie ran somewhere in the spectrum between goofy and petrified.

The talent show began with an impressive fifth grader wowing the audience with magic tricks. Various music and dance performances followed, including a skit with a young boy who juggled. My boys were scheduled as the first skit in the second act. During the intermission, I walked them to the bathroom, then gave them a snack-pack of Oreos to split. Most theatre teachers would balk at them eating in costume, but a sugar spike trumped a few crumbs. Plus, I'd kept their makeup light—only a bit of color for their cheeks and tinted ChapStick—so after their cookies, touch-ups were easy.

We moved to the right wing and stayed tucked behind the curtains. I rubbed my hands together. "I'm ready to laugh," I told the boys.

They each repeated their opening lines, and the emcee walked out to announce the second act. I smiled wide as the stage manager ushered them onto the stage. Then I stopped and watched.

The curtain opened, and the spotlight found Rutherford. His eyes widened, and he looked back at Frankie and Cole. Then he turned to the audience, cracked a hammy smile, and delivered his line. It was pure gold.

He set the tempo for the other two boys, and they did not disappoint. Beat after beat they hit their cues, pausing for laughter and then picking up at the optimal moments. At the end of their seven-minute skit, they exited with flair, and the audience continued to laugh after the curtain pulled closed.

"Well done!" I jumped in giddiness alongside them, clapping my hands. "You guys nailed it!"

"We were funny, weren't we, Miss Kasie?" Frankie asked.

I held up my hand for a high five. "You were hilarious." I gave all the boys a hand smack, then shushed them as we moved offstage so the next performance could begin.

We talked in excited, hushed whispers and waited for the girl dancing on stage to finish her routine before slipping out a side door. The front left section of chairs had been reserved for the participants, and the boys each snagged a seat in the first row. I settled into a chair behind them, soaking in the euphoria of a successful performance. Piano pieces were played, several singers belted out tunes, a baton-twirling phenom ended by catching her baton while doing the splits, and the final act involved a boy and his well-trained dog completing an obstacle course on stage, where the dog jumped through a hula hoop wrapped in foil flames to look like fire circled the hoop.

The emcee stood. "How about another round of applause for all of this great talent!" The audience obliged, and the emcee acknowledged the judges. She held up a standard certificate. "Each student will get a participation award, and we have a few additional accolades."

Reading down the program, the emcee called each act onstage. They crowded together, and she handed them their participation certificates before turning back to the audience. "What a great night of entertainment we've had. The judges have tallied their votes." One of the judges handed her another stack of papers, and she began to read off the specific awards.

As she read through the pile, it became apparent that each act would receive a more specific award. Most Acrobatic went to the baton twirler, and variations of Most Musical, Best Solo, and Best Show Tune went to all the singing and instrumental acts.

Frankie, Rutherford, and Cole began to whisper, looking back at the emcee with questioning eyes. She grinned at the three boys and read the paper in her hand. "Best Comedy goes to Sherlock's Mystery!"

Frankie whooped, Rutherford pumped his arms in the air, and Cole stepped forward to accept the award. The fire alarm could have begun blaring and the boys wouldn't have heard it. They crowded around Cole, grinning wide and tracing their fingers along the letters proclaiming they were the biggest clowns around. The lights brightened, and families gathered for pictures.

"Here, Miss Kasie!" Cole stood on his tiptoes with a bouquet wrapped in crinkly cellophane. "Thank you for helping us." The three boys, their families, and Tucker and Noah all stood near as Cole handed me the flowers.

"And we won an award!" Frankie said with a grin.

"You boys were amazing. You deserved an award, and you deserve ice cream." I pointed to the line at the back of the auditorium, where ice-cream sundaes were being doled out.

"Can we go now, Mom?" Rutherford asked Marylou.

"Yes, but don't make yourself sick," she said. She turned back to me. "You did a great thing for them."

"I honestly enjoyed it," I said. "They were excited, and that makes a world of difference."

"Well, thank you," Emmaline said. "Come by the restaurant sometime, and your meal is on the house."

"You went out of your way, and it showed," Hope said. "Cole will always treasure this memory. I'm grateful, Kasie. Truly."

I lifted the flowers a little higher. "I'll hold on to this memory too."

Noah vocalized his desire to get ice cream. Tucker winked his accolades, then nodded his head toward the back. I chatted with the other parents a bit more before the promise of treats pulled everyone else away.

"Hey," a voice whispered from behind me. I turned to find Andrew leaning near, his hands clasped behind his back. He revealed a large bouquet of white lilies and yellow and pink carnations. "These are for you." He held a plastic grocery sack in his other hand.

"Thank you." I took the flowers and smelled the fragrant blooms. A third bouquet from Andrew set some sort of record. "I didn't see you arrive."

"I came in when the magician was performing." He leaned forward and kissed my cheek. "You're amazing," he said.

"They did a great job." I was so pleased with the boys' performance.

Andrew cocked his head to the side. A sly, dimpled smile appeared. "But *you* did great too." He reached forward and took my hand. "They killed it because you taught them and worked with them and prepared them."

I shrugged. "You can't beat being well rehearsed."

Andrew rubbed his thumb over my knuckles. "You're missing my point, and I'm not sure if you're doing it on purpose. Don't keep dismissing yourself, Kasie. I took you for granted once, and you walked away. I regret it every day."

I opened my mouth to respond, but no words escaped. Desire filled me. Desire to be near Andrew, to throw my arms around him and never let him go. I needed to tell him . . . soon.

"Excuse me, Kasie Foster?" A woman with a cute bob cut and a business-casual gray suit approached. I'd seen her around during the performance and earlier in the week for rehearsal.

"Hi." I turned from Andrew and offered my hand. "You're the principal, right?"

"Nicole Moreno. It's nice to meet you." She looked over her shoulder and pointed to where Cole sat with Frankie and Rutherford, eating their ice-cream sundaes. "You did an amazing job with those boys."

"I was just telling her the same thing," Andrew chimed in. Pride laced his words.

I shot him a smile and shook my head.

"So here's the thing," Nicole said. "We've had crazy budget cuts I have been fighting tooth and nail. I hope to get some programs reinstated, and I found out this afternoon that we got approved for funding in the arts."

"Congratulations," I said.

"I'm very pleased." She looked between Andrew and me. "Could I borrow you for a moment?"

Andrew hooked his thumb toward the Nottinghams. "I need to go tell Cole congratulations, and I got the boys a treat. Snickers bars." He held up the bag in his hand. The perfect gift. "It was nice to meet you, Ms. Moreno."

Nicole smiled, and Andrew walked away. She turned her sure gaze on me. "Mrs. Nottingham told me your background is in theatre?"

"My degree is theatre studies with a minor in writing," I said.

"Which explains why you did so well managing those boys," she said, motioning toward the stage.

"I can't take all the credit," I said. "They really wanted this. I just helped them fine-tune and rehearse."

"Well, this grant is wonderful news, but there are some pros and cons." Her eyes never broke contact. "We get the funds, but it has to be framed as an after-school program, which means not all students will take advantage of this opportunity. Some will miss out."

"That's tough. I wish everyone could have an opportunity to be exposed to theatre and various art programs," I said.

"The plus side is that if it's after school, the instructor doesn't need to be a licensed educator." A smile spread across Nicole's face. "I know you're here with the military, which means you won't be here for long, but depending on your timeline, I wondered if you might be interested in heading up this program."

My shock must have been apparent.

"From what I've seen, you're good with kids, you're organized, and you know your craft." Nicole gave a soft smile. "We could brainstorm and go lots of ways with this."

"You want me to teach?" The concept crunched in my mind, and I couldn't straighten it out.

"I guess it's essentially teaching, but I'm really looking for someone to manage and craft and create. I think the budget would allow for a salary for you and an assistant. Since it's after school, it would be part time, but I think we also have some flexibility there. Depending on interest, we could recruit volunteers or maybe even find some additional funds." Someone called for Nicole from across the room. Nicole looked over her shoulder and held up a finger indicating she'd be there in a minute. She turned back to me and pulled a business card from her pocket. "Take some time. Think it over and give me a call in a week or so. We can talk about any questions you have and flesh out some more ideas."

I mumbled a response, and Nicole walked across the auditorium. Her offer settled on my mind, and I didn't quite know where or how to catalog the conversation.

Andrew sat at a table, talking to Cole with animated expressions. I moved to the chair across from them and set my two bouquets on the table.

"Everyone liked our skit," Cole said.

"The crowd was cracking up!" Andrew threw his hands to the side, then placed them on his stomach. "My stomach hurt 'cause I couldn't stop laughing."

"I could hear them clapping too." Cole grinned wide.

"Cole!" Rutherford ran up. "My mom wants to take a picture of us on stage."

Cole jumped out of his seat and skipped after Rutherford.

Andrew moved around the table and sat in the chair next to me. He laced his fingers through mine. "You've made three boys really happy."

I looked to the stage, where Cole, Rutherford, and Frankie were striking poses like seasoned models, albeit sporting goofy grins. "They did well." My focus shifted back to Andrew. His dimples peeked from the corners of his cheeks, and the magnetic pull drew me in. I leaned forward and pressed my lips against the small indent on one side.

His eyes lit with delight, and my heart swelled. I loved this man. I loved feeling special when he held my hand. I loved the sincere emotion emanating from his smile. I loved the security I felt in his presence, knowing he wanted a future with me. A forever.

Our connection sparked in my mind, a time-lapsed image of a match striking red phosphorus, a tiny flicker growing to a bulbous, unstoppable flame. I'd been praying for answers. Praying for clarity. Praying to know if a possible pathway existed and whether I should take it.

After a performance, when final bows were made and the curtain fell for the last time, closure came—a silent peace associated with the completion of something beautiful and grand. Before, I had felt confusion, fear. But now a familiar solace filled me, not from the three boys bouncing around the stage or the clutches of flowers on the cafeteria table but from the man sitting across from me and from the answer to my prayers that had manifested in a conversation with the principal.

CHAPTER 15

I DIDN'T SHARE MY EPIPHANY with Andrew that night. I wanted to pray one more time and let the rightness of it all settle into my soul. Andrew had a study group Saturday morning, and we planned to picnic after Sunday services. I would talk to him then.

We sat together in church, and I enjoyed sitting side by side. The lessons from the pastor and in Sunday School highlighted that God answers prayers, and I wondered if prayer truly was the purpose of their prepared messages or if the topic simply resonated with me because the subject had been twining through my thoughts.

When Sunday School dismissed, Andrew confirmed our plans. "I'll pick you up at one o'clock?"

"Sounds good," I said.

"Oh, I forgot to tell you, or ask you, rather." He scrunched his nose and looked too adorable for me to worry about whatever he had forgotten. "Is it okay if Cal and Ricky join us on our picnic? They asked if I had plans, and they wanted to come. They'll probably bring a football to throw around, and I think they wanted to bring a couple of friends." He grimaced. "Dates." He ran a hand through his hair. "But I can tell them no."

I had hoped we might have time alone together to talk. Answers finally felt tangible, and I wanted to share my feelings with Andrew, to tell him I was ready to give us a shot. But I hadn't seen him flustered very often. Control and cool usually oozed from him. "It's fine," I said. I reached forward and wrapped my fingers around his wrist. "It'll be fun." I would tell him afterward.

Relief settled over his face, like a calming mist. "Thanks, Kasie. It won't be weird, right?"

"It'll be great." I gave him a quick hug. "I'll see you soon."

I stopped by the nursery and visited with Wendy, helping her tidy up the toys and run the roller vacuum over the flat carpet.

"Let's do lunch this week," she suggested.

"I'll have a plus one." I pointed to Noah snuggling against Tucker's shoulder.

"If you'll share your date, we'll be just fine," she said.

We planned to meet Tuesday at a small café in town.

I drove home with Tucker. Noah crashed, and by the time I'd changed out of my dress, Tucker's snores sounded from where he had passed out on the couch. I gently closed the front door and walked to Andrew's car, where he already waited for me.

The river wasn't far from the base, about ten minutes toward the Mexican border. "I asked Google where to go and found a nice grassy area," Andrew said.

"As long as there's shade, I won't be picky." Summer had rolled into Del Rio with full strength, hot and humid.

Andrew turned south on the main intersection through town and then wove through some houses to reach Moore Park. We circled the full parking lot twice before we found a family loading up to leave. Andrew waited, then parked in the space they'd vacated. "I guess everyone wanted to come to the river today."

All the tables and standing barbecues had been claimed. I turned to ask Andrew if he had a blanket just as he pulled one from his trunk, along with a canvas bag filled with food. He told me he'd take care of the meal, and when I tried to peek, he maneuvered the bag so I couldn't see the contents. The crowds gravitated toward the cool banks of the river, but he led me in the opposite direction.

We stepped onto the sidewalk, and a horn blared behind us.

"Hey, Stoll! Where ya going?" Cal hung his cropped head of blond hair half out of his sports-car window.

Andrew pointed to the wide trunk of an oak tree. "Headed for the shade," he hollered back.

Cal held up a palm and continued around the parking lot.

The grass could hardly be called sod. Patches of dirt and weeds tangled with the few smears of actual green.

"Maybe we should have eaten at my place," Andrew said. We spread the blanket across the ground, and he set the food down.

"It's nice to have a change of scenery," I said. The base did present excellent landscaping, but I welcomed the change. "We can stay however long you want."

"We at least have to go see how cold the water is." He began unpacking the food, and I watched with exaggerated interest.

"Hey, guys!" Cal walked up with his arm around a pretty woman.

Andrew and I stood.

"This is Ashley," Cal said.

Ashley's long black hair was pulled into a ponytail. She had beautiful teeth and a beautiful smile. Cal stepped back to make room for Ricky and his date.

"And this is Suzanne," Ricky said. Suzanne had dyed-blonde hair that framed a perfect heart-shaped face.

"Nice to meet you both," Andrew said. "This is Kasie."

I offered a smile hello and a wave and moved backward on the blanket near where Andrew had set our food. I sat down. Suzanne held a bag of Subway sandwiches, and Ricky passed fountain drinks to the four of them. I crossed my legs to try to give everyone more room. "How do you all know each other?" I asked. "I mean, besides pilot training?"

"Cal and I met at Julio's," Ashley said.

"Is that in Del Rio?" I asked. "I'm not familiar with it."

"It's the bar on Main Street," Ashley said, which explained why I hadn't heard of it.

"She totally scammed me," Cal said, lying on his side across the short end of the blanket.

Ashley swatted his arm. "I did not."

Ricky took a huge bite of his sandwich. "She thrashed him at pool," he said around the bite in his mouth.

Ashley pouted at both men, then looked at me. "I told him I would beat him, and he didn't believe me. I can't help it if I proved him wrong."

"Cleaned the table off the break," Cal said with a grin.

"Nice!" Andrew said. "Someone needs to humble Cal."

We all laughed.

Andrew set a plate resembling a charcuterie board between us and then handed me a single-serving bottle of Martinelli's apple cider.

"Thank you," I said.

"Look at you, all snazzy," Ricky said to Andrew, pointing to the plate.

"Now, that's romantic," Suzanne said softly.

It was romantic and looked far more appetizing than the hoagie sandwiches the others were eating. As if to prove my point, Cal squeezed his bag of chips, making them open with a *pop*.

"How did the two of you meet?" Ashley asked.

"We went to college together," I said.

"And you've been dating ever since?" she asked.

"Whoa, did you two date before? I thought you just knew each other from school." Cal pushed himself up and sat cross-legged. "That explains a lot." He started to unwrap his sandwich.

"We dated in college but broke up to go our separate ways. Neither of us knew the other was here until we ran into each other a few months ago," Andrew said.

"And you decided to give it another chance?" Ashley said. "How did you end up in Del Rio?"

I explained Tucker's situation. "I'm here to help him for a while."

"That's super sweet," Ashley said.

"It's loaded," Cal said. "Your girl's bro is also your IP."

I took a steadying breath. "Tucker doesn't combine his work with my private life. He draws a line and doesn't bring things home."

"You're one lucky punk," Cal said to Andrew. "Your cousin and Tuck both got your back."

Andrew chuckled, but I felt him tense beside me. "Yeah, right. Bowman can't even fly with me, and Tuck . . . remember, he hooked me on my eighty-eight ride?"

"Had no choice, right?" Ricky asked.

Andrew nodded. "Sure. I mean, I oversped the flaps, but if anything, I bet he evaluates me on a steeper curve."

Ricky bobbed his head. "That's true. He's a solid IP. Who's your next check with?"

"Spitfire," Andrew said.

"What are they even talking about?" Suzanne asked Ashley.

Ricky explained the air force terminology, and I glanced at Andrew to make sure my situation—*our* situation—hadn't put him on the spot. He placed his hand over mine.

Time for a subject change. "Do you work?" I asked Ashley.

She explained how she ran the front desk for the local dentist. "Suzanne is one of the hygienists," she said. "We met at work and became friends."

"I should get the number from you. I haven't even had time to think about dental care," I said.

"What would you be doing if you weren't helping your brother?" Ashley asked.

"My major is theatre studies. I hope to go work in London for a while and build my résumé. I just completed a script, and I've submitted it to a few places. My ultimate goal is to direct my own work," I said.

Cal finished his sandwich and crinkled the wrapper in his hands. "But directing is a long shot, right?"

I bristled. "What do you mean?"

He shrugged. "I know several guys who make films. Every one of them says they want to be a director, but that seems pretty far-fetched. I mean, there's only so many who actually make it. I would think theatre would be similar." He looked at me with a challenge in his eyes. "You basically follow a script, and the actors do their thing, right? I would guess those who actually get a break are few and far between."

I opened my mouth, unsure what I would say but ready to defend the arts and educate Cal on the insane amount of hours, devotion, and commitment required to bring a script to the stage.

Andrew squeezed my hand. "Kasie's major required far more work than my BS in geography. I had classes during the day and random ROTC events. She attended class, then worked late into the night to meet production deadlines." He glanced at me, all goodness and warmth. He smiled, and my world righted. "I didn't know what dedication was until I met her."

"Until you got to UPT," Ricky said with a laugh.

"That's when I had to put all she taught me to the test. UPT's been a beast. You guys know how close I came to washing out." Andrew released my hand and began assembling a tower of salami, crackers, and cheese. "Let's talk about something other than flying. My brain needs a break."

My heart swelled. Andrew turned and winked when the others weren't watching. I'd faced opinions like Cal's ever since high school. Some people didn't get theatre. Some didn't care to try. But others—Andrew—took time to listen. They asked questions and opened themselves up to new experiences. Musicals, plays, adaptations, readings, comedy, classics. I firmly believed everyone could find something to appreciate in the medium of theatre if they were humble enough to acknowledge that the world held space for creative expression.

We tossed a football for a bit, then walked over to check the temperature of the water, but when Suzanne and Ashley wanted to wade farther into the river, Andrew and I made our excuses and left.

As we pulled back onto base, I said, "Thank you . . . for deflecting Cal."

"He can be a bit hard-nosed." Andrew fished his wallet from his pocket, and the guard verified his ID card, then asked for mine.

It was always hit or miss whether I had to show my credentials to get on base. Something about the threat-con level, which Tucker had told me was short for *threat condition*. The military liked the phonetic alphabet, and *alfa* meant a low threat. *Delta* was the highest. Today the sign posted at the gate showed the base sat at threat-con Charlie.

"Is something going on?" Andrew asked the guard.

"We're running an exercise," the guard said before handing back my ID card. He saluted Andrew, and we turned left toward base housing.

Andrew picked up our previous conversation. "I don't think Cal's intentionally abrasive. He just tends to speak before he thinks."

"I'm not so sure. I think he was trying to get a rise out of me." I hadn't missed the challenge in Cal's eyes.

"I believe that too. He's super competitive. It serves him well at UPT, but the class likes to razz him about it." Andrew took my hand again. "Don't let him get to you."

"I won't. At least, not after I get a good night's sleep." I smiled at Andrew to let him know I wasn't bothered. In fact, he'd been my knight in shining armor; Wendy was right, and I wasn't about to let him ride off into the sunset without me.

"Let's go swing at the park," I said. "Do you have time?"

My favorite dimpled smile appeared. "For you? Always."

Andrew drove past my street and turned onto the following block. The park sat empty. He pulled up to the curb and slowed, and the moment the wheels stopped I pushed open my door. "Race you to the swings."

"Not fair," Andrew called, but his vain protest died as he gave a valiant effort to catch me.

I laughed and plopped myself into the small swing, giving a big push, then pumping my legs to gain height. Andrew settled into the swing beside me, and it didn't take long for both of us to max out the length of the chains. "I forgot how much you love to swing," Andrew said.

"I'm sure it's nothing like being in the cockpit, but it's how I fly." I stopped pumping my legs and closed my eyes, enjoying the back-and-forth pendulum motion, the wind brushing my cheeks, and the knowledge that Andrew swung beside me.

"Flying is actually a similar sensation to swinging, only the clouds are closer in the plane."

I opened my eyes to see Andrew's momentum had stalled. His feet touched the ground, and his swing moved slightly beneath him. His eyes remained trained on me.

"What?" I asked, laughing lightly.

"It's crazy to think training is almost over." He stood and put his hands in his pockets.

"And you did it." I dragged my feet through the wood chips to stop my movement.

"Almost." He grinned. "In large part thanks to you." He reached for my hand and pulled me to my feet, our fingers twining together. He grinned and tugged me closer, taking my other hand in his. "I don't know how to explain it, Kasie. I prayed and prayed and ended up track-selecting to choose heavies instead of fighters. I'm seriously happy to fly anything. In heavies I could be stationed somewhere exotic, like Japan or Germany, but I've come to realize that hasn't been my dream lately."

Curious hope wormed through me, and I stood silent.

Andrew's lips twitched. "Prayer is funny like that, huh?" he said.

"I know exactly what you mean." And I did. The focus of my prayers often turned to needs, a combination of my own needs and those of people I loved. When a difficult decision loomed, my pleas shifted to specifics, asking God to guide my decision or fulfill a particular request. But I should know better than to assume Deity might conform to my script. God's ways were higher than my ways. I knew this. I trusted He knew better, but time and time again I would think I had it figured out. Thankfully, God was patient. "You know I've been praying about us," I said.

Andrew cocked his head to the side. His eyes narrowed a bit, as if he could read my mind before I revealed it. "I have too."

"And . . . did you get an answer?" I asked.

He inhaled and glanced skyward. "I never wanted to break up, Kasie." His words were nothing new. He'd told me before. He pulled my hand to his lips and kissed it. "But I couldn't convince you to stay, and I did want you to find happiness." He looked at the place his lips had touched. "I thought chasing this dream would help me move on. UPT has kept me busy, but I've still thought of you every day." His thumb brushed over the back of my hand. "But then you showed up here, and I think I understand now why I didn't choose fighters."

Emotion pierced my heart, and my eyes filled with joyful tears. "You think God's given me—given us—a second chance?" I asked.

Andrew dropped his hands to my waist. I wrapped my fingers around his solid biceps. "I think He knew, long before either of us did, that you'd end up here. But I meant what I said before. I will never ask you to give up your dream so I can live mine. I love you too much to ask that."

"Andrew?" My heart felt near to bursting, and his sincerity coddled me just enough that I could breathe.

"I love you, Kasie. That hasn't changed. I want to be with you, but not if it means you're the only one sacrificing." He held my gaze.

"You've made sacrifices," I said. "You may not have known why, but you had the faith to follow the answer you received too."

"I get it now, and I have no regrets."

He leaned forward. I knew he meant to kiss me, but I needed to tell him about the answer I had received. "The grant money." The words burst from my mouth.

Andrew pulled back. His face softened, and his lips tugged up in a smile.

I hurried to explain. My fingers tightened around his arms with every word I spoke. "Nicole Moreno. Remember when she pulled me aside at the talent show? She told me the school got a grant, and it's for the arts—specifically, she wants to focus on theatre arts."

Questions laced the corners of his eyes, tentative hope mixed with uncertainty. "What are you saying?"

"She wants me to run the program. It would be a way to use my degree and stay here with Tucker and Noah—"

"And me?" Andrew's blue eyes illuminated, a hopeful smile tugging at his lips.

My grin matched his. "And you."

His eyes crinkled. "I thought you didn't want to teach," he said.

"I don't want to be confined to a classroom and state-mandated curriculum, but I enjoyed working with the boys, more than I thought I would. I need to find out more, but talking with Nicole, it sounds like there's flexibility in how to use the funding. There are lots of ways to structure the program, and I would have control."

Andrew pulled me tight against his chest. He wrapped his arms around my middle and lifted me off my feet. He laughed and spun in a circle before setting me back down. "Oh, Kasie! This makes me so happy." He squeezed me close again.

The grant offered me a way to stay. Uncle Sam still held all the cards where Andrew was concerned. "You have possibilities around the world," I said. "I don't want you to give that up, but if you choose to stay here, in Del Rio—"

His arms slid around my back, and he kissed my temple above my left ear. Then he whispered. "I choose you. If you're here, then yes. This is where I want to be."

CHAPTER 16

Mom did a happy dance on video chat when I told her about the offer to help with the theatre program at the school. Then I told her about my conversation with Andrew.

"I told him I'm ready to try again," I said.

"You're different this time," she said.

"What do you mean?" I asked.

"Don't take this the wrong way, but before, you were all about you. Now you're looking outward."

Her words surprised me. "So I was being selfish to want to go to London?" It surprised me how much the thought hurt.

"Now, don't go switching up my words," Mom said. "London was a good goal. And it could have been the right thing." She paused to formulate her thoughts. "Do you remember when Stacy first received her cancer diagnosis and Tucker kept it all to himself?"

When Mom, Dad, and I had finally found out, emotions had been high. We were heartbroken for Tucker and Stacy but also sad that Tucker hadn't trusted us enough to tell us.

"He finally confessed because I pushed him to," Mom said. "Mother's intuition kicked in, and I knew something wasn't right. He tried to carry the burden all by himself, but that's not how families work. You did the same thing."

"With Andrew?" I asked.

"Yes. You had a plan and figured it was the right thing, but you didn't bother to ask anyone else their opinion. You opted to go it alone."

"I did pray about it," I said sulkily.

"And God is the most important person to turn to, but you also have us. Now, I'm not saying I would have told you to stay home. I never would have guessed Stacy would be taken to heaven so soon, but I would have told you something seemed off."

"What do you mean?" I asked.

Mom tapped a finger against her lips, considering her answer. "You were full of confidence, but you didn't seem at peace."

"That's exactly how I felt," I said. "Everything felt turbulent. I was trying to balance final projects. Andrew was asking for more, and while I loved being with him, the thought of more was unsettling. I thought that was my answer."

"It may have been," Mom said. "I believe God speaks to each of us differently. I know that final semester was a stressful time. Breaking up with Andrew didn't make you happy . . ."

It had shattered me. I'd hated going to sleep knowing that when I woke I would spend another day without him.

"And then Stacy got sick," I said.

"Exactly. It was a difficult year."

"For you too," I said.

"Yes. But I could tell you were aching. You were wandering around in the dark, searching for a light that kept eluding you."

"Mother's intuition?" I guessed.

"Absolutely," Mom said. "One day you'll understand." Her smile returned. "And that same intuition tells me you're in a better place now. Maybe now you're ready to make decisions you weren't prepared to make before."

"I found the light switch?" I asked.

"Or maybe someone was patient enough to wait for you to stop flailing in the dark so they could take your hand to lead you outside to the sunshine."

My mother was extremely wise.

The flight students entered their next phase. They had another round of academics and flights, and then the *drop* would follow. Tucker had told me the drop ceremony ranked almost as high as the students being awarded their wings. In the week before the drop, each student was ranked by how they had performed during training. Each pilot training class received a list of follow-on assignments to include an airframe and a base. If there were twenty students, there were twenty possible assignments. Every student submitted a drop sheet listing their first choice to their last. Then the commander went down the list and matched number one with their choice, number two with theirs, and so on, until every student received their orders for their next duty station.

The date of the air show fell right in the middle of the training flights, which would be put on hold so the performers could practice. I knew the students were anxious to complete training and learn where they were headed next, but I thought the break would be nice. Tucker agreed.

Andrew and I hung out only a couple of nights during the week of academics because he was too close to the end to mess up now. I refused to be a negative distraction, and he studied hard, hitting the books and attending cram sessions with his classmates before test days. He aced the written tests and the emergency procedures.

"He has to check for visual flight rules and instrument flight rules," Tucker explained as he pulled his toolbox out from under the kitchen sink. "IFR allows him to fly in bad weather as well as on the clear days."

"I thought he already had those flights." Right when I thought I understood the process, I learned how much more I didn't know.

"He had an IFR phase in the T-6, but he has to do it again for the T-1." Tucker found the screwdriver he wanted and stood.

"So, basically, you learn it for any plane you fly?" I asked, handing him the toy of Noah's that needed the batteries replaced. My nephew lay sleeping peacefully in his crib.

"If you want to be completely checked out in the aircraft, yes." Tucker had shown a lot of patience, but I wondered if he secretly enjoyed me asking questions and learning more about what he did.

He swapped out the batteries and pressed the button on the fire truck Noah preferred over all of his other car toys.

"Bravo," I said. "Now we can once again be assailed by the sounds of a dramatic rescue."

Tucker grinned. "I know you would do anything for him."

"You're right. I would." I stuck out my hand for the fire truck.

Tucker handed me the toy. His expression turned serious, and he planted his hands on his hips. "I can't tell you enough how much we appreciate you, Kas."

I smiled. "I know. And you *have* told me." I walked to the living room and dropped the fire truck into Noah's basket of toys.

Tucker followed me. "I mean it. I can't even imagine trying to find someone I trust to watch Noah while I'm at work. They would see him more than I do, and if I have to share that privilege with someone, I'm glad it's with you."

I sobered and turned back to my brother. "I'm glad too. I know it's been hard, Tucker. And I miss Stacy too." Emotion flooded through me. Raw grief. It rocked me, and I simply stood in place, feeling it all. I wiped the tears from my eyes. "I know you miss her even more." Tears pricked Tucker's eyes, and his face wilted with sorrow. "I think you're really brave. And I'm glad you're my big brother."

Tucker's shoulders began to shake, and tears rolled down his cheeks. I hugged him, squeezing so he would know I was there for him. My strength could be his, for however long he needed it. I mourned on a different level, but I would mourn with him. We stood like that for a long while. I didn't move until Tucker's tears slowed and the rhythm of his ragged breaths steadied.

He stepped back and collapsed onto the couch. "Thanks a lot, Kas," he said with sarcasm, but he forced a smile. He wiped his eyes and shook his head. "I never know when it's going to hit."

I flopped back against the cushions beside him. "Whew."

"Kas?" Tucker said.

"Yeah?"

"I don't know exactly how to say this . . ."

I wasn't sure I could take more heaviness, but I also wanted Tucker to be able to share whatever he needed to share. We sat, collecting our emotions and trying to stymie our grief.

Tucker unfolded himself and sat upright. "I . . . I have to ask." He looked at me. "Do you like Andrew?" He scrubbed a hand through his hair. "I mean, do you love Andrew?"

Not the direction I thought he would go. I wanted to give him an honest answer. "Do I like Andrew? Yes. I can say that I like him. Love?" I blew out a breath, and the confirmation came again. "I do love him," I said.

Tucker propped his arms on his knees and pressed his fingertips together.

I could tell he had more on his mind. "Why?" I asked him.

"When I told you I'm grateful you're here, I was telling the truth. But you gave up a lot to come, and I don't want you to feel like you have to stay. Not for me, anyway. Or Noah. If you need to leave, I'll figure something out." Tucker stared at me so directly, I could feel the sincerity of his words.

"Okay," I said.

"When Andrew has drop night, he could be assigned anywhere in the world—"

"Or he could be assigned to stay here," I said.

Tucker thought on that. "I don't want you to stay here for me or Noah or Andrew, unless you're sure it's for you. If you stay and give up your plans, it needs to be for the right reasons. And I don't want Noah and me to be the reasons. I don't want to hold you back when you've already given so much. Only you know your feelings, and I'm sure you've already prayed about what's right. I just want you to know the choice needs to be yours. Wherever in the world that leads you." He cocked his head to the side. "Do you get what I'm saying?"

My heart felt near to bursting. "I do. It's different this time with Andrew. I don't know why, but it feels . . . right. I can't say with 100 percent certainty that I'm staying or going, but I do want to figure this out, and right now Andrew and I are trying to do that together." I touched Tucker's knee. "Thank you for caring enough to say something." I smiled. "Noah may be what got me here, but if I stay, it'll be because I want to."

Cole's birthday fell on the last day of May, which also happened to be the last day of school. He had a half day, and Hope had promised him a water party and ice cream. We were invited to attend, and Noah and I showed up early to help tie balloons and cut up fruit. The kids arrived and headed straight for the sprinklers, and Noah gravitated to the bubble machine.

Hope exited the house, carrying a large platter filled with fruit, and set it on the patio table, next to cut-up wedges of PB and J sandwiches. She called to the kids to come get a snack, then sat beside me in the shade. "This summer's gonna be a long one."

"I enjoyed the warm weather of California, but this humidity is something else," I said.

"That's the South for ya." Hope laughed. She popped a sandwich into her mouth, and suddenly her expression shifted, focusing on me. "Ian said Andrew's been extra chipper lately. Did y'all work out what's going on between the two of you?"

I smiled, something I'd been doing more and more lately. "We're hoping we can make it work."

Hope clapped her hands together. "Oh, I'm so, so glad. You know, from the beginning I wanted you two to connect."

I called Noah over and handed him a sandwich.

"Oh," Hope said. "Has Tucker talked to you about the game?"

I shook my head. "What game?"

She explained that there was a softball game last week of class; it would be students versus instructors, and all family members were invited to participate. "Technically, you could be on either team."

"I'd probably be more of a hindrance than an asset," I said. "I do okay at sports, but I'm not gonna be anyone's first pick."

Hope waved her hand. "Ah, I love a good softball game. It's a fun time, and it's for the families. I don't know if I like the socializing or watching the competitiveness of these military types. They don't like to lose. I honestly think they encourage the families to play because it would get too serious if it were only the students versus the IPs."

We also chatted about the air show the following weekend. Hope said she would sign me up to work the same shift as her. "I already talked to Ian about taking the kids. It'll be a nice reprieve. Plus, Ian loves showing off the planes to Becca and Cole."

The temperature continued to climb, and I found myself walking through the sprinklers with Noah to keep cool. I'd pushed back his naptime, and he lasted till late afternoon. By the time we'd dried off and changed, we were both ready to crash.

Our naps made Noah and me groggy and a bit grouchy, so Tucker agreed to order takeout. We sat around the table, and he told me about one of his failed check rides when he'd been in training. "It was my IR flight, and I felt so stressed. In the plane I'd run the checklist perfectly, but during the debrief the IP asked me about the EPs, and I mixed up the order of the boldface even though I'd practiced it again and again and again. Stacy would review it with me, and I must have said it three hundred times, but for some reason, my mind went blank, and instead of saying, 'Controls neutral,' I said, 'Controls neutered.'"

I laughed, and because I laughed, Noah did also. And then I realized I'd understood everything Tucker had said. Acronyms and terminology—it had all made sense to me. Maybe I could do this air force life after all.

I prayed that night, asking God to comfort the men and women fighting in conflicts around the world. I prayed for leaders to seek peaceful solutions and for the families of soldiers to know of God's love for them. Then my prayer turned inward. I told God that my foggy confusion had begun to clear. My destination wasn't clear, but when I considered the next step with Andrew, opening my heart considering a future with him, peace consumed me. If I was making a wrong choice, I prayed God would let me know, that the solace I now felt would evaporate and a different path would be shown.

I rose from my knees and climbed under my covers. Awareness filled my senses. Awareness of my body, my breath, the lightness and joy filling my heart. I was aware of the past and at peace with the future. I was aware that

God loved me and that now He blessed me with faith to move forward with Andrew. Absolute joy washed over me, and tears of joy wet my pillow before I fell into contented sleep.

CHAPTER 17

The day before the air show proved to be its own entertainment. The performing aircraft zoomed over the runway, practicing their maneuvers. Other aircraft, planes larger than the trainers usually seen around base, landed in between the rehearsal flights. Tucker had been tasked to help with the setup, and Hope spent most of the day outside with her kids, watching all the airframes come in to land. She'd text when something extra special happened, and Noah and I had wandered out to the yard a few times. Having a front-row seat was one of the benefits of living on base, but the screaming engines of the fighter planes didn't hold Noah's attention for long, so we wandered back inside. He got a good nap, despite the noise, and I chatted with Annabelle, asking about her next project and updating her on all things Andrew.

Later Tucker called. "Hey, Kasie, do you have a plan for dinner?" He explained that a friend of his was bringing his C-17 in for the air show, and Tucker wanted to invite him over. "I haven't seen Jake in forever, and I'd love to catch up, but we could grab something if you don't want to cook."

I thought for a minute. "If he doesn't mind my imitation tacos, compliments of a seasoning packet, I can cook. If he wants authentic Del Rio food, then we can go takeout."

"I don't think he'll be picky." Tucker confirmed a time. "Oh, and do you have the stuff to make Oreo pie?"

"Yep."

"Then, let's do that too. I can help when I get home." Tucker asked about Noah, and I told him how Noah and I had read the animal sounds book for almost an hour.

"Each time he pushed the button with the pig, he couldn't stop laughing. I think he finally wore himself out, because he's still asleep." I pulled the phone away from my ear to verify the baby monitor remained silent.

"I'm excited to take him to the air show," Tucker said, and I didn't have the heart to tell him Noah's attention span lasted all of two minutes, unless he was pushing a button making oinking sounds.

Jake arrived promptly at 1800. He stepped through the door behind Tucker, with a four-pack of deluxe cream soda. "I didn't want to arrive empty-handed," Jake said.

Tucker introduced me, then explained, "Jake and I were at UPT together."

"So glad to be done with that." Jake had short blond hair and impressive blue eyes. "How is it being back?" he asked.

"It's much better sitting in the right seat. I like to be the one giving the downgrades," Tucker said. Noah toddled over, and Tucker picked him up. "And this is Noah."

"Hey, buddy!" Jake waved, and when Noah held out his hand for a high five, Jake complied.

"Did I tell you Paige and I are expecting?" Jake said.

Tucker grinned wide. "I'm happy for you, man!"

"When's the baby due?" I asked.

"The week of Thanksgiving." Jake beamed. "We find out the gender next month. I can't wait."

I offered my congratulations. "You guys hungry?"

During dinner Tucker and Jake chatted nonstop. I listened in, happy for my brother. Other than church and the few times visiting the stables, Tucker didn't socialize, so I was grateful he had a friend in Jake.

I monitored Noah, encouraging him to take bites and not throw his taco meat onto the floor.

After eating too much Oreo pie, I put Noah down for the night. I waited outside the bedroom door to verify he had fallen asleep, and Jake's voice floated down the hall. "I'm so sorry about Stacy," he said. "Such a shock. You know we all loved her."

Stacy had been stationed with Tucker when he went through training. I hadn't made the connection that Jake had known her.

Emotion filled Tucker's voice. "I appreciate all you did for us. I didn't know whether I should call, if it was too soon after your mom's passing."

"No, man," Jake said. "I get it. It sucks. It hurts. And sometimes you just need . . ." Jake paused to swallow down his own cup of sentiment. "You just need someone. I've been there, and if it weren't for Paige . . . well, let me say I know the feeling. I'm glad you called."

When Stacy had received her cancer diagnosis, she and Tucker had kept it a secret for three weeks. Once Mom had gotten Tucker to confide the load he'd been trying to carry on his own, she'd flown out that very night. Dad had gotten things settled at work and joined her the next day. Tucker had a hard time telling people, and everything had happened so fast. I had wondered who else knew, who Tucker had to lean on. I was grateful for this moment to witness Tucker's vulnerability, to get to know the friend he had in Jake.

I waited a few minutes before joining them in the living room. The conversation turned from somber to nostalgic as they reminisced about their time together in training. They didn't ignore me intentionally, but they had connections I didn't—shared experiences and shared friends.

"Remember the time Gabe tried to convince Cappy to let us out before release time?" Jake asked with a laugh.

Tucker shook his head. "He could charm the tail feathers off a peacock."

"But he was the nicest guy. I don't think he even realized the potential he held." Jake rubbed his hands together. "He would have gotten away with it, too, if L.J. hadn't shown up."

"L.J.?" I asked.

"Little John," Tucker said.

"There was nothing little about him." Jake laughed.

"Picture this, Kas," Tucker said to me. "This guy was bulked out. All muscle. And he was at least six foot four. But he was so mellow."

Jake nodded in agreement. "One of the nicest guys I've ever met."

"And his name was John?" I clarified.

"Yeah. When Gabe tried to convince one of the female IPs to let us go home early, Little John couldn't play along. He stood up"—Tucker chuckled at the memory—"walked over to where Gabe sat—"

"More like hulked over there." Jake grinned.

Tucker reenacted the scene. He stood, flexed his biceps, and stomped toward Jake. Then his voice turned soft. "Now, Gabe. Don't get Cappy in trouble. She's not supposed to let us go for another hour. I heard you missed two on the last test. Why don't you let me help you study." Tucker could barely finish for the laugh bursting out.

Jake leaned back and covered his forehead with his hand. "The look on Gabe's face."

Tucker sat back down and held up a finger. "But he did pass the next test with a perfect score." He dropped his hand. Tucker looked happy, and it filled my soul. "I got Gabe's wedding invitation," he said.

"Mine came two days ago," Jake said. "He looks happy. Being married to a military member is not easy." He looked at me. "It's great you can help your brother. It's different from being a spouse, but I'm sure you understand."

"She may understand even better pretty soon." Mischief touched Tucker's eyes.

"Really?" Jake drew out the word. "Someone here at Laughlin?"

"One of my students," Tucker said, and Jake whistled.

"That's a short explanation, and an incomplete one," I said, challenging my brother. "Andrew and I dated in college. We didn't know we'd end up here together."

"Hey." Jake held up his hands. "When it's right, it's right. There're all kinds of crazy things that bring people together. I met my wife after almost hitting her in the grocery store parking lot."

Tucker snort-laughed, and I pressed Jake for an explanation. He told me how Paige was returning her cart and he rounded the end of the aisle too quickly and almost hit her. "She looked ready to punch me, and in that moment I saw how pretty she was, standing there, glaring at me. I realized she had spunk, and I couldn't let her just walk away, so I drove around again and asked her to go to dinner with me."

"And she agreed?" I asked.

"Not at first, but after some persuasion—okay begging, I gave her a time and a place and let her decide." He gave a cocky grin. "She showed up, and now we're living our happily ever after."

Jake and Tucker turned to talk of deployments and air force manning. I pondered on Jake's statement of happily ever after. He radiated happiness. Once upon a time, Tucker had too, until life had shifted. It seemed some people found their happily-ever-after ending and others waded through the muck. Andrew's happy eyes, his dimples, and his contagious smile danced through my mind. Along with the hope that we could achieve our own happily ever after.

CHAPTER 18

A PAIR OF AIRPLANES SCREECHED loud overhead. Many aspects of the air show were fun, but a headache had been building for the last two hours, and it was time to pull out the medicine.

Hope placed one hand on my back and leaned near so I could hear her. "You okay, hon?" she asked.

"Yeah." I nodded. "I just don't want it to get worse."

I returned to my task, packing cups with the snow-cone ice Hope continued to create with the machine the military spouses had rented from a store in Del Rio. There hadn't been a break in the line in the sixty minutes I had been working. My hands were chilled, but a few minutes later I swapped out with my replacement, a lovely woman named Gloria.

Hope insisted I take a snow cone with me. "It's hot on the tarmac, and if you don't want it all, you can share with Andrew." She pointed behind me. Sure enough, he stood in his flight suit, looking all sorts of handsome.

"Are you done soon?" I asked Hope.

"Heavens no, thank goodness," Hope said with a laugh. "If I'm here, Ian has the kids. This is my break."

I laughed. "If we get anything good to eat, I'll bring something by." I waved and ducked out the back of the booth to meet Andrew.

"Open wide," I said, scooping a bite of blue snow cone from my cup. He obediently opened his mouth, and I spooned the ice in.

"Mmm, good," he said.

I took a bite of my own, then handed him the cup. "It's yours. I'm all iced out."

"Thanks." He finished off the snow cone while we walked toward the static displays of the planes. "That's a C-130. And there's an A-10 Warthog," he said.

"What's the giant one?" I asked.

"The C-17," Andrew said. "The largest airframe in the air force."

"I think that's Jake's plane. Jake's a friend of Tucker's I met last night. They were in UPT together."

"That's awesome," Andrew said. We walked over and followed the crowds up the huge ramp. Seats lined both sides of the aircraft, and the floor was striped with various markings and anchors to tether cargo. Jake stood near the flight deck, talking to an eager teenage boy and his parents. Jake pointed to something in the cockpit, and the boy headed up to check it out.

Jake turned and saw us. "Hi, Kasie. Enjoying the air show?"

"I am," I said. "But I don't know how you stand out here all day. I can at least run home to my AC for a few hours."

Jake laughed. "They have a greenroom set up in one of the squadron buildings, and I've been switching off with my copilot."

Andrew extended his hand. "Hello, sir. Andrew Stoll."

"How's Laughlin treating you?" Jake asked.

"I'm beginning to see the light at the end of the tunnel," Andrew said.

"It's a tough year. What are you hoping to fly?" Jake asked.

"This one's a beauty," Andrew said, looking around Jake and motioning to the cockpit. "I love flying with the heads-up display on the T-1."

"The HUD is great. The updated avionics make a huge difference," Jake said. He and Andrew fell into pilot-speak and I tuned out. Andrew continued talking, and his hand reached for mine. I slipped my fingers into his grip, admiring the contours and edges, where his hand wrapped around mine and we joined together with such a simple effort.

". . . so I think I might try to stay here a bit longer." Andrew's words caught my attention.

"Taking one for the team, huh?" Jake chuckled. "You'll get a lot of hours, and they usually try to give you your choice of follow-ons."

"That's what I'm hoping for, sir." Andrew turned to me and his face lit.

Jake slapped a hand across his back. "Best of luck to you, man."

We wandered up to the flight deck, then waved goodbye to Jake before heading back down the ramp. Andrew glanced at his watch. "I have about an hour before I have to go to our booth. Want to grab some food?" The line for Tristie's Street Tacos extended farther than that of any of the other food trucks. "There's the obvious choice," Andrew said.

Slowly we inched forward, the smells of grease and funnel cakes making my stomach pinch with hunger. "What did Jake mean about the follow-on assignments?" I asked.

Andrew's brow scrunched for a moment until he made the connection. "Oh. Most pilots don't want to be assigned to a training base, especially right out of UPT, because they want to train on a new plane and start getting hours so they can upgrade. The hours for a UPT instructor are somewhat regular, and because of the mission, there's not really a chance of deployment." The line moved forward again.

"That's why Tucker asked to transfer here," I said.

"Exactly. It works perfectly for his situation. He gets to fly, and he gets to be with Noah." A formation of three stunt planes roared past, and the announcer introduced the stunt team from Dallas. Andrew craned his neck to follow the aircraft as they zoomed north.

"So most people don't want to be here?" I got that. I had come, but I hadn't exactly chosen to be here either. But my next questions were important. "What about you? Do you want to stay at Laughlin for your next assignment?"

Andrew and I needed to be honest with each other, honest in sharing our desires. A future in the air force involved a large commitment, and if we were to promise forever to each other, Andrew's contract with the military became my contract too. I knew to expect a lot of change. I knew we would have separations and possible deployments. But I also needed to know that through it all, I could look into Andrew's eyes and never question whether he had regrets.

His gaze turned from the sky to me. Slowly his lips turned up and his dimples appeared. He leaned forward and gave me a quick kiss on my cheek. "I want to fly airplanes, and I want to be with you, Kasie. If staying here allows me both, then I consider it a blessing."

Daily I received further confirmation that Andrew and I were meant to move forward together. Andrew's words assured me he felt the same. My gratitude and surety of our situation climbed a steep upward trajectory.

"You sure you want to stay?" I teased. "Texas is really hot."

Andrew smirked. "And so are you."

Nicole Moreno agreed to meet with me on Wednesday afternoon. Simple decor filled her principal's office—a stale utilitarian desk and a small sofa and chairs that had probably been ordered in mass by the district—but she had spruced it up with glitzy silver frames on her desk and colorful artwork tiled along the walls. Gray and teal pillows with bright white accents sat on the chairs and couch.

"I'm so glad you're considering this," Nicole said, motioning for me to sit on the sofa. She sat on a nearby chair. "These children are so eager to learn, and I want to expose them to every possibility I can."

"I hadn't planned to stay in Del Rio past January, but some things have changed, and I may be here longer. I'll know better after Saturday," I said.

"I understand." Nicole paused, her mouth forming a tight circle as she considered what to say next. "I know you're here with the military, which means things could change. However, the grant money is accessible now. Would you be willing to give me one day a week over the next month so we can sketch out a program? I can offer a member of the faculty an additional stipend. I have the perfect teacher in mind, and if the three of us work together, we can get the bones of the project in place. We can learn from your experience, and whenever you move on, we'll still have something to work with."

The idea made sense, and a surprising twinge of excitement stirred at the prospect. Creating a program from scratch would be difficult, but it also meant freedom to explore and imagine and experiment. We could have units on scriptwriting, creative storytelling, movement, design, costumes, makeup, and even stage combat. An array of ideas flowed through my mind on a happy current of possibilities.

Nicole and I swapped a few basic ideas and set a time to meet the following week. My availability would depend on finding someone to help watch Noah, but I figured Wendy might be willing to take a shift or two, and Hope would probably help as well.

The opportunity thrilled me, and I couldn't wait to tell someone about it who could celebrate with me. I called Andrew the moment I stepped outside the school. The call rang to voicemail. I wasn't surprised he couldn't pick up, but for some unexplainable reason, it felt important for my first call to go to him.

The realization settled over me like a peaceful transition from exhaustion to sleep. The person I wanted to call, the person I wanted to see, was Andrew, my best friend and the man I loved. I couldn't deny it, and I didn't want to. The rightness of our relationship, the transition from dating to friends to a combination of both, rooted us together, unified and solid.

I looked heavenward and smiled, silently thanking God for knowing better than me and showing me that the path to true happiness didn't lead to London or Laughlin Air Force Base. It led to God, and God had led me back to Andrew.

CHAPTER 19

Any large indoor event was hosted at either the base theater or Skyward Hall. Graduation ceremonies were held in the theater, but the venue for the drop was the ballroom at Skyward Hall. A handful of dedicated spouses had strung twinkly lights back and forth across the high ceilings of the rectangular space. A large screen set at the front played a loop of pictures the UPT students had submitted from the past year, and a table set with a buffet of vegetables, dips, and sweets ran along the back wall with a huge congratulatory cake as the centerpiece.

Wendy had offered to watch Noah so that Tucker and I could attend the drop for Andrew's UPT class. Everything pilots did in training culminated in the drop ceremony at the end of the year. Each test, each flight, each debrief had been evaluated and ranked. Now it was a simple match-and-eliminate process. Tonight, June 21, every student would learn which plane they would be assigned to fly and which duty station they would be transferred to.

Nervousness bubbled through me, and I kept glancing at the door, waiting for Andrew to arrive.

"You okay?" Tucker asked.

"I think so. I mean . . . it'll all work out, right?" I rubbed my hands together. They were sticky with sweat.

Tucker put his arm around me and pulled me close, but he didn't say anything, and his silence made me wonder if he knew something.

Andrew had earned the number thirteen spot out of nineteen. With both fighter planes and cargo planes in the drop sheet, some options were eliminated from the get-go. He could choose the C-130 in Little Rock or Alaska or the refueling tanker, the KC-135. The C-17s were a popular choice, but he'd thought those ranking above him would grab those slots. There was also a C-21 to Scott Air Force Base and the option to be an instructor pilot and fly the T-6.

Andrew had wanted me to look at the list with him. "I want your input on the final dream sheet," he had said. "We're talking about a future together; this needs to be a joint choice."

"This is your choice," I had replied. "You've worked hard, and I don't want to sway you." My conviction ran deep. Andrew and I felt good, but this decision was between him and the Lord. My future plans were still in flux. Andrew had a minimum of six weeks left at the base, all depending on this night—his future assignment. He had mentioned choosing to stay in Del Rio and asked if I would like that. Truthfully, if he remained here and I had the opportunity to work on a theatre program, I would be tempted to stay, but he needed to make the decision that was best for him. If his dreams were outside of Texas, then he should follow them.

He never told me what his final list entailed, but a goofy, adorable grin had filled his face every time I had seen him for the last forty-eight hours. Still, my nerves had not settled.

Tucker glanced at his watch. "We start in six minutes."

"Tuck," another IP called from across the room. "Come help me for a sec."

Tucker looked at me. "Go," I said. "I'm fine." And I was, because a breath later Andrew walked through the door.

He found me immediately, pulled me to him, and placed a kiss on my forehead. Then he stepped back, firmly holding my hand. "You look nice," he said.

Three discarded outfits sat on my bedroom floor. I'd settled on a denim skirt, a graphic tee with gold letters encouraging one to follow their dreams, and slip-on shoes. "Thanks. You look good too."

Andrew laughed and looked down at the flight suit he'd worn nearly every day for the past year.

"Laugh all you want," I said, "but the uniform looks good on you." Though, tonight my attraction to him probably had just as much to do with his contagious smile.

He slipped his hand through mine. "Are you ready for this?"

I paused and considered the implications of drop night. Calm filtered through me, like warm bath water or the peacefulness of a star-filled sky. "Yeah," I said. "I am."

The microphone zinged resonance. "That's Lieutenant Colonel Haggar," Andrew said.

He looked exactly as I had imagined, sturdy and authoritative, with dark hair. He asked everyone to find a seat. Andrew, still holding my hand, led me to where Tucker held two seats for us, and Ian stood up front with several other IPs.

Lieutenant Colonel Haggar began by welcoming families and spouses. He then gave a quick recap of the various aspects of pilot training all the students had completed. "They're here tonight because we know they're ready to join the elite fighting force that is the United States Air Force," he said. "Now, I know you don't want to see me, so let's get on with it."

Whoops and cheers sounded, and the pilot who had called for Tucker earlier took the mic. "Thank you, Spitfire. You all ready for this?" she asked. More hollers answered her question, and she moved to stand to the side of the large screen.

"That's Major Espinoza, Sphinx," Andrew whispered, pointing to the woman running the show.

A picture of Lieutenant Brasher appeared on the screen, along with his name and call sign. "Number one in the class 24-05 is Brash." Cheers and catcalls rang out. "Brash, come on up," Major Espinoza said.

Brash walked to the front and sat in a chair with his back to the screen. Major Espinoza read off a list of humorous likes and dislikes, and everyone laughed along with Brash. "And now for his assignment." She lifted a gold envelope from the podium. "Brash, you will be flying . . ." She paused for dramatic effect. "The F-15 Eagle in Kadena, Japan!"

The screen behind Brash lit up with a video of the F-15 soaring through the clouds and the words *Kadena, Japan* flashing bold. Brash jumped up from his seat and pumped a fist in the air. Everyone applauded as he jumped off the raised platform to meet Janie in the aisle and scoop her into a big hug.

"Come back here, Brash." Major Espinoza waved a hand for him to return to the stage.

Brash kissed his wife and with a huge grin jumped back onto the raised platform. Major Espinoza awarded him with the Top Flight award for ranking first in the class and presented him with a lei. She held another lei in her hand. "And this is for that special someone in your life who supported you through this past year."

Brash accepted the lei. He turned to the crowd, held his hand up again, and then walked to his seat while more cheers and clapping ensued as he placed the lei over Janie's head.

"Your turn, Bowman." Major Espinoza passed the mic to Ian.

"Next up, Harper Nash, aka Bazaar," he said. A female pilot walked to the stage, and on it went, with Major Espinoza and Ian trading off for every student and announcement. Encouraging whoops and applause followed each one, and my nerves escalated with every reveal as the count moved closer and closer to number thirteen.

My phone buzzed in my pocket. I was grateful I had remembered to set the ringer to silent.

Major Espinoza finished congratulating Hector Evans, a foreign-exchange pilot from Germany. She passed the mic to Ian, who announced the next assignment. My phone buzzed again. Then, instead of returning the mic to Major Espinoza, Ian placed his hands on the podium, and a wide grin crossed his face. "Next up at number thirteen . . . Andrew Stoll."

I squeezed Andrew's arm as he stood, and I clapped exuberantly as nervous energy bounced through my chest. Andrew walked forward, nodded to Ian, and then turned and sat in the chair. His lips twisted upward, but it was not the unadulterated grin I had grown to love. His nerves were on display.

"Many of you know Stoll is my cousin," Ian said. "I'm proud of all of you, but I'm especially proud of the fight Stoll put up to get to sit in this seat." Applause ensued. Ian then recounted Andrew's UPT journey. He talked of Andrew's excellence in academics, then spoke bluntly about the struggles Andrew faced in the cockpit. "He got to his '89 ride and was assigned to fly with Spitfire." Ian motioned to where Andrew sat. "And because he's sitting here, we know that ride was successful." He continued through the last few months of Andrew's training and teased him about a time he started dozing off during a debrief. "But I can say without reservation that Stoll got no favors from me."

"Home-cooked meals!" someone yelled from the back, and everyone chuckled.

My phone continued to hum with notifications of texts and calls. I worried something might have happened with Mom or Dad or Noah, so I peeked at my screen. It was filled with congratulations and well wishes. Confusion flooded through me. I glanced up at the stage.

Ian laughed and held up a hand. "My wife is a good cook, and she wasn't about to allow my cousin to go hungry, so you'll have to take that up with her." After some scattered laughter, the room quieted. "Let me just say, well done, Stoll." Ian read off a list of Andrew's likes and dislikes. He paused and grinned. "It's only fair we add Kasie Foster to your list of likes."

Andrew nodded while cheers rang out.

My phone buzzed again in my hand. I looked down and read a text from Annabelle. *LONDON!! Way to go, Kasie! You'll rock it! Congratulations!!!*

London? My body disconnected from reality, as if I were living in an alternate universe. I glanced quickly at a few of the other texts. Those messages mirrored Annabelle's. I'd been accepted to the England Academy of Dramatic Arts. My eyes lifted to where Andrew sat on the stage. He looked directly at me, though his smile had been replaced with concern.

Acrid bile churned in my stomach.

Ian clicked the slide forward. "Lieutenant Stoll, you have been assigned to fly . . . your first choice, the T-6 Texan II. Duty station, Laughlin Air Force Base, Texas!"

Applause erupted around me. I'd heard Ian's words. They anchored in my mind, latching there, where I knew this thing, this proclamation, should be something to celebrate. Andrew had gotten his first choice, Laughlin, Texas. The enthusiasm around me made tears swell in my eyes, because rather than being happy in this moment, I was crushed.

Andrew stood.

"Kasie?" Tucker whispered. "What's wrong?"

The clapping hands around us, the expectation, the worry washing over Andrew's face as he stepped off the stage and walked toward me—it was too much. I pushed out of my seat and ran for the door.

I heard Andrew's voice rise above the din. "Kasie!"

His call pushed me forward faster.

Tears streamed down my cheeks. Questions pounded in my head, matching the rhythm of my feet. *Why? Why now, God?*

"Kasie!" Andrew called again.

Then I heard Tucker's voice. "Lieutenant Stoll!"

I don't know what happened after that. I didn't look back. I only ran.

Honky snorted at me before he turned away to explore the back corner of his pen. I wasn't sure why I'd ended up at the stables, but I was grateful to be alone.

Bugs swarmed in clusters around the barn. I wiped the moisture from my cheeks and paced back and forth while my breathing slowed. When I could finally inhale deeply without choking on a sob, I dared pull my phone out.

It had continued to vibrate with messages. There were multiple texts and missed calls from Tucker and Andrew plus all the other notifications I had received while at the drop ceremony. I closed my messaging apps and opened my email. Sitting at the top of my inbox was the crux of my dilemma: an email from the England Academy of Dramatic Arts.

> Dear Ms. Foster:
>
> We are pleased to offer you a slot in our Movement and Adaptation course. The session will run from 3 May to 30 October. You are responsible for your lodging and meals while in residence.

The moment I'd seen Annabelle's text, I'd known my name was on the list, but the application had been so long ago and my time had been so occupied with Noah and the talent show and Andrew that I had nearly forgotten about submitting it. Now here the acceptance sat in my inbox.

The email included links for recommended housing and details on the cost and deadlines for accepting the offer. Emotion knocked the air from my lungs. I slid down and sat in the dirt in front of Honky's stall.

The excitement of earlier that evening had fled. Defeat pooled in my stomach as deep as a reservoir. What was the purpose of seeking God's will if every time I got an answer, I got the wrong one? First, breaking up with Andrew, then giving up London to stay in the States to help Tucker. When Andrew and I had crossed paths again, I'd trod so carefully. My fear of getting it wrong, of messing up, of missing what God would have me do, had felt like restraints, forcing me to crawl when I'd wanted to sprint. But I had taken it slow; I had prayed. I had humbled myself to accept that either I had messed up in the past or God's will had changed. And right when I thought I'd found the direction He wanted me to go, I was accepted into a prestigious program in the city of my dreams.

My soul ached.

I tilted my head against the wood of the stall. "What am I supposed to do?" I asked God aloud.

I didn't expect an answer. Tires crunched on the gravel drive. I stood and brushed the dirt from my skirt as best as I could. Tucker's frame soon came into view.

"How did you find me?" I asked.

He held up his phone. "We share locations, remember?"

Oh yeah.

He walked slowly near and stuck his hands on his hips. "That was quite the exit." He wasn't angry. His face held a combination of sorrow and concern. "Want to tell me what's going on?"

My chest constricted and tears welled in my eyes. "I got accepted to the England Academy of Dramatic Arts residency program."

Tucker's eyes narrowed. Hesitancy laced his voice. "Is that a good thing?"

"I applied months ago. I never really thought I'd get in." I wiped my nose with the back of my hand. "They only accept fifteen people each session."

Tucker started riffling through the various pockets on his flight suit, and after a moment he pulled out a crumpled tissue. "You're an overachiever. Of course you got in." His attempt at humor quickly faded. He handed the tissue to me. "So *is* this a good thing?"

I wiped my eyes and a sob wrenched free. "It should be, but I thought I had a good thing here too. I thought God wanted me to stay in Del Rio longer." My breath hitched. "I thought this was a second chance for me and Andrew, and I was offered the arts position at the school . . ."

"And now London." Tucker frowned. He walked over and pulled me into a hug. "I'm sorry, Kas."

The zippers and patches on his uniform scratched against my cheek. I stepped back and let the tears fall. "I just want to know what to do," I said.

Tucker blew out a breath. "I don't know what to tell you."

"Is Andrew okay?" I asked.

"Truthfully? No."

My heart splintered. I had never intended to hurt him. Again.

"I think you both should talk."

"I'm sure I'm the last person he wants to see. I ruined his huge night." I stared at the hay scattered around the barn floor.

"You know, you can be pretty stubborn sometimes," Tucker said. I looked at him. "Andrew would have chased you all the way here if I hadn't called him back. When I pulled rank and demanded he return to the ceremony, he got pretty belligerent and told me I could take his wings or kick him out, but he was coming after you."

I held my breath. "What happened? Did you fight?"

Tucker's face softened and he chuckled lightly. "You do know I've been in intense combat situations, right? I know how to keep my composure, and I wasn't about to slug your boyfriend."

"So what did you do?"

"I stopped talking to him as his instructor and talked to him as your brother," Tucker said. "I promised to find you and ensure you were okay. He's worried about you."

I finally exhaled.

"You need to talk to him, Kas." Tucker pulled his car keys from his pocket.

"I know," I said. "I just couldn't in that moment. I needed to process." I blew my nose, and Honky snorted.

"Are you ready now?" Tucker asked.

"Not really."

"Kas?" Tucker said softly. "Do you love him?"

"I do," I answered without hesitation. When the words left my mouth, peace washed over me. Rightness. Confusion still pricked like an annoying burr in my brain, but it felt as if the anchor had been lifted from my heart.

"Then, let's go find him so you can tell him that." Oh, Tucker. Such a wise older brother.

CHAPTER 20

Tucker pulled up to the stucco building where drop night was held. Andrew sat on a large boulder near the entrance, his elbows propped on his knees and his head in his hands.

"You can take my car, and I'll catch a ride back with Ian," Tucker said. He left the engine running and climbed out. "Hey, Stoll," he called.

Andrew lifted his head, then jumped to his feet. I got out of the car, my heart thrumming. Andrew ran over, his eyes quickly scanning my body, then focusing on my face.

"You two have some things to talk about," Tucker said. He clapped a hand on Andrew's shoulder.

Andrew ignored my brother. "Are you okay?" he asked me. He reached for my hand. I squeezed his fingers, then let go.

"We should talk." I forced my legs to move, walking around the car and then climbing into the driver's seat. Andrew sat beside me and fastened his seat belt. "Do you care where we go?" I asked.

He shook his head. "I'm just glad you're okay."

I scoffed internally at the thought of being okay. Everything I felt did not align with the word, but at the same time, I couldn't deny the peace lumbering through me. It had been massaging my soul ever since Tucker had asked if I loved Andrew.

I turned randomly, left and right, then right again. Andrew stared out the window, his breath slow and sad. Del Rio didn't offer scenic vistas or prominent viewpoints, so when the neighborhood park came into view, I pulled up to the curb and cut the engine.

"Are you sure you're okay?" Andrew's voice was soft, tender, cutting through the thick emotion between us.

"Physically, I'm fine," I assured him. I released my seat belt. "Should we go sit on a bench?"

He nodded. "Whatever you want, Kas."

The air was sticky and hot. The sun would linger low on the horizon for another hour. Andrew followed protocol and pulled his flight cap from his leg pocket and adjusted it on his head. I walked around the play structure to the far side of the circular park and sat down. Andrew sat near, our arms nearly brushing. I turned to face him.

"I've been praying," I began, "asking God to tell me if I got it wrong the first time. You were so certain this was our second chance, so maybe before, the timing was just off. Lately I've felt such peace with you and with the offer from Nicole to run the program with the grant funding." My tongue was running fast, but I couldn't help it. The dam had burst, and every emotion, every thought, concern, hope, and desire came flooding out. "It all felt so solid."

Confusion touched Andrew's eyes.

I needed to tell him about the rock that one hour ago had shattered the perfect stained-glass mosaic. "I got accepted to the England Academy of Dramatic Arts," I said.

I thought Andrew's face would deflate, that he would frown or frustration would lace the corners of his eyes. Instead his face lit and he grabbed my hands. "Kasie, that's wonderful!"

"You're not angry?" Peace massaged my heart a bit more.

Andrew's smile fell. "Why would I . . . ?" His words drifted into the sticky evening. "I'm happy for you."

"But you were assigned to stay at Laughlin. The academy is in London." The pieces of shattered glass would never be perfectly restored.

"Why don't you tell me about it," he said.

I explained that the residency program ran for six months. "It focuses on adapting works to stage through movement," I said. "They selected me for the program starting May 3 of next year."

"It sounds awesome," Andrew said, his smile genuine.

"But you're staying here." My chest tightened. "And I thought . . . I thought I might too. When I prayed, it felt right, and now . . . I don't understand what I'm supposed to do." My eyes welled with tears.

Andrew closed the distance between us and cocooned me in his arms. He rested his head atop mine. "There's a common saying in the air force," he whispered near my ear. "'Flexibility is the key to airpower.'"

I pulled back so I could see his face. His thumb stroked a tear off my cheek. "Can we be flexible?" he asked. "You and me, together? We can make this work. I know we can."

"Are you saying God's answer is to stay?" I asked.

"I think we're supposed to be together, Kasie. And when I pray about that, it feels right," Andrew said.

The peace in my heart pulsed outward. "I feel the same way." I leaned in to his touch, and he pressed a kiss to my forehead. "I'll deny the offer."

Andrew jolted back. "Why would you do that?"

"But you just said . . ."

"I said we should be together, *and* we can be flexible. The timing is perfect." His dimples appeared.

Hope began to fill my heart. "How?" I asked.

"Ms. Moreno asked you stay a year, right?" he asked. I nodded. "Now, I know May isn't quite a year, but it's pretty darn close. You will have implemented the program, have it up and running, and be set to hand off the reins."

"But what about us?" I asked.

"That's where the flexible part comes in." Andrew took my hands and stood, pulling me up with him. "Kasie, I love you. Of course I don't want to be apart from you, but being in the military involves deployments and separations. I've heard absence makes the heart grow stronger, though I can't imagine loving you more than I do now. And I don't know if you realize I'll get quite a bit of leave. I could probably come visit you in London for a week, maybe even two."

"You think we can make both work?" My heartbeat quickened. Was there really a way?

"The residency would be like your own deployment. That's part of the deal if you're a military spouse."

"Spouse?" I asked.

Andrew released my hands. "I'd envisioned this happening in an entirely different way." He reached down to unzip one of his leg pockets. When he straightened again, he had a ring box in his hand. "I was going to pull you up on stage, and I had Ian slip a slide into the presentation."

"Andrew!" I covered my mouth with my hands, afraid that if I breathed, the moment would disappear.

"I know you thrive with a crowd, but it's probably better this way." Andrew knelt on one knee. He fumbled to open the black satin ring box. For some reason, his trembling fingers settled me. Nerves fled and giddiness overflowed, and I couldn't stop smiling. Nor could I look away from Andrew, his eyes pleading for an answer to the question he had yet to ask. His dimples made a slow showing. "Kasie," he said softly. "I've loved you for a long time, and I want to love you for longer still, even if that means we may be apart sometimes. I promise to love you forever. Will you marry me?"

"Yes!" I launched myself forward. His flight cap flew off his head as I knocked him backward and landed on top of his chest. I did, after all, have a flair for being dramatic. "I would love to marry you," I said. "Forever."

Andrew laughed and kissed my cheek, and in the next moment we were sitting in the dirt side by side. "Kasie?" he said. "Did you see where the ring went?"

I gasped and jumped to my feet. "Oh, I can't believe I did that!" I frantically ran a circle around where I had tackled Andrew.

Andrew stood and started to laugh.

"How is this funny?" I asked.

"Marriage to you is going to be so much fun," he said, still chuckling. He turned slowly, his eyes scanning the ground. "Here it is." He walked five steps and plucked the ring box from where it had landed near the slide. "May I?" he asked, coming to stand before me.

The simple gold band was thin and delicate, with a small round-cut diamond. Andrew slipped it from the ring box and onto my finger. He lifted my hand to his lips and kissed it. "I love you, Kasie Foster."

"I love you too."

Andrew and I called my parents together that night. They already knew about the proposal because Andrew had called to ask for their blessing. The night ended with a delicious kiss before I dropped Andrew back at his car.

I knelt next to my bed that night and thanked God for His goodness. I couldn't say why Andrew and I needed to connect this way. I would probably never know. What I did know was that my soul felt peace. My heart beat strong. My faith secured me to God, and I would be forever grateful for His hand in my life.

After church the next day, Tucker and I made our regular video call to our parents. After Noah got bored with the conversation, I had some one-on-one time to chat with them. "I know this is soon, but have you talked about a wedding date?" Mom asked.

Andrew and I knew we wanted a short engagement. "Do you know when you and Dad will be returning to the States?" I asked.

I could sense Mom's resistance through the phone. "We've been praying. We're making a difference here, and well, since you're going to be near Tucker and Noah, we feel like we should extend our mission."

"Oh," I answered quickly, and almost immediately tears pricked my eyes. They were doing a good thing, but I was getting married. I needed my mom.

As if Mom could sense my disappointment, she jumped in. "But Dad talked to the director because we wanted to get the details, and we found out that if we extend, they'll fly us back to the US for two weeks."

My heart lifted. "Really?"

"We thought it might be nice to be there for Christmas. The director said December would be a good time to go." Mom's voice held an apology.

"December sounds like the perfect time for a wedding," I said.

"You don't mind?" Mom asked.

"Two weeks won't give you a lot of time to get to know Andrew, but I know we both want you and Dad there." Wedding excitement bubbled inside me. I couldn't picture an exact scene, but I could well imagine the warmth and joy of being surrounded by my family as Andrew and I promised forever to each other. "He has survival training, and then he'll be in San Antonio for instructor training, so it should work out."

"Do you think so?" Mom asked, hesitation evident in her voice. "I want it to be your perfect day, and already I'm being selfish."

"Mom, you're anything but selfish. You're asking because you're willing to remain in a third-world country and serve those in need." Sure, it would take some adjusting, and maybe I would have otherwise chosen March instead of December, but Mom and Dad were doing good.

"Andrew won't mind?" Mom asked.

"I'll ask him for sure, but I think he feels the same way I do. We just want you to share our special day with us, and if that means a Christmas wedding, then a Christmas wedding sounds delightful."

Mom insisted she would buy my wedding dress and that she and Dad wanted to contribute to the cost of the festivities. "And you have to call me when you pick out invitations and flowers and"—her voice clogged with emotion—"all the things." I could tell sentiment had won despite her effort not to cry.

"I'll call you for all of it," I said. "I promise."

I hung up and dialed Andrew, but after one ring, I hung up. I wanted to see him in person. Ten minutes later I bounced with excitement, waiting for him to answer his door. He pulled it open, still dressed in his button-down from church, with his tie loose around his neck. "This is a lovely surprise," he said.

Exuberance had me jumping at him as he laughed and caught me in his arms. "I talked to my mom," I said as he pulled me close. "How does a Christmas wedding sound?"

"Too far away," Andrew teased.

I laughed. "Are you suggesting we forget about our families and elope?"

He held my shoulders and leaned back. His eyes lit with the idea, and he raised his brows to question whether I was serious.

"No!" I swatted his arm.

He stuck out his bottom lip with all the drama of a two-year-old. "Why not?"

I lifted the end of his tie. "You still have a month of training, and I have a theatre program to plan." I smirked and tugged him toward me. "Along with a wedding, of course."

"Which will be my favorite thing," Andrew said, planting a kiss on my lips.

I kissed him again. "Mine too. Now, will you hurry up and get your pilot's wings already?"

CHAPTER 21

Annabelle had been trying to call me since Saturday. She too had been accepted to attend a course at the England Academy of Dramatic Arts, though we'd been assigned to different sessions. We finally connected late Sunday night via video chat, and I told her about the emotional roller coaster of drop night.

"Engaged!" Annabelle shouted and jumped from her chair and out of the camera's view. I watched her pace in front of her computer for a hot second before she sat back down and wagged a finger at me. "I knew you were getting serious but not this serious."

"Is it possible to be shocked and not shocked at the same time?" I asked. "Because that's how I feel."

"Well, first, I need to see your ring."

I held my hand to the screen, rotating my wrist so the diamond twinkled under the light.

"Andrew did well," Annabelle said. "It totally fits you." She paused for a long beat. "What about England?"

I dropped my hands to my lap. "We're gonna make it work."

Annabelle lifted her eyebrows and began to grin. "Really?"

Andrew's support meant the world to me, and I told Annabelle how great he'd been. "I guess the idea of a long-distance relationship doesn't scare me so much anymore."

"I'd imagine the fact that you're not dating but you're actually ***married*** might help."

"It's crazy, huh?" My grin grew.

"Absolutely."

"You know what's not so crazy?" I asked.

"What?" Annabelle said.

I leaned closer to the screen and pointed at Annabelle. "I know Christmas is a crazy time of year, but we've decided to just have a small ceremony on Christmas Eve."

"That sounds dreamy," Annabelle said.

"We'll probably get married in California, and if you can come, I'd love to pay for your flight—and I'll pay extra so you can fly out that night or Christmas morning to be wherever you want for the holiday."

"You don't have to pay for my flight, Kasie," Annabelle said.

"Well, I really want to because . . . I would like you to be my maid of honor. What do you think?"

She clutched her hands over her heart. "I would love to."

The final phase of Andrew's training included another round of academics, simulator flights, training flights, including a cross-country flight, and then the final check ride and awarding of official pilot's wings. Andrew would complete his cross-country flight the last week of June, then on July 13—UPT graduation.

The week after the drop, the cross-country flights were set. Andrew and his fellow students would leave on Monday for destinations all around the country to test their planning, their ability to fly into various airports and through various conditions, and the skills they had acquired over the last eleven months.

I tucked Noah into bed and sat down with Tucker to watch a reality show in which teams competed in marksmanship.

Tucker told me about the cross-country flight and how it had been one of the best things he'd done during his own training. "Andrew is assigned to fly with Bentley," he said.

"Is that good?" I asked.

Tucker muted the TV. "Yeah. Bentley's the perfect IP for a cross-country. She's a good instructor, but she's also chill."

"Bentley's a she?" I asked. "Did I meet her at drop night?"

Tucker rubbed a hand down the side of his face. "Ah, no, she couldn't be there. She had a family emergency and just got back. But don't worry about it, Kas. Andrew will fly with another student, and they'll all have their own rooms and stuff."

I smacked his arm. "Duh. I'm not worried about that. The name confused me."

"Okay, fair," Tucker said. "They call her Bentley because she's picky about funny things, like she wants fancy chocolate stocked in the snack bar. Ritzy-flavored water too. But she drives a beat-up Corolla." He gave a playful shrug. "She has expensive taste in the cheap things."

I loved hearing the backstory of call signs. Wait. "Does Andrew have a call sign? Everyone calls him Stoll. Is that his call sign?" I asked.

"He hasn't told you?" Tucker asked.

"No. What should he tell me?" My mind circled through possibilities.

"Maybe you should ask him." My brother moved to unmute the TV, but I snatched the remote from his hand and turned off the show. "Come on, Kas."

I pegged my brother with a look that said I would not budge. "Tell me."

"He didn't exactly have one before. Everyone called him Stoll before the two of you got engaged."

"And now?" I asked.

Tucker heaved a dramatic breath. "Now they call him Crush."

"Crush?" I repeated, totally confused. "Like he 'crushes' it?" I used air quotes.

Tucker smirked. "'Cause he's totally crushing on you."

My cheeks colored. How would Andrew feel having his peers address him as Crush every day? Tucker could sense my worry. "Don't worry, Kas. He grins whenever someone calls him Crush. He eats it up. He totally owns it."

I settled into the couch and turned the show back on. When the contestants took their shots, some called their performance *skill* and others called it *luck*. I didn't pay attention to the bull's-eyes. I could only think of how I felt like the luckiest girl of all.

Andrew's cross-country flight sounded more like a vacation than training. He paired with Cal, and their flight plan took them over the Grand Canyon and Zion National Park. They headed north to Washington and Montana before returning to Texas via Colorado and New Mexico. Tucker planned to be gone the same time as Andrew. His students were Harper and Ricky, and they planned to fly east, across the southern states to Florida. They even did some touch-and-go maneuvers at the base in Puerto Rico.

Hope had me and Noah over for dinner during the week while the men were away, and I invited Wendy to come over another night for a marathon watching of the 1995 *Pride and Prejudice*. "I'm not familiar with Jane Austen," she had told me, but she was willing to give her a try. By the end of the fourth hour, she proclaimed herself an Austen fan. We finished at two in the morning, and Wendy decided to stay the night and crash on the couch.

Noah got extra television time the following day, but he also took an extra-long nap, so I felt somewhat rejuvenated by the time Tucker got home that evening. He told me about his flight and how nice the weather was, and I told him silly stories about Noah.

I got a text from Andrew not long after. *We just landed. Still have to debrief, but I can't wait to see you. I've missed you.* I texted back that I couldn't wait and changed into jeans and a Cal State Northridge T-shirt.

Andrew knocked on the door an hour later. The cross-country flight had consisted of long hours in the cockpit, and he looked exhausted. We sat on the front step, and he shared the highlights of his trip.

"Are you glad it's done?" I asked.

"It's nice to check another thing off and be that much closer to graduation, but it was fun, and I know I'll sleep well tonight." He reached for my hand. "I missed you, Kas."

"I missed you too. But . . ." I paused, wanting to make sure I got the words right.

He squeezed my fingers and dipped his head to make me look at him. "What is it?"

"It wasn't as hard as I thought . . . being apart." I shifted so I could better face him. I hoped he could sense the peace I was trying to convey. "I'm not expressing myself well. What I mean is, before, I was scared of long-distance. I worried that if we couldn't be together, we couldn't make it work. And I'm not scared of that anymore. I missed you, but it was okay."

Andrew leaned forward and pressed his lips to my temple. "I think I get what you're trying to say."

"I don't know what the difference is between our breakup and now, but I'm not afraid. This trip was nothing compared to a deployment or attending the course in London, but where before it all felt off, now it feels right. So very right." It was a calm I felt in my soul. A knowledge that Andrew loved me and I loved him and God was cheering for our success.

CHAPTER 22

The first weekend in July was the hyped IPs-versus-students softball game.

Both Andrew and Tucker had vied for me to play on their teams, but in the end I chose to play with the IPs because I needed Hope's cheery moral support. I could function in sports, barely. I understood the rules and could apply basic physics, but I did not excel. It sounded like a fun afternoon, with the game, a barbecue, and homemade ice cream. I looked forward to bettering friendships with people I had met, and I wanted to participate; I just didn't want to look like a fool.

Tucker dug out two baseball gloves from a box in the carport storage. I packed sunscreen, water, and all of Noah's favorite snacks, along with the two bags of chips Tucker had signed up to bring. We pulled up to the softball field in our air force blue T-shirts. The IPs had one more week with the students, and as a reminder that they held the cards, they'd insisted the students wear their PT gear: gray T-shirts and blue shorts. They had dubbed it the blue vs. gray game.

The IPs, families, and students visited for a while, Tucker and me tag-teaming conversations while chasing Noah around the playground. I got to meet Lieutenant Colonel Haggar, who proved to be every bit as pleasant as Hope had indicated.

"Congratulations on the engagement," Lieutenant Colonel Haggar said. "I've heard your name, and it's nice to finally meet you."

I think my mouth fell open.

He chuckled. "Don't worry. Your brother sings your high praises, and Lieutenant Stoll . . . well, he's been smiling a lot lately. When he came to me and asked what I could do, I wasn't sure it would work out. But it made sense to ask, given the unique situation. I'm glad we could switch things around to get him the assignment he wanted."

Lieutenant Colonel Haggar must have seen the confusion on my face. “Oh,” he said. “Perhaps he didn’t tell you.”

“I’m sorry,” I said. “I’m still figuring out all this air force stuff. But yeah, I have no idea what you’re talking about.”

He chuckled. “I’ll just say Lieutenant Stoll’s original assignment was not to Laughlin Air Force Base. It wasn’t even an option on our drop sheet. But he approached me with the request, so I made a few calls. There’s always a need for new IPs. I’m glad we could make it happen.”

“Me too,” I mumbled, realizing the implications of what I’d just learned. My heart swelled with love for Andrew. When he said he would fight for us to be together, he’d meant every word, and I couldn’t wait to start our happily ever after.

Lieutenant Colonel Haggar’s wife walked up, and he gave her a quick kiss on the cheek. He turned back to me and offered an introduction. “This is Angeline,” he said. “The military is packed with good people, and there’s lots of support and options available.”

“And I’d be happy to answer any questions you have,” Angeline said.

“Thank you,” I said.

Lieutenant Colonel Haggar glanced around the park. “I think I’d better get this game started,” he said. “Good luck out there.”

I thanked him for mentoring Andrew. I was especially grateful for the steps he had taken to help Andrew remain in Texas. He took his wife’s hand and called to the crowd. “Gather with your teams and figure out your positions. And, remember, this is a family-friendly game!”

Some whoops and hollers followed. Amy, one of the IP wives, who was thirty-three weeks pregnant, had offered to watch the kids on the playground so Hope, Ian, and Tucker could participate. The students were first at bat. Hope had proven herself at previous games and now played second base. I was relegated to right field, way beyond where a reasonable person could hit the ball. Lieutenant Colonel Haggar may have labeled it a family-friendly game, but there were too many teasing taunts for anyone miss the underlying competitiveness.

No balls were hit my way. Ricky made it to third, but when Pluto hit a grounder and Ricky took off for home, our catcher tagged him, and he became the final out of the inning. Hope and I stood behind the chain-link fence, cheering for the top of our lineup. Lieutenant Colonel Haggar bat first.

“Let’s go, Spitfire,” someone shouted.

Lieutenant Colonel Haggar swung and popped a fly ball to left field. It was caught, and he shook his head in apology as he returned to the bench.

Ian batted next, and Hope cheered loudly when he hit a line drive and claimed second base. Sphinx got a single, and Tucker got tagged out. We scored one run before another fly secured our third out. The next inning, Andrew hit a high ball that dropped behind the second baseman, and he scored the tying run. By the bottom of the second, the students were up four to three.

Hope and I didn't enter the batting lineup until the third inning. Bentley's husband, Tim, batted before me, and he advanced the runners and made it safely to first. The bases were loaded, and as luck would have it, Cal played catcher. His cocky grin screamed the opposite of family friendly. We were playing slow pitch, so I knew I'd get an easy, underhand pitch. Now my bat just needed to connect with the ball. I didn't care if I got out, but I didn't want to strike out.

"You've got this, Kasie." Hope clapped as Tucker selected a bat and handed it to me.

My stomach felt like a family of frogs bounded around inside. I hadn't felt my nerves this elevated since the first time I'd taken the stage, for my fifth-grade play. I would have preferred to watch all the kids at the playground over the pressure I felt standing in front of Cal and the other flight students. I avoided making eye contact with Andrew because, although I had chosen to play with Tucker, I still worried I might embarrass him.

Harper pitched for the students, and she lobbed a pitch directly over the plate. The ball neared, and I swung and missed. "Whoops," Cal said under his breath.

I ignored him, gritted my teeth, and gripped the bat. The second pitch came, and I swung again. The bat connected, but the ball fouled somewhere behind me.

"Whoa, slugger," Cal said, through his catcher's mask. "That's strike two."

I knew Cal's words were meant to be playful. He'd made similar comments to all the batters, but my pride demanded I show him I could hit the ball. What I really wanted to do was slug the ball to Mars, but I would settle for a hit.

"Bend your knees more," Tucker said from behind the fence.

I shifted my stance and lifted the bat over my shoulder. The pitch came, I swung—and struck out.

Cal didn't say anything, and my team gave me lots of positive *nice try* comments. It still stunk.

Hope knew her way around the ball, and she brought in a run with her base hit. We scored once more before the inning ended.

I grabbed my glove to jog back to right field. Andrew ran in from his position as rover and veered toward me. He jogged close, leaned forward, and kissed my cheek. "Love you," he said.

"Hey, Crush, no PDA with the opposing team!" one of his teammates called.

"You're just jealous," Andrew called back. I guess I hadn't embarrassed him too badly.

The game continued, the lead bounced between the IPs and the students, and we started the ninth inning two runs down, in the middle of our batting lineup.

"Can I get a pinch hitter?" I asked Hope as my turn to bat grew closer.

"You'll do fine," she said.

I did not share her confidence. The frogs in my belly had graduated to kangaroos. Bentley got on base, and her husband hit the ball hard and long. Bentley scored, and they played the ball to Cal, holding Bentley's husband to third.

My turn. Tucker again handed me a bat. He chuckled. "No pressure, Kas. Have fun."

"Yeah right," I said. I might have glared at him.

"Tying run's on third," Cal said before squatting over the base.

I gripped hard enough that my knuckles turned white. I wanted this hit. Pluto had swapped Harper out as pitcher. He tossed the ball, and the moment I swung, I knew I was early. The ball thwacked into Cal's glove, and he stood and threw it back to Pluto.

Cal pulled up his catcher's mask. "Let's go," he shouted. "Final inning."

"I love you, Kasie!" Andrew screamed from across the grass.

Head shakes followed, and a few chuckles. My grip relaxed, and the tension in my shoulders eased a bit.

Cal pulled his mask back down and squatted again. "Let's see what you've got, drama girl," he said.

I bent my knees and shifted my weight to my back foot. Pluto bent forward, then tossed the ball. The urge to swing surged with the approaching ball. I waited a second more. Then I cranked the bat around as hard as I could. A loud crack sounded, but the tinging noise and the position of the bat was all wrong. Instead of hitting the ball, I'd swung through and connected the bat with Cal's face mask. The mask skewed to the side of his face, and he fell backward in the dirt.

The bat dropped from my hands. "Cal!" I ran to his side, my fists clenched. I panicked. How could I help him? "Are you okay? I'm so sorry!"

Cal moaned, and my team rushed from the dugout. "Ahhh!" Cal pulled the catcher's mask off. Blood ran from his nose. He dropped the mask in the dirt and then lifted his shirt to stop the blood. "Dang, girl," he said. "You've got a wicked swing."

"Use this." Ian thrust a wad of tissue into Cal's hand. "Someone get some ice," he called.

By this time, both teams had gathered to the scene of my humiliation. "I am so sorry, Cal. I only meant to hit the ball."

"Well, I didn't think you were aiming for my head." He chuckled and winced at the same time.

"It's a big enough target," one of the students said, making everyone laugh.

Everyone but me. I'd thought striking out was the worst thing that could happen. Knocking my bat into Cal's face was far worse.

Andrew appeared at my side. "You okay, Cal?" he asked, looking him over.

"I'm so sorry, Cal," I said again.

Ricky watched Cal, putting an arm under his elbow as he stood to make sure he remained steady as he climbed to his feet. "You good?" Ricky asked.

Cal folded the tissues in his hand, then pressed them back to his still-bleeding nose. "Yeah. But remind me not to get on Kasie's bad side," he said. I didn't know what to say. Cal looked at me, and his face softened. "Hey, I'm just teasing," he said. "The mask did its job. And I've broken my nose before."

Ian handed Cal a bag of ice, and Cal placed it on the side of his face, over the tissues.

My hands twisted. "Can I help in any way?"

"It was an accident. We're all good," Cal said lightheartedly, adjusting the ice. "It's just blood."

"Why don't you head over to the clinic and get that checked out," Lieutenant Colonel Hagger said.

"Want me to drive you?" I asked.

"Nah," Cal said. "Ricky here will take me." He raised his free hand in the air. "Win this one for me, team!"

Everyone clapped and cheered in support of Cal. Ricky patted him on the back, and they turned to walk to the parking lot.

"Sorry!" I called again.

Andrew put his arm around my shoulder. "It looks like he's okay."

"I'm glad," I said. "But don't expect me to pick up a bat again. I'm retiring from softball and sticking with theatre."

CHAPTER 23

Andrew and I stood at the fence at the end of the runway, watching the flashing lights of the planes taxiing, circling, and taking off. "How's Cal's nose?" I asked.

"You can't even see the swelling now. He didn't even mention it," Andrew said.

"That bad, huh?" I asked.

Andrew laughed and stepped behind me, wrapping his arms around my shoulders. "That means he let it go. Cal's not reserved. If he had something to say, he would have said it."

"I still feel bad," I said, layering my arms over Andrews.

"It was an accident. He knows you didn't mean to hit him." Andrew nuzzled his chin on my shoulder. "What a crazy year," he said after a pause.

"But you did it." I looked at a plane flying low overhead. "You graduate in four days. Doesn't it feel great?" It was Wednesday evening. Andrew's parents flew in on Friday, and graduation was Saturday.

"I guess I was thinking more about us. A year ago, I didn't think this could be a possibility." Andrew tightened his arms more snugly around me. "I'm glad pilot training is done, but more than that, I'm glad I get to hold you in my arms and count down the days until we can be married."

"That does make for a pretty good year," I said, leaning my head on his arms.

A plane turned at the end of the runway and pushed up the throttle. The engine noise filled the space around us until the plane lifted from the runway and climbed into the clouds. "One hundred and sixty-eight days," Andrew said.

"What?" I asked, turning in his arms to face him.

"One hundred and sixty-eight days until our wedding," he said. It warmed my heart that he knew the number.

"One-hundred and sixty-eight days until I become Mrs. Stoll," I said. And I couldn't wait.

The day before UPT graduation, Andrew's parents, Aaron and Rhonda Stoll, arrived. We had called to talk to them about the wedding twice before on video chat, and thankfully, they were both gracious and kind. Hope and Ian hosted them since Andrew had only one room. That night we visited with them, and Hope fed us all biscuits and gravy.

The student pilots' graduation festivities started early the next day. The base photographer set up to take pictures of families near the aircraft. Andrew smiled first with his parents, and then he took a picture with me, and finally we all stood together with the T-1 behind us.

"What a great picture," his mom said. "It might make for a lovely wedding invitation."

Andrew grimaced. "I'm not sure that's what Kasie has in mind," he said. Gosh, I loved him.

Everything reminded me of Tucker's graduation, and I missed Stacy. On graduation days, the simulators were reserved for the students and their families. Andrew had reserved several time slots, and his dad flew with him first. His mom and I visited while Aaron steered the T-1 around a virtual Texas. Rhonda flew for a short five minutes before she started feeling nauseous.

During my time in the cockpit, Andrew focused on steering the plane and checking the altimeter. "Now, let's try to land it," he said.

I turned the yoke as he directed and lined up with the runway. "Keep the nose about two degrees above the horizon."

"And should I lower the flaps?" I teased.

He laughed. "If you want to hook. We need to slow down more."

He flipped some switches and then pointed to one overhead. "Here's your flaps," he said. "Go ahead."

I reached up and pushed the switch over. Andrew's soothing voice directed me as we grew closer and closer to the ground. He took care of the pedals and the throttle and the radio calls. I tried to focus on adjusting the yoke as he instructed. "It's going to pull as we come in. Hold it steady."

The simulator jarred as the imaginary rear wheels made contact. "Now the nose will ease down," Andrew said.

I assumed he meant I should push the yoke forward, and Andrew noticed my mistake too late. "Pull back!" he said.

With all my might I yanked the yoke toward me, and the simulator pitched upward. The video showed us skidding sideways across the runway, and the screen flashed red. A silent beat passed, and then we broke into laughter.

"I guess it takes a year to master," I said.

Andrew leaned across the controls and kissed my cheek. "I'm glad you're here, Kasie. You make a great copilot."

We separated and headed home to dress for the graduation ceremony and banquet. I had yet to see Andrew in his full dress blues, and I couldn't wait. I wore my tea-length blue dress with the string of tiny white pearls my parents had given me when I'd graduated from college. I straightened the random kinks from my hair.

Tucker had to leave early to help set up, and Wendy came to tend Noah. He cried for his dad, and Wendy bounced him on her hip. She had also agreed to watch Cole and Becca, and Hope dropped them off as I slipped on my heels. The kids headed for Noah's toy box.

"You look lovely," Hope said.

I gave her a big squeeze. "Thank you," I said. "I'm so grateful for you."

Noah continued to cry, Cole found the siren button on the toy fire truck, and another knock sounded at the door. Hope turned and opened it. Andrew stood on the other side with the most tempting dimpled smile, and I whistled.

"You look like a pilot," I said.

"And you look like a pilot's fiancée." He stepped inside, holding two corsages. He slipped a white-and-green arrangement over my wrist, then lifted my fingers to kiss the back of my hand. He held the other corsage box. "This one's for my mom."

Becca stood with an open-mouthed stare.

I leaned low and whispered to Becca, "He's cute, huh?"

Becca closed her mouth and gave a shy, blushing smile.

Andrew bent at the waist. "Have a lovely evening, Miss Becca," he said.

She giggled.

Hope swept in for one more hug from her kids. I opted to slip out with Andrew rather than cause more problems by announcing to Noah that I was leaving. Wendy had her hands full enough.

We walked next door, where Andrew presented his mother with her corsage, and we were soon on our way to the base auditorium. Andrew left to find his classmates, and his parents, the Nottinghams, and I walked into the main room. Families chatted and mingled in the aisles. Excitement pulsed through the air. The culmination of dreams and a difficult year had finally arrived.

I met Cal's parents and apologized for breaking his nose. His mother laughed and waved a dismissive hand. "He's had a crooked nose since he was little. You probably knocked it back into place."

Tucker stood near the podium, talking to Sphinx. I tried to catch his eye, but he exited the stage and sat in the front row.

The rest of us found seats, and somehow, in unison, everyone quieted.

Sphinx stood at the mic. "We would like to welcome our graduates of UPT class 24-05."

Music played, and all the students walked in. Andrew came into sight and my heart lifted. This was it! He'd earned his wings.

Sphinx continued. "Please stand for the arrival of the official party and remain standing for the National anthem." She announced the names and titles of three officers who entered, one woman and two men, and a woman with fiery red hair moved to the mic and sang a beautiful rendition of "The Star-Spangled Banner." Applause followed, and we were asked to be seated.

The program continued with a short message from Lieutenant Colonel Haggar and another motivational presentation from the wing commander. Brash had maintained the number-one slot, and he'd earned the Esteemed Graduate award. Music once again streamed through the speakers, and each student pilot's name was read. They crossed the stage, where they were presented with the piece of paper proclaiming their accomplishment.

"Andrew Curtis Stoll," Sphinx said.

My clap could not convey my joy. His father walked near the stage to take his picture, and I kept applauding. Andrew saluted his commander and then found me in the audience. I smiled wide, wishing I could shout my feelings aloud. His dimples faded, and he mouthed, *I love you.* Simple. Silent. And true.

I did not doubt.

The final student crossed the stage. "Ladies and gentlemen," Sphinx said. "The class of 24-05 has been awarded the aeronautical rating of pilot, effective 9 July 2024." She called Brash back to the podium.

"It is now time for the traditional breaking of the wings," Brash said. "Today class 24-05 has earned the right to be called pilots and pin on their first set of wings. Years ago, when the army air corps started issuing wings, the tradition began for aviators to break their first set of wings. This first pair is not to be worn. As the tradition goes, the pilot should break the wings into two parts, one half to be kept by the pilot, the other to be given to the pilot's loved one. The two halves should never be brought together while the pilot is still alive. After death, the two halves are once again united with the pilot for good fortune in the next life. I am honored to lead class 24-05 in this tradition. Pilots, please stand with your wings in hand and face your families. One the count of three, you will break your first pair of wings."

The new pilots turned, and Brash counted down. "Three. Two. One." Pairs of wings snapped in two, and applause erupted around the room. "We'd like to thank our families and friends for all their support. We will reconvene in the reception hall directly," Brash said.

Hope leaned forward. "We're gonna sneak out and go make sure everything is ready at the reception. We'll see you over there." Hope and Ian squeezed past a handful of guests and hurried to the exit.

Andrew's parents and I filed slowly from our seats, following the flow of people. Andrew's mom met him first. She wrapped him in a big hug. "I'm so proud of you!" she said.

Andrew grinned. "Thanks, Mom." He opened the palm of his hand and handed her half of his broken wings. "I'd like you to have this."

Her eyes flicked to me and back to Andrew. "Are you certain?"

He leaned close and whispered something into her ear. The concern melted from her face. "Well, thank you." She held the broken piece in her palm and pressed it against her heart.

Andrew's dad looked near tears. "Well done, son."

"Thanks, Dad," Andrew said, and they gave each other a long embrace.

Andrew stepped away from his father and opened his arms to me. I skipped the two steps forward and jumped into his embrace. My heart felt near to bursting. "Ah, my handsome pilot!" I giggled as he spun me around. He set me back on my feet. "How does it feel?" I asked.

Andrew paused to consider my question. "I came in with one ideal, and along the way, something changed. And I'm okay with that." He took my hand in his. "I think I'm where God wants me to be."

"Lieutenant Stoll," Tucker said, walking up the aisle. "Two things. First off, congratulations."

"Thank you," Andrew said. I had a feeling he would be grinning for a long time.

"Second, Lieutenant Colonel Haggar would like to have a word with you," Tucker said.

Andrew's brows pulled together. "Right now?"

Sphinx walked up to where we stood.

"He asked me to have you report to his office," Tucker said.

Sphinx turned to me and Andrew's parents. "I'd be happy to escort your guests to the reception, and you can meet them there when your business is concluded."

I squeezed Andrew's fingers. The request seemed odd, but he had his certification in hand and his wings on his uniform. The day had been all good things, and I had no reason to think a conversation with Lieutenant Colonel Haggar would change that.

Andrew leaned over and kissed my cheek. "I'll see you at the reception."

"We can head out this door," Sphinx said, motioning the rest of us down the aisle to a side exit.

Andrew and Tucker walked the opposite way.

"Is everything all right?" Andrew's mom asked Sphinx.

Sphinx offered the perfect diplomatic smile. "I'm sure there's nothing to worry about."

We walked across the lawn to Skyward Hall. A long table held a buffet of appetizers, finger sandwiches, and various flavors of empanadas. Drinks were served in the corner, and a giant cake with scrawled words of congratulations and all the graduate's names filled another table. Music streamed through boulder-sized speakers, and people were already celebrating on the dance floor.

Hope found us. "Hey, y'all. That was such a nice ceremony." She paused. "Where's Andrew?"

"His commander asked to see him," his dad said.

Hope grimaced. "Hmm, I wonder what that could be about." The same thought pounded in my brain, but beyond curiosity, I felt peace.

"I hope it won't take too long," Andrew's mom said. "We have to fly out in the morning."

"The empanadas are delicious. Why don't we grab some food before the line gets longer." Hope pointed to the buffet table. Andrew's dad guided his wife over, and Hope walked beside me. "I just got off the phone with Wendy. Everyone's doing fine. She's about to put Noah down to bed, and my kids are set to watch a movie."

"Thanks," I told Hope. "Have you seen my brother?" I scanned the dimly lit room.

She nudged my arm. "There he is." She pointed toward the main door. "Oh, and Andrew too." Tucker stood with Andrew, and they appeared to be having a serious conversation.

My feet moved forward with the urgent need to be a part of whatever they were discussing. I crossed the room quickly, and Andrew's eyes connected with mine. He said something to Tucker, then closed the distance between us.

I opened my mouth to ask what his commander had wanted, but before I could speak, Andrew kissed my lips. It started as a simple kiss—we were in the middle of a crowd, after all. He pressed his mouth to mine again, lingering.

I smiled against his lips. "Andrew?" I said his name, and he clasped my hand in his and led me to the dance floor.

He spun me in a circle and wrapped his arms around my waist, pulling my body to his. Despite the pumping tempo of the song, we swayed in our own rhythm.

"I have the best news," he said, his dimples on full display. "Well, let me start at the beginning so you know how amazing this is."

"Okay," I said. My arms rested on his, our hips moving in unison, left and right.

"As things grew more serious between us, I talked with Spitfire." A large group joined the dancing, pushing us into the crowd.

Andrew glanced over his shoulder and smoothly danced us to the edge of the dance floor.

I leaned close to his neck so I could whisper into his ear. "He told me you asked him about an assignment change," I said. Andrew looked confused. "At the softball game," I clarified. "He told me you asked him to make a change about something."

The lightbulb went off. "Ah," Andrew said. "The initial drop sheet had an IP slot to Columbus. One of the other UPT bases. I asked Spitfire about it, and he said he'd never seen an IP slot in a drop to a different base. I told him I had hoped to take the spot, but I wanted to stay at Laughlin, so he said he would make some calls. In the end, it was a mistake and they straightened it out."

"So that's what he wanted to talk to you about?" I asked.

"No." Andrew's eyes sparkled like the strobe light over the dance floor. "Kasie, you know military life has a lot of change, right?"

"Yeah," I said, my stomach twisting in confusion. "You're making me nervous."

Our movement slowed, and the music and tempo no longer mattered. "I figured by the time we finish our assignment here, Lieutenant Colonel Haggar will have gotten his permanent change in station. Since he was willing to help me before, I asked if he'd help me again." Andrew appeared eager, but his words confused me.

"Did you ask him to change your assignment to something else?" We had stopped moving, but my mind kept rotating around and around.

He shook his head. "I asked if he would help me secure our follow-on assignment."

"For after Laughlin?" I asked.

"Yes." Andrew grabbed my hands. "Usually you don't receive your follow-on assignment until you've been at a base for three years, so we normally wouldn't know for a while what comes after Del Rio, but Spitfire has some connections at Randolph Air Force Base, where they make the assignments." Andrew couldn't hold still. He bounced on the balls of his feet. "England, Kasie!" he said, grinning wide. I froze, working to process his words. "I know it's three years away, and I know it's not London. But we can live there, and you can travel into London, and—"

I grabbed his face in my hands. "We're going to England?"

"Mildenhall Air Force Base, to be exact. I looked it up on the way from Spitfire's office. It's about a two-hour drive from the base to London. I thought maybe we could live halfway in between. I'll be flying the KC-135, and you can—"

This kiss was all mine. My lips found Andrew's. Warm. Soft. Sweet. I wanted to stay there all night.

"No PDA on the dance floor!" someone shouted, and I couldn't help the laugh that erupted, dancing over our tangled lips.

Andrew took my right hand, and with a few fancy steps, he had us moving around the wooden floor, dancing a pseudo salsa. My dress flared with the turns, and my heart swelled with love. I doubted I could be happier anywhere else in the world, because the man who brought me joy grinned at me while showing off his moves.

The song ended, and Andrew leaned me back in a low dip. When he lifted me to stand straight again, I laughed with delight. A popular slow song began, and Andrew released my hands and reached into his jacket pocket. "I gave my mom half of my broken wings. I want to give this to you." He pulled out a silver chain. A tiny pair of pilot's wings dangled at the end of the necklace. He released the clasp and stepped near to secure the gift around my neck. His fingers brushed my skin below my hairline. "I thought you deserved your own set of wings," he said, tracing the lines of my shoulders. He pulled me close and kissed my forehead. "I'm grateful to have you as my copilot for the rest of my life."

I fingered the dainty silver charm. "I love it," I said.

"And I love you." Andrew kissed me softly, and we began once more to sway with the music.

I rested my cheek against his chest. "Thank you, Andrew," I said. "For making all of my dreams come true."

ABOUT THE AUTHOR

Chalon Linton is an air force spouse, a mother of four, and a fan of all things romance. Jane Austen has long been a favorite because who can resist handsome men in tailcoats? Manners, wit, and true love, combined with a faith in God, guide her stories to a happily ever after. She has met friends from around the globe and is grateful for each experience that adds to her own faith in the goodness of people.

You can learn more about Chalon's books at chalonlinton.com or follow her on social media.

Instagram: lintonloveslife

Facebook: Author Chalon Linton